THE EERIE ADVENTURES OF THE
LYCANTHROPE
ROBINSON CRUSOE

OTHER WORKS BY PETER CLINES

THE EERIE ADVENTURES OF THE

LYCANTHROPE
ROBINSON
CRUSOE

Daniel Defoe and H.P. Lovecraft

Abridged by
PETER CLINES

A PERMUTED PRESS BOOK

ISBN: 978-1-61868-633-6

THE EERIE ADVENTURES OF THE LYCANTHROPE
ROBINSON CRUSOE
© 2016 by Peter Clines
All Rights Reserved

Cover art by Christian Bentulan
Interior design by Neuwirth & Associates

PERMUTED
PRESS

Permuted Press, LLC
275 Madison Avenue, 6th Floor
New York, NY 10016
http://permutedpress.com

For Professor Robert Payson Creed,
who taught me classic literature could be fun.

A Woodcut of Robinson Crusoe, circa 1700. The engraver's patron insisted elements of the image be changed or removed "for the sake of goodness and decency."

Foreword

Throughout history, it's been the nature of storytellers to make their tale fit the audience, no matter what the truth of that tale may be. Most people are horrified to read the unedited fairy tales that were popularized by the Brothers Grimm. Many college students are stunned by the action-packed tale of *Beowulf* printed in its true form as a long epic poem. Even the epics *The Odyssey* and *The Iliad* are dry on the page without a skilled translation.

In a like manner, when writing out the biography of Robinson Crusoe, budding writer and pamphleteer Daniel Defoe decided on several edits to the assembled journals and accounts that made up the manuscript. While there were numerous popular tales of shipwrecked mariners at the time, Crusoe's experiences were so singular and unnatural that they far outshone the tales of contemporary castaways such as Alexander Selkirk and Henry Pitman. Still, Defoe felt certain changes needed to be made if Crusoe's story were to receive any sort of audience (indeed, if it was even to see print).

Chief among these changes, alas, was a personal bias. Defoe, a Presbyterian dissenter who once debated becoming a minister, felt the need to include numerous passages on Christianity, faith, and devotion in the manuscript, contrary to Crusoe's well-documented dislike of organized religion (having been raised in England during the religiously-conflicted reign of Charles I, at a time shortly after the Spanish Inquisition had burned almost a dozen people for witchcraft in Europe). In an angry 1721 letter to Jonathan Swift, rebutting that author's latest criticism of *Robinson Crusoe*, Defoe justifies the excessive additions by the belief it was impossible for a man to spend so much time in isolation without turning to Jesus Christ in some regular form or another.

In a similar vein, Defoe also decided that Crusoe *must* have tried to escape the island. This belief, however, posed the problematic question of, if such a capable man had built a boat, why did he remain stranded for over a quarter-century? Thus, Defoe's account shows Crusoe repeatedly building canoes and boats, yet through a series of flimsy constructions never once reaching the nearby island of Trinidad.

As a historical note, Crusoe was enraged by the random omissions and additions to his biography, which made him alternately appear to be a bumbling fool, a zealot, or a senile old man. At least one account says he was infuriated by the idea he spent 27 years on his island carrying a parasol to block the sun. Over the irreverent matter of "the dancing bear" inserted at the end of Defoe's text, Crusoe was driven into a rage and threatened the writer with bodily violence at least three times. The writer was intimidated enough by the old man that he did not attempt to publish the work until a few months after Crusoe's reported death at the then-remarkable age of 87.

To his credit, when Defoe first edited the journals and accounts of Crusoe, he took great pains to maintain the original (and often creative) spellings and grammar that his worldly-yet-uneducated subject had used. For example, like so many dabblers at writing, Crusoe thought commas were not so much placed as scattered like ashes. He was also, if Defoe's manuscript is to be believed, the creator of the run-on sentence.

In the three centuries since, countless publishers and scholars have "improved" the manuscript. Misspelled or inconsistently spelled words have been replaced and grammar adjusted to modern standards with little regard for the flavor of the original tale. This has resulted in hundreds of varying editions being produced over the years.

Faced with the decision of which edition was to be judged "correct," I've done the same as many scholars before me and satisfied my own ego, falling back on the interpretation of the tale I was first familiar with. While this version is not as raw as the original manuscript, it still contains far more of Crusoe's original spellings and phrasings than many readers are used to. I have also taken the liberty of dividing the book into chapters, of a sort, where the narrative seemed most inclined for a break.

All of this does, of course, skirt around the elephant in the room, as it were. This edition of *Robinson Crusoe* has been drawn from the original accounts and journals, few copies of which are known to exist. These original documents reveal Crusoe's exile, and indeed much of his life, to be a far darker and more ominous tale than most editions have shown. Seen in this new light, some of these facts will have the manuscript dismissed as a work of pure fiction at best and trite fantasy at worst, even though many of the corroborating elements have always remained in Defoe's more popular version.

This version of that manuscript was first found amidst the papers of writer, historian, and bibliophile Howard P. Lovecraft a few years after his death in 1937. Lovecraft had footnoted an amazing amount of the manuscript and cross-referenced it with certain texts and histories available at the Old College Library of the University of Massachusetts at Amherst and the Curwen Rare Books Library of Miskatonic University. Those footnotes have allowed me to simplify some of Crusoe's more poetic and elaborate descriptions in this abridged edition, and also to put names to many things Defoe found unnameable.

It may also be noted that this edition contains several more proper names than previously published versions. Thanks here must again go to Lovecraft and his extensive research. The writer spent countless hours sifting through historical documents in several languages for birth records, death notices, and other hints at the numerous identities Crusoe himself was oblique about, and Defoe's changes only concealed more.

The issue of time and dates throughout the manuscript should also be acknowledged. At this point in history, England was still using the Julian calendar while many European countries (most notably Spain and Portugal, which figure heavily into the tale) had switched to the modern Gregorian calendar, and there is evidence Crusoe switches freely between the two. While logs, harbor records, and shipping manifests allow us to pinpoint certain moments in the narrative (Lovecraft notes a special thanks to the Cape Cod Maritime Museum), Crusoe's years on the island are documented only by himself. He gives numerous dates throughout his records, yet they very rarely match with one another and inconsistencies are common. At one point in the manuscript October comes just seven months after the previous November, and mid-December follows just two weeks later. Some see this inaccuracy as a sign of Crusoe's degenerating sanity, using the rest of the manuscript as evidence thereof. Lovecraft himself notes the time inconsistencies only occur during Crusoe's years on the island, and sees it as a sign of just how dangerous that place is.

As a final historical note, this view was shared by the Royal British Navy and the modern Trinidad and Tobago Defense Force. After the rediscovery of Crusoe's island in 1890, and the subsequent investigation and explorations, the British fleet began an unofficial blockade that lasted through World War II. When Trinidad and Tobago became an independent nation in 1962, this blockade became a state-mandated 10 mile quarantine zone around the island. To this day two TTDF coast guard large patrol craft are always on maneuvers there.

—P. C.
Los Angeles, March 1st, 2010

THE EERIE ADVENTURES OF THE
LYCANTHROPE
ROBINSON CRUSOE

My family, my nature, my first voyage

I was born on the last day of the full moon in the year 1632, in the city of York, of a good family, tho' not of that country, my father being a foreigner who had fled the Prince-Archbishopric of Bremen and settled first at Hull. He got a good estate by merchandise, and leaving off his trade, lived afterwards at York, from whence he had married my mother, whose relations were named Robinson and from whom I was called Robinson Kreisszahn. By the usual corruption of words in England we are now called, nay we call ourselves, and write, our name Crusoe.

I had two elder brothers, both of the same bloodline and inheritance as myself. One was lieutenant-colonel to an English regiment of foot in Flanders, commanded by the famous Colonel Lockhart, and was killed at the battle near Dunkirk when he was run thru with a silver saber. What became of my second brother I was never told, though I was led to guess he had succumb'd to the life of the beast afore I was old enough to know him.

Being the third son of the family, and bred with the wild blood of my sire, my head began to be fill'd very early with rambling thoughts. My father had given me a competent share of learning and designed me for the law. But I would be satisfied with nothing but going to sea. My inclination led me so strongly against the commands of my father, and against all the entreaties and persuasions of my mother and other friends, that there seemed to be something fatal in that propension of nature, tending to the life of misery which was to befall me.

My father, a wise and grave man, gave me serious counsel one morning against what he foresaw was my design. He asked me what reasons more than a mere wandering inclination I had for leaving his house and my native country, where I had a prospect of raising my fortune by application and industry, with a life of ease and safety. Mine, he said, was a life of legend hidden by necessity. One ruled by the Moon and her brilliance, one which he had found was best suited to a quiet life of stability and routine. He bid me observe it and I should always find the calamities of life were shared among the upper and lower part of mankind. The middle station had the fewest disasters. Peace and plenty were the handmaids of a middle fortune. This way men went silently and smoothly through the world and comfortably out of it. Not embarrassed with the labours of the hands or of the head. Not harassed with perplexed circumstances, which rob the soul of peace, and the body of rest. Nor hunted by the mobs of townsfolk and churchmen. Not enraged with the animal passion of the beast or the secret hunger for flesh.

After this he press'd me earnestly, and in the most affectionate manner, not to play the young man, not to precipitate myself into miseries which the life I was born in provided against. He would do well for me and endeavour to enter me fairly into the station of life which he had been just recommending to me. To close, he told me I had my elder brother for an example, to whom he had used the same earnest persuasions to keep him from going into the Low

Country wars, but could not prevail, his young desires prompting him to run into the army, where he was killed. Tho' my father said he would not cease to pray for me, yet he would venture to say to me that if I did take this foolish step God would not bless me, and I would have leisure hereafter to reflect upon having neglected his counsel, when there might be none to assist in my control or recovery.

I observ'd, in this last part of his discourse, the tears run down his face very plentifully, especially when he spoke of my brother who was kill'd. When he spoke of my having none to assist me, he was so moved he broke off the discourse and told me his heart was so full he could say no more to me.

I was sincerely affected with this discourse, as indeed who could be otherwise? I resolv'd not to think of going abroad any more, but to settle at home according to my father's desire. But, alas! a few days wore it all off. In short, to prevent any of my father's further importunities, a few weeks after I resolv'd to run quite away from him.

It was not till almost a year after this I broke loose, tho' in the mean time I continued deaf to all proposals of settling to business, and frequently expostulated with my father and mother about their being so determined against what they knew my inclinations prompted me to. Being one day at Hull, where I went casually, and without any purpose of making an elopement at that time, one of my companions, Jakob Martense, then going by sea to London, in his father's ship, prompted me to go with them with the common allurement of seafaring men— it should cost me nothing for my passage.

I consulted neither father nor mother any more, not so much as sent them word of it, leaving them to hear of it as they might. In an ill hour, God knows, on the first of September, 1651, the day after the last night of the moon, I went on board a ship bound for London.

Never any young adventurer's misfortunes, I believe, began sooner or continued longer than mine. The ship was no sooner gotten out of the Humber but the wind began to blow and the waves to rise in a most frightful manner. As I had never been at sea before, I was most inexpressibly sick in body and terrified in mind. I began now seriously to reflect upon what I had done, and how I was overtaken by the judgment of Heaven for leaving my father's house and abandoning my duty. All the good counsel of my parents, my father's tears and my mother's entreaties, came now fresh into my mind. My conscience reproached me with the breach of my duty to my father.

All this while the storm encreas'd and the sea went very high, tho' nothing like what I have seen many times since. But it was enough to affect me then, for I was but a young sailor. I expected every wave would have swallowed us up, and every time the ship fell down in the trough or hollow of the sea I thought we should never rise more.

In this agony of mind I made many vows and resolutions. If it would please God here to spare my life this one voyage, if ever I got once my foot upon dry land again, I would go directly home to my father, and never set it into a ship again while I liv'd. Now I saw plainly the goodness of his observations about the middle station of life. How easy, how comfortably he had liv'd all his days and nights, and never had been exposed to tempests at sea or troubles on shore. I resolv'd I would, like a true repenting prodigal, go home to my father.

But the next day, as the wind was abated and the sea calmer, I began to be a little inured to it. The sun went down clear and rose so the next morning. I had slept well in the night and was now no more sea-sick, but very cheerful, looking with wonder upon the sea that was so rough and terrible the day before, yet could be so calm and so pleasant in a little time after.

And now my companion, Jakob, who had indeed enticed me away, came to me and said, "Well, Bob," clapping me on the shoulder, "how do you do after it? I warrant you were frightened, wa'n't you, last night, when it blew but a cap-full of wind?"

"A cap-full do you call it?" said I. "It was a terrible storm."

"A storm, you fool," replied he, "do you call that a storm? Why it was nothing at all. Give us but a good ship and sea-room and we think nothing of such a squall of wind as that. But you're but a fresh-water sailor, Bob. Come, let us make a bowl of punch and we'll forget all that. Do you see what charming weather it is now?"

To make short this sad part of my story, we went the old way of all sailors. The punch was made, I was made drunk with it, and in one night's wickedness I drowned all my repentance and all my resolutions for my future. I had, in five or six days, got as complete a victory over conscience as any young fellow who resolv'd not to be troubled with it could desire.

But I was to have another trial for it still, and Providence resolv'd to leave me entirely without excuse. For if I would not take this for a deliverance, the next was to be such a one as the worst and most hardened wretch among us would confess both the danger and the mercy.

The sixth day of our being at sea we came into Yarmouth Roads. The wind having been contrary and the weather calm, we had made but little way since the storm. Here we were obliged to come to anchor and here we lay, the wind continuing contrary for seven or eight days, during which a great many ships from Newcastle came into the same roads, as it was the common harbour where the ships might wait for a wind for the River.

We had not, however, rid here so long but the wind blew too fresh, and after we had lain four or five days, blew very hard. However, the Roads being reckon'd as good as a harbour, and our ground tackle very strong, our men were unconcerned. But the eighth day in the morning the wind increased. We had all hands at work to strike our top-masts and make every thing snug and close so that the ship might ride as easy as possible. By noon the sea went very high indeed. Our ship rode forecastle in and we thought once or twice our anchor had come home, upon which our master ordered out the sheet anchor. So we rode with two anchors a-head and the cables veer'd out to the better end.

By this time it blew a terrible storm indeed, and now I began to see terror and amazement in the faces even of the seamen themselves. The master, tho' vigilant in the business of preserving the ship, yet as he went in and out of his cabin by me I could hear him softly say to himself several times, "God, be merciful to us! We shall be all lost. We shall be all undone!" So soft were his words that the Lord's name came to my ears as "Gon," though I knew it was not.

During these first hurries I cannot describe my temper. I could ill reassume the first penitence which I had so trampled upon. I thought the bitterness of death had been past, and this would be nothing like the first. But when the master himself came by me, as I said just now, and said we should be all lost, I was dreadfully frighted. I looked out, but such a dismal sight I never saw.

The sea went mountains high and broke upon us every three or four minutes, and in the deep water tween the waves I glimpsed great shapes, like pale eels, each the size and length of a goodly cottage. Our men cried out a ship which rid about a mile a-head of us was overrun by shoggoths, which I took to mean the high waves. Two more ships, being driven from their anchors, were run out of the roads to sea with not a mast standing.

Towards evening, the mate and boatswain begged the master of our ship to let them cut away the fore-mast, which he was very unwilling to do, but the boatswain protested to him if he did not the ship would founder. He consented, and when they had cut away the fore-mast the main-mast stood so loose and shook the ship so much they were obliged to cut her away also and make a clear deck.

Anyone may judge what a condition I was in at all this, who was but a young sailor. But if I can express the thoughts I had about me, I was in tenfold more horror of mind upon account of my former convictions, and having returned from them, than I was at death itself. These, added to the terror of the storm, put me in such a condition I can by no words describe it.

But the worst was not come yet. The storm continued with such fury the seamen themselves acknowledged they had never known a worse. We had a good ship, but she was deep laden and wallowed in the sea. The seamen every now and then cried out she would fall to the shoggoths. It was my advantage, in one respect, that I did not know what they meant by shoggoths. However, the storm was so violent, I saw what is not often seen; the master, the boatswain, and some others more sensible than the rest, at their prayers, though the words and language of their prayers were unknown to me. When the boatswain saw me intruding upon their time with their Lord and master, I was given a heated glare and sent away.

In the middle of the night one of the men cried out we had sprung a leak. All hands were called to the pump. At that very word my heart died within me and I fell backwards upon the side of my bed where I sat. However, the men roused me and told me I who was able to do nothing was as well able to pump as another. I stirred up and went to the pump and worked very heartily.

While this was doing, the master, seeing some light colliers who would not come near us, ordered us to fire a gun as a signal of distress. I was so surprised I thought the ship had broke or some dreadful thing had happened. We worked on but it was apparent the ship would founder. Tho' the storm began to abate a little, it was not possible she could swim till we might run into a port, so the master continued firing guns for help. A light ship who had rid it out just ahead of us ventured a boat out to help. It was with the utmost hazard the boat came near us, till at last the men rowed very heartily, and ventured their lives to save ours. Our men cast them a rope over the stern which they took hold of. We hauled them close under our stern and got all into their boat.

We were not much more than a quarter of an hour out of our ship but we saw her sink. Then I understood for the first time what was meant by shoggoths. I must acknowledge I had hardly eyes to look up when the seamen told me she was overrun. The shapes, like pale worms or catter-pillers, tore at the hull and twisted upon the deck. From that moment, my heart was dead within me, partly with fright, partly with horror of mind, and the thoughts of what was yet before me. They rode the ship beneath the waves, and the boatswain said another prayer to the Lord, whom he also muttered as "—Gon."

While we were in this condition, the men yet labouring at the oar to bring the boat near the shore, we could see a great many people running along the strand to assist us. We made slow way towards the shore, nor were we able to reach it till, being past the light-house at Winterton, the shore falls off to the westward so the land broke off a little of the violence of the wind. Here we got all safe on shore and walked afterwards on foot to Yarmouth, where, as unfortunate men, we were met with great humanity by the magistrates of the town, who assign'd us good quarters and had money given us sufficient to carry us either to London or back to Hull, as we thought fit.

But my ill fate pushed me on now with an obstinacy nothing could resist. Tho' I had several times loud calls from my reason to go back to Hull, I had no power to do it, even with the moon a week upon me. Certainly, nothing but some such decreed, unavoidable misery which was impossible for me to escape could have pushed me forward against the calm reasonings and persuasions of my most retired thoughts, and against two such visible instructions as I had met with in my first attempt.

My comrade, Jakob, who had helped to harden me before, and who was the master's son, was now less forward. The first time he spoke to me after we were at Yarmouth, which was not till two or three days, for we were separated in the town to several quarters, it appeared his tone was altered. Shaking his head, he asked me how I did, telling his father who I was and how I had come this voyage only for a trial, in order to go farther abroad.

Master Martenese turn'd to me with a very grave and concerned tone. "Young man," said he, "you ought never to go to sea any more. You ought to take this for a plain and visible token you are not to be a seafaring man."

"Why, Sir," said I, "will you go to sea no more?"

"That is another case," said he. "It is my calling, and therefore my duty. But as you made this voyage for a trial, you see what a taste Heaven has given you of what you are to expect if you persist. Perhaps this has all befallen us on your account, like Jonah in the ship of Tarshish. Pray," continued he, "what are you, and on what account did you go to sea?"

Upon that I started that he may be experienc'd in the ways of knowing the beast in mortal form, for it was four days fore the first night of the moon and the signs were most definitely upon me. Yet I was not certain of his meaning, for he seem'd not afraid. So I told him but some of my story, of my defiance of my father, and of my inclinations against his wishes.

At the end he burst out with a strange kind of passion. "What had I done," says he, "that such an unhappy wretch should come into my ship? I would not set my foot in the same ship with thee again for a thousand pounds." This indeed was, as I said, an excursion of his spirits, which were yet agitated by the sense of his loss, and was farther than he could have authority to go. However, he afterwards talked very gravely to me, exhorting me to go back to my father, and not tempt Providence to my ruin. "And young man," said he, "depend upon it, if you do not go back, wherever you go, you will meet with nothing but disasters and disappointments, till your father's words are fulfill'd upon you."

We parted soon after, for I made him little answer, and I saw Jakob and his father no more. As for me, having some money in my pocket, I traveled to London by land. On the road I had many struggles with myself. By the sun I dwelt on what course of life I should take, and whether I should go home, or go to sea. And by night, I let the beast come upon me as it has been wont to do since the first moon of my tenth year, and it kill'd many sheep and a cow.

My second voyage, my third voyage, my life among the Moors

I remained some time uncertain what course of life to lead. As I stayed a while, the remembrance of the distress I had been in wore off. As that abated, the little notion I had in my desires to a return wore off with it, till at last I quite laid aside the thoughts of it and looked out for a voyage.

That evil influence which carried me away from my father's house hurried me into the wild notion of raising my fortune, and impressed those conceits so forcibly upon me as to make me deaf to all good advice. I went on board a vessel bound to the coast of Africk, or, as our sailors call it, a voyage to Guinea.

It was my great misfortune that in all these adventures I did not ship myself as a sailor. I might have learnt the duty and office of a foremast-man. I might, in time, have qualified myself for a mate or lieutenant, if not for a master. But as it was always my fate to choose for the worse, so I did here. Having money in my pocket and good cloathes upon my back, I would always go on board in the habit of a gentleman, and so I neither had any business in the ship or learnt to do any.

It was my lot first of all to fall into pretty good company in London, which does not always happen to such loose and unguided young fellows as I then was. I fell acquainted with the master of a ship who had been on the coast of Guinea. He was resolv'd to go again, having had very good success there. Hearing me say I had a mind to see the world, he told me if I would go the voyage with him I should be at no expense. I should be his messmate and his companion. If I could carry any thing with me, I should have all the advantage of it that the trade would admit.

I embraced the offer and entered into a strict friendship with this captain, who was an honest and plain-dealing man. I went the voyage with him and carried a small investment with me, which, by the honesty of my friend the captain, I increased very considerably. For I carried about £40 in such toys and trifles as the captain directed me to buy. This £40 I had mustered together by the assistance of some of my relations whom I corresponded with, and who, I believe, got my father, or at least my mother, to contribute so much as that to my first adventure.

This was the only voyage which was successful in all my adventures, which I owe to the integrity and honesty of my friend the captain. Under him also I got a competent knowledge of the mathematics and rules of navigation, learnt how to keep an account of the ship's course, take an observation, and, in short, to understand some things that were needful to be understood by a sailor. In a word, this voyage made me both a sailor and a merchant, for I brought home five pounds nine ounces of gold-dust for my adventure, which yielded me in London at my return almost £300. This fill'd me with those aspiring thoughts which have so completed my ruin.

Yet even in this voyage I had my misfortunes too. I was continually sick, being thrown into a violent calenture by the excessive heat of the climate, our principal trading being upon the coast, from the latitude of 15 degrees north even to the line itself. I also pass'd no less than six moons on board, and while four were hid in my cabin by the fierce fever which even quell'd the beast, two I spent in the deep bowels of the ship's brig clapped in irons. True, plain iron could not contain the beast, but my father had shewn me, as a lad, how a few silver coins can be placed within knots and against locks, and thus they are render'd incorruptible before the beast's fearsome strength.

I was now set up for a Guinea trader. My friend, to my great misfortune, dying soon after his arrival, I resolv'd to go the same voyage again and I embarked in the same vessel, once again after the last night of the full moon. Alas! I fell into terrible misfortunes in this voyage.

Our ship, making her course between the Canary Islands and the African shore, was surprised in the grey of the morning by a Turkish rover of Sallee who gave chase to us with all the sail she could make. We crowded as much canvas as our yards would spread or our masts carry, but finding the pirate gained upon us, and would come up with us in a few hours, we prepared to fight.

He came up with us, bringing to just athwart our quarter, and we brought eight of our guns to bear on that side and poured in a broadside upon him. This then made him sheer off after returning fire and pouring in also his small-shot from near 200 men which he had on board. However, we had not a man touched, all our men keeping close.

He prepared to attack us again and we to defend ourselves. Laying us on board the next time upon our other quarter, he entered sixty men upon our decks who fell to cutting and hacking the sails and rigging. We plied them with small-shot, half-pikes, powder-chests, and such, and cleared our deck of them twice. During this fighting, I wish'd I could call out the beast as my father has told me his father could, but alas! I was still young and foolish, and the nights of the full moon were still more than a week away.

However, to cut short this melancholy part of our story, our ship being disabled, three of our men killed and eight wounded, we were obliged to yield. We were carried into Sallee, a port belonging to the Moors. I was not carried up to the emperor's court, as the rest of our prisoners were, but was kept by the captain of the rover as his proper prize and made his slave.

At this surprising change of my circumstances, from a merchant to a miserable slave, I was perfectly overwhelmed. I looked back upon my father's prophetic discourse to me, that I should be miserable and have none to relieve me. Now the hand of Heaven had overtaken me and I was undone without redemption. But this was but a taste of the misery I was to go through.

As my new patron, or master, had taken me home to his house, so I was in hopes he would take me with him when he went to sea again, believing it would sometime or other be his fate to be taken by a Spanish or Portugal man of war and then I should be set at liberty. But this hope of mine was soon taken away, for my patron, it seem'd, knew the signs of my nature and had kept me thus for himself. The day of the first moon, stout manakles, plated with silver, were brought, and in my patron's courtyard I was strip'd naked and chayn'd to a fountain. Many wise men and vizeers came to view me and study me, for they had heard of *almustazeb*, which was their word for the beast.

The moon rose and the mantle of the beast came upon me. When this happens, my flesh is burned with unseen fire and great aches and pains fill my limbs and jaw. The world is as if seen thru a lens darken'd with smoke, and heard as if a heavy woolen blanket wrapt round my head. Yet always I have no more freedom than a helpless passenger on a storm-wrack'd ship with a mad captain, and that captain is the beast. I could see the wise men as they discust my change and the beast before them, but their words were but noise, and to my intoxicated mind they look'd like good, succulent meat does to a starv'd man. I could remember they did feed the beast a young lamb, but also prickt its flesh and pluckt its fur and sketch'd it for their scrolls.

The three nights pass'd, and I was left chayn'd thru-out, yet during the day my needs were cared for. I was given wine and shayde and fish and good flat bread which they call'd *peetah*. Here I meditated nothing but my escape and what method I might take to effect it, but found no way that had the least probability in it.

On the morning after the third night of the moon, I was freed of the silver manakles, which had left welts and blisters on my flesh, and my cloathes return'd to me. I was then order'd by my patron to look after his little garden, and do the common drudgery of slaves about his house. When he came home from his cruise, were he absent for a time, he order'd me to lie in the cabin to look after the ship.

Thus it was for four weeks, until the moon was close again. Then the manakles appear'd once more and I was chayn'd naked yet again where the other slaves could not see me. Two of the wise men return'd to witness my changes again, and with them three new scholars and a new vizeer I had not lay'd eyes on before.

This, then, is how each of my months pass'd in Sallee. The wise men would study the beast each night of the moon, and I would feel the pain and rage of it at being chayn'd and unable to run free as was its nature. The scholars would discourse with me during the day, and many of them spoke Spanish, of which I spoke only a little, and good King's English, of which I could of course speak freely, and they would ask many questions, viz. what was my name and my age and for how long I had carry'd the beast within me, and of my history and family, and if they carry'd the beast as well. But my father had long instructed not to speak of family, and so these questions I would not answer.

Many times in these conversations would come mention of a great book or work, which they called *Nekri Nomikan*. I asked of the nature of this work, but depending on which of the wise men I asked, each would give a different answer. One vizeer call'd it a book of history which told of things like the *almustazeb*, while another spoke of it as like a Bible, but for the worship of dark, heathen gods. Still another told it as a book of magick written by a sorcerer who had been driven mad by the writing of it.

After about two years of this life, an odd circumstance presented itself which put the thought of making some attempt for my liberty again in my head. My patron used once or twice a week, sometimes oftener, to go out into the road a-fishing. He always took me (when it was between moons) and a young Moresco with him. We made him very merry, and I proved very dexterous in catching fish, insomuch that sometimes he would send me with one of his kinsmen and the youth to catch a dish of fish for him.

Having the long-boat of our English ship, he ordered the carpenter of his ship to build a little cabin in the middle of the long-boat, like that of a barge, with a place to stand behind it to steer. She sail'd with a shoulder-of-mutton sail, and the boom gibbed over the top of the cabin, which lay very snug and low, and had in it room for him to lie and a table to eat on, with some small lockers.

It happened he had appointed to go out in this boat with two or three Moors of some distinction and had therefore sent on board a larger store of provisions than ordinary, and had order'd me to get ready three fuzees with powder and shot, for they design'd some sport of fowling as well as fishing.

I got all things ready as he had directed and waited the next morning with the boat washt clean, her ensign and pendants out, and every thing to accommodate his guests. By and by my patron came on board alone and told me his guests had put off going, upon some business that fell out. He order'd me with the man and boy, as usual, to go out with the boat and catch them some fish, for his friends were to sup at his house, and commanded as soon as I got some fish I should bring it home to his house.

This moment my former notions of deliverance darted into my thoughts, for now I found I was like to have a little ship at my command. My master being gone, I prepar'd to furnish myself for a voyage.

My first contrivance was to make a pretence to speak to this Moor, to get something for our subsistence on board. I told him we must not presume to eat of our patron's bread.

He said, "That is true." So he brought a large basket of rusk, or bisket of their kind, and three jars with fresh water into the boat. I knew where my patron's case of bottles stood and I conveyed them into the boat while the Moor was on shore, as if they had been there before for our master. I conveyed also a great lump of bees-wax into the boat, which weighed above half a hundred weight, with a parcel of twine or thread, a hatchet, a saw, and a hammer. His name was Ismael, whom they call Moley. So I called him. "Moley," said I, "our patron's guns are on board the boat. Can you not get a little powder and shot? It may be we may kill some alcamies for ourselves, for I know he keeps the gunner's stores in the ship."

"Yes," says he. "I'll bring some." Accordingly he brought a great leather pouch which held about a pound and a half of powder, and another with shot, and put all into the boat. At the same time I had found some powder of my master's in the great cabin, with which I fill'd one of the large bottles in the case, which was almost empty, pouring what was in it into another. Thus furnished with every thing needful, we sailed out of the port to fish. The castle, which is at the entrance of the port, knew who we were and took no notice of us.

We were not above a mile out of the port before we hauled in our sail and set us down to fish. The wind blew from the north, which was contrary to my desire. Had it blown southerly, I had been sure to have made the coast of Spain and at least reached to the bay of Cadiz. But my resolutions were, blow which way it would, I would be gone from that horrid place where I was prickt each moon and leave the rest to fate.

After we had fished some time and catched nothing, I said to the Moor, "This will not do. Our master will not be thus served. We must stand farther off."

Ismael, thinking no harm, agreed and set the sails. As I had the helm I run the boat out near a league farther, and then brought her to as if I would fish. Giving the boy the helm, I stept forward to where the Moor was and I took him by surprise, with my arm under his waist, and toss'd him clear overboard.

He rose immediately, for he swam like a cork, and begged to be taken in. He swam so strong after the boat he would have reached me very quickly. I stept into the cabin and, fetching one of the fowling-pieces, I presented it at him. Said I to he, "You swim well enough to reach to the shore and the sea is calm. Make the best of your way to shore and I will do you no harm. But if you come near the boat I'll shoot you through the head, for I am resolv'd to have my liberty."

So Ismael turned himself about, and swam for the shore, and I make no doubt but he reached it with ease.

When he was gone I turned to the boy, whom they called Xury, and said to him, "Xury, if you will be faithful to me I'll make you a great man. But if you will not swear by Mahomet and your father's beard to be true to me, I must throw you into the sea too."

The boy smiled in my face and spoke so innocently I could not mistrust him. He swore to be faithful to me and go all over the world with me.

While I was in view of Ismael, I stood out directly to sea with the boat, rather than stretching to windward, so that they might think me gone towards the Straits' mouth (as indeed any one that had been in their wits must have been supposed to do), for who would have supposed we were sailed on to the southward to the Barbarian coast, where whole nations of Negroes were sure to surround us with the canoes, and destroy us? Where we could never once go on shore but we should be devour'd by savage creatures, or more merciless savages of human kind?

But as soon as it grew dusk in the evening, I changed my course, and steered south and by east, bending my course a little toward the east, that I might keep in with the shore. Having a fair, fresh gale of wind, and a smooth, quiet sea, I made such sail that I believe by the next afternoon, when I first made the land, I could not be less than 150 miles south of Sallee, quite beyond the Emperor of Morocco's dominions, or indeed of any other king thereabout, for we saw no people.

My flight along the coast, Xury's terror,
my salvation

S uch was the fright I had taken at the Moors, and the dreadful apprehensions I had of falling into their hands, I would not stop or go on shore or come to an anchor. The wind continuing fair till I had sailed in that manner five days, I concluded if any vessels were in chase of me they also would now give over. So I ventured to make to the coast and come to an anchor in the mouth of a little river, I knew not what, or where. Neither what latitude, what country, what nation, or what river. I neither saw, nor desired to see, any people. The principal thing I wanted was fresh water. We came into this creek in the evening, resolving to swim on shore as soon as it was dark and discover the country. But as soon as it was quite dark, we heard such dreadful noises of the barking, roaring, and howling of wild creatures, of we knew not what kinds. The sounds carry'd no fright for me, for animals can smell the beast beneath my skin and will most always shy away from my kind, but the poor boy was ready to die with fear and begged of me not to go on shore till day.

"Well, Xury," said I, "then I won't. But it may be we may see men by day who will be as bad to us as those lions."

"Then we give them the shoot gun," says Xury, laughing, "make them run wey." Such English Xury spoke by conversing among us slaves. However I was glad to see the boy so cheerful, and I gave him a dram (out of our patron's case of bottles) to cheer him up. After all, Xury's advice was good, and I took it. We dropped our little anchor and lay still all night. I say still for we slept none. In two or three hours, we saw vast great creatures of many sorts come down to the sea-shore and run into the water, wallowing and washing for the pleasure of cooling themselves. They made such hideous howlings and yellings that I never indeed heard the like, even from the beast.

Xury was dreadfully frighten'd, and indeed so was I too, for I bethought myself that the animals of Africk may not be aware of the beast and would not avoid it. But we were both more frighten'd when we heard one of these mighty creatures come swimming towards our boat. We could not see him, but we might hear him by his blowing to be a monstrous huge and furious animal. Xury said it was a lion, and it might be so for aught I know. Poor Xury cried to me to weigh the anchor and row away.

"No, Xury," said I. "We can slip our cable with the buoy to it and go off to sea. They cannot follow us far." I had no sooner said so but I perceived the creature (whatever it was) within two oars' length, which something surprised me. However, I stepped to the cabin-door and taking up my gun, fired at him. He turned about and swam towards the shore again.

But it is impossible to describe the horrible noises and cries and howlings that were raised upon the noise or report of the gun, a thing I have some reason to believe those creatures had never heard before. This convinced me there was no going on shore for us in the night upon that coast, and how to venture on shore in the day was another question too. To have fallen into the hands of any of the savages, which would not know the beast, would have been as bad as to have fallen into the hands of lions and tygers, and we were equally apprehensive of the danger of it.

Be that as it would, we were obliged to go on shore somewhere or other for water, for we had not a pint left in the boat. When or where to get it was the point. Xury said if I would let him go on shore with one of the jars, he would find if there was any water and bring some to me. I asked him why he would go? Why I should not go and he stay in the boat? The boy answered with so much affection that made me love him ever after. Said he, "If wild mans come, they eat me, you go wey."

"Well, Xury," said I, "we will both go, and if the wild mans come, we will kill them. They shall eat neither of us."

So I gave Xury a piece of rusk bread to eat and a dram out of our patron's case of bottles. We hauled the boat in as near the shore as we thought was proper, and so waded to shore, carrying nothing but our arms and two jars for water.

I did not care to go out of sight of the boat, fearing the coming of canoes with savages down the river, but the boy seeing a low place about a mile up the country, rambled to it. By and by I saw him come running towards me. I thought he was pursued by some savage, or frighted with some wild creature, and I ran forward towards him to help him, but when I came nearer I saw something hanging over his shoulders, which was a creature he had shot, like a hare but different in colour and longer legs. However, we were very glad of it and it was very good meat, but the great joy poor Xury came with was to tell me he had found good water and seen no wild mans.

But we found afterwards we need not take such pains for water, for a little higher up the creek we found the water fresh when the tyde was out, which flows but a little way up. So we fill'd our jars and feasted on the hare we had killed and prepared to go on our way, having seen no footsteps of any human creature in that part of the country. My hope was if I stood along this coast till I came to that part where the English traded, I should find some of their vessels upon their usual design of trade that would relieve and take us in.

By the best of my calculation, this place where I now was must have been that country which lies waste and uninhabited except by wild things. The Negroes having abandoned it and gone farther south for fear of the Moors. The Moors not thinking it worth inhabiting by reason of its barrenness. Both forsaking it because of the prodigious numbers of tigers, lions, and leopards, and other furious creatures which harbour there. The Moors used it for their hunting only, where they go like an army, two or three thousand men at a time. Indeed for near a hundred miles together upon this coast we saw nothing but a waste, uninhabited country by day, and heard nothing but howlings and roaring of wild creatures by night.

We made on to the southward for ten or twelve days, living very sparing on our provisions, which began to abate very much, and going no oftener into the shore than we were obliged to for fresh water. My design in this was to make the river Gambia or Senegal, that is to say, any where about the Cape de Verd, where I was in hopes to meet with some European ship. If I did not, I knew not what course I had to take, but to seek for the islands, or perish there among the Negroes. I knew all the ships from Europe which sailed either to the coast of Guinea, to Brasil, or to the East Indies made this Cape or those islands. In a word, I put the whole of my fortune upon this single point. Either I must meet with some ship, or must perish.

Several times I was obliged to land for fresh water, and once in particular, being early in the afternoon, we came to an anchor under a little point of land which was pretty high. I was fill'd with concern for Xury, as this was to be the first night of the full moon, the first since our escape from the Moors. Several times during our voyage I had ask'd what he knew of the visiting wise men and vizeers, but the boy knew only that they came to study with our former patron, and not at all of my nature or my part in these studies. So I told him that I must go ashore for the night, into the higher country, and he was to wait for me on the boat and not follow. I would return in the morning.

This upset Xury a great deal, and more so when he heard I would take no arms with me, for I did not want to risk losing my gun while the beast ran free. He cried and spoke dire warnings and said I would not be safe without him. I assur'd him I would be fine and had him remember I would be back on the shore in the morning. It upset him but I knew he would obey my commands, so great was his love for me.

As the sun set I waded into shore and bade the boy to sleep well. I wander'd till the shore was quite out of sight, and Xury could not see me as well. Here I remov'd what cloathes I had, which was precious little as I still wore the cloathes of my servitude to the Moors, viz. breeches, waistcoat, linen shirt, and kerchief. These I placed in a tree atop a high branch and walked still farther, expos'd now, were any other man there to see.

The sun went down and it was but a few hours later that the moon rose and the beast came upon me with great savage glee, for it sensed from deep within my skin it was not to be chayn'd this night. As a rule, the first night of the moon is gentle as that heavenly orb becomes full and true, but not this time, for after two years of silver chayns so quick it rush'd out that I did scream from the pain of it before its nature made me numb and distant.

I know the beast took great joy that night, for it had never been amidst such savagery, and I knew its pleasure through the smoky haze of my dream in the same way a man knows his horse or dog is happy and satisfied. It ran and kill'd and ate and howled and ran more and kill'd more and ate more. This was a danger my father had taught against us, for to appease the beast makes it stronger and gives it a better purchase upon one's thoughts and immortal soul.

I awoke the next day on a patch of soft grass that had been press'd down and made a most serviceable bed. A few scratches marr'd my arms and legs, but I was well rested and had no hunger, a fact I chose not to dwell on. It took but a short time to locate the tree with my cloathes, left on the high branch just as I had plac'd them. I walked back to the shore, where Xury greet'd me with joyous cries, for he told me the howls and screams of the night before had been far worse than any we had heard, and he feared I had met whatever fearsome creature he had heard, not knowing it was now within my skin while we spoke. "He eat you at one mouth," said Xury. One mouthful he meant.

We made our way south for the day, and that night we again dropp'd anchor and I went ashore. Xury wailed again at my leaving, but not as much as before, and I once more spent the night in the high country of Africk. The beast spent another night of savage debauchery beneath the moon, and when I came upon my own natures again, I was so deep in the forest I could not see the sun to acquaint myself with the cardinal directions. It was most unpleasant to me to spend hours walking uncloathed in the forest like a savage. After some time I found a clearing and did orient myself, yet it was still well into the second half of the day when I locat'd the tree with my cloathes, but was most put out to discover they had fallen from the tree and my good linen shirt was soiled by some creature.

It being too late to return to the boat, I call'd out to Xury from shore. The boy was in a state and from the sand I saw tears in his eyes. He cried out in joy and begg'd me not to leave him again, for he was sure a great creature had eaten me up. I told him I must spend one more night in the high country, but in the morning we would resume our journey. He was most displeas'd at the thought of another night alone, and wailed for me to let him join me on the shore. I told him he could not, for he was small and the creatures of Africk truly would "eat him at one mouth."

I left him in tears on the boat and travel'd back away from the water. I was in process of storing my cloathes in the tree again, but not my good linen shirt, which I had abandoned upon finding it soiled and foul, and had not yet removed my breeches when the sun set and the nature of the beast came over me. I did try to fight it off, for the binding of cloathes angers the beast, but it was too eager to be free in the high country again. Through the smok'd lens I watched it struggle and fight with the breeches, and become more and more savage by their simple constrictions.

The beast kill'd many creatures that night, and in my dreams were the dim memories of a dreadful monster that it fought with for close on an hour afore it fell to the inhuman power of the beast's claws and teeth.

I woke in the shade, and the first thought was I was not in the high country, for there was white sand beneath me. I still wore my breeches, though they were rent and torn to be all but useless to me. They too had been soiled, as was my good linen shirt, though these by the beast.

I started at once, for next to me on the sand was a terrible great lion, on its side as if still asleep in the morning sun. I felt great fear for a moment but then saw it was dead and could not hurt me. Indeed, one leg was torn right off as one would tear apart a roast fowl, and much of the meat of its stomach was gone. The claw marks and teeth marks were most familiar to me, and left me with no question that the beast had dispatched this great lion.

I stood up and now saw the lion had been felled and lay between myself and the coast, and there was my boat just off shore, and there was little Xury staring with wide eyes and trembling with a great fear in him. He stood upon our boat's little deck holding in his hands our biggest gun, which was almost musket-bore. He stair'd at me as one does at awful things, and I knew in his eyes his kind and goodly master now was an awful thing, for I could but suppose what he had seen in the night and now come the morning.

I waved to him and spoke kind words and told him to be not afraid, but still he shivered and held the fuzee. At last, I order'd him to shore and to bring the hatchet from the cabin. This firm tone help'd calm him and, taking the little hatchet in one hand, he swam to shore with the other hand, coming close to me, though still his eyes were wide.

I bethought myself that perhaps the skin of the lion might one way or other be of some value to us. I resolv'd to take off his skin if I could. Xury and I went to work with him, but Xury was much the better workman at it, for I knew very ill how to do it. Indeed it took us both up the whole day, but at last we got off the hide of him, and spreading it on the top of our cabin, the sun dried it in two days' time. It afterwards served me to lie upon. Xury would no longer sleep near me, nor did he smile or talk.

I made forward for about three days more, without offering to go near the shore, till I saw the land run out a great length into the sea, at about the distance of four or five leagues before me. The sea being very calm, I kept a large offing, to make this point. At length, doubling the point, at about two leagues from the land, I saw plainly land on the other side to seaward. I concluded, as it was most certain indeed, this was the Cape de Verd and those the islands called, from thence, Cape de Verd Islands. However, they were at a great distance and I could not well tell what I had best to do, for if I should be taken with a gale of wind I might neither reach one nor the other.

In this dilemma, as I was very pensive, I stepped into the cabin and sat me down, Xury having the helm. On a sudden, the boy cried out, "Master, master, a ship with a sail!" The foolish boy was frightened out of his wits, thinking it must be some of his master's ships sent to pursue us, when I knew we were gotten far enough out of their reach. I jumped out of the cabin and saw it was a Portuguese ship, and was bound to the coast of Guinea for Negroes. But when I observ'd the course she steered, I was soon convinced they were bound some other way and did not design to come any nearer to the shore.

With all the sail I could make, I found I should not be able to come in their way. They would be gone by before I could make any signal to them. But after I had crowded to the utmost and began to despair, they saw me by the help of their perspective glasses. So they shortened sail to let me come up. I was encouraged with this, and as I had my patron's ensign on board, I made a waft of it to them for a signal of distress and fired a gun, both which they saw. Upon these signals they very kindly brought to and lay by for me.

In about three hours' time I came up with them. They asked me what I was in Portuguese, and in Spanish, and in French, but I understood little of them. At last, a Scotch sailor who was on board called to me and I answered him and told him I was an Englishman, and I had made my escape out of slavery from the Moors at Sallee. They then bade me come on board and took me in and all my goods.

I immediately offered all I had to the captain of the ship as a return for my deliverance, but he told me he would take nothing from me. All I had should be delivered safe to me when I came to the Brasils.

"For," said he, "I have saved your life on no other terms than I would be glad to be saved myself. Besides," continued Captain Amaral, for that was his name, "when I carry you to the Brasils, if I should take from you what you have, you will be starved there, and then I only take away that life I have given. No, no, Seignior Inglese," (Mr. Englishman,) said he, "I will carry you thither in charity, and these things will help to buy your subsistence there and your passage home again."

As he was charitable in this proposal, so he was just in the performance. He ordered the seamen that none should offer to touch any thing I had. Then he took every thing into his own possession and gave me back an exact inventory of them, that I might have them, even so much as my three earthen jars.

As to my boat, it was a very good one, he saw, and told me he would buy it of me for the ship's use and asked me what I would have for it. I told him he had been so generous to me in every thing I could not offer to make any price of the boat, but left it to him, upon which he told me he would give me a note of hand to pay me eighty pieces of eight for it at Brasil. When it came there, if any one offered to give more, he would make it up.

Captain Amaral offer'd me also sixty pieces of eight more for my boy Xury. I was very loth to sell the poor boy's liberty who had assisted me so faithfully in procuring my own. Alas, the boy still often stair'd at me in fear, and had seem'd much relieved at the sight of other men, even those not of his kind. However, the captain offered me this medium, that he would give the boy an obligation to set him free in ten years, if he turned Christian. Upon my savior's kind nature, and Xury saying he was most willing to go to him, I let the captain have him.

My fortunes reverse, my plantation,
my foolishness

W e had a very good voyage to the Brasils, and arrived in the Bay de Todos los Santos, or All Saints' Bay, in about twenty-two days, and two before the first night of the moon. Xury had tried numerous times to tell his new master and the crew of the beast within my skin, but his poor slave's English allow'd me to brush aside his words as those of a small boy scared by the creatures of Africk. I was once more delivered from the most miserable of all conditions of life, and what to do next with myself I was now to consider.

The generous treatment Captain Amaral gave me I can never enough remember. He would take nothing of me for my passage, gave me forty ducats for the lion's skin which I had in my boat, and caused every thing I had in the ship to be delivered to me. What I was willing to sell, he bought of me. In a word, I made about two hundred and twenty pieces of eight of all my cargo, and with this stock I went on shore in the Brasils.

I had not been long here before I was recommended to the house of a good honest man who had an ingeino as they call it, that is, a plantation and a sugar-house. I lived with him some time and acquainted myself with the manner of planting and making of sugar. Seeing how well the planters lived, I resolv'd that if I could get a license to settle there, I would turn planter among them, endeavouring, in the mean time, to find out some way to get my money, which I had left in London, remitted to me. To this purpose, I purchased as much land as my money would reach and formed a plan for my plantation and settlement.

I had a neighbour, a Portuguese of Lisbon, but born of English parents, whose name was Wells, and in much such circumstances as I was. My stock was but low, as well as his. We rather planted for food than any thing else for about two years, and oft did he ignore the howls and roars that came from my estate at the time of the full moon. However, we began to increase and our land began to come into order. The third year we planted some tobacco, and made each of us a large piece of ground ready for planting canes in the year to come. But we both wanted help.

I was, in some degree, settled in my measures for carrying on the plantation before my kind friend, Captain Amaral, went back to England. When telling him what little stock I had left behind me in London, he gave me this friendly and sincere advice.

"Seignior Inglese," said he, for so he always called me, "if you will give me letters with orders to the person who has your money in London to send your effects to Lisbon, and in such goods as are proper for this country, I will bring you the produce of them, God willing, at my return. Howe'er, since human affairs are all subject to changes and disasters, I would have you give orders for but one hundred pounds sterling, which, you say, is half your stock, and let the hazard be run for the first, so if it come safe, you may order the rest the same way."

The merchant in London, vesting this hundred pounds in English goods such as the captain had wrote for, sent them to him at Lisbon and he brought them all safe to me at the Brasils. Without my direction, for I was too young in my business to think of them, he had taken care to have all sorts of tools, iron work, and utensils necessary for my plantation, and which were of great use to me.

When this cargo arrived, I thought my fortune made, for I was surprised with the joy of it. Captain Amaral had also laid out five pounds to purchase and bring me over a servant, under bond for six years' service, and would not accept of any consideration, except a little tobacco which I would have him accept, being of my own produce.

But as abused prosperity is oftentimes made the very means of our adversity, so was it with me. I went on the next year with great success in my plantation. I raised fifty great rolls of tobacco on my own ground, more than I had disposed of for necessaries among my neighbours. These fifty rolls, being each of above a hundred weight, were well cured and laid by against the return of the fleet from Lisbon.

You may suppose, having now lived almost four years in the Brasils, and beginning to thrive and prosper very well upon my plantation, I had not only learned the language, but had contracted an acquaintance and friendship among my fellow-planters, most of whom had accept'd my unusual and monthly hermitages. In my discourses among them I had frequently given them an account of my two voyages to the coast of Guinea, and how easy it was to purchase for trifles not only gold dust and elephants' teeth, but Negroes for service in great numbers.

It happened, being in company with some merchants and planters of my acquaintance, three of them came to me the next morning and told me they had been musing very much upon what I had discoursed with them of the last night. They came to make a secret proposal to me and, after enjoining me to secrecy, they told me they had a mind to fit out a ship to go to Guinea. They had all plantations and were straitened for nothing so much as servants. As it was a trade that could not be carried on, because they could not publicly sell the Negroes when they came home, they desired to make but one voyage to bring the Negroes on shore privately and divide them among their own plantations. The question was whether I would go in the ship to manage the trading part upon the coast of Guinea. They offered me that I should have an equal share of the Negroes without providing any part of the stock.

This was a fair proposal, it must be confessed, had it been made to any one that had not a plantation of his own to look after, which was coming to be very considerable and with a good stock upon it. But for me, that was thus entered and established, and had nothing to do but go on as I had begun for three or four years more, and could scarce have failed of being worth three or four thousand pounds sterling, and that increasing too, to think of such a voyage was the most preposterous thing that ever man in such circumstances could be guilty of.

But I who was born to be my own destroyer could no more resist the offer than I could restrain my first rambling designs, when my father's good counsel was lost upon me. I told them I would go with all my heart if they would undertake to look after my plantation in my absence, and would dispose of it to such as I should direct if I miscarried. This they all engaged to do, and entered into writings or covenants to do so. I made a formal will disposing of my plantation and effects in case of my death, making Captain Amaral my universal heir.

In short, I took all possible caution to preserve my effects and to keep up my plantation. Had I used half as much prudence to have looked into my own interest, and had made a judgment of what I ought to have done and not to have done, I had certainly never gone away from so prosperous an undertaking and gone a voyage to sea, attended with all its common hazards, to say nothing of those needs and hazards posed to one such as myself.

But I hurried on and obeyed blindly the dictates of my fancy rather than my best reason. Accordingly, the ship being fitted out, and the cargo furnished, and all things done as by agreement by my partners in the voyage, I went on board in an evil hour again, the 1st of September, 1659, being the same day eight years I went from my father and mother at Hull in order to act the rebel to their authority, and the last day of the full moon at that.

My fourth voyage, the unlock'd door, shipwrecked

O ur ship was about one hundred and twenty tons burden, carried six guns, and fourteen men, besides the master, his boy, and myself. We had on board no large cargo of goods except of such toys as were fit for our trade with the Negroes; beads, bits of glass, shells, and odd trifles, little looking-glasses, knives, scissars, hatchets, and the like. I had explain'd to the ship's master through polite discourse my occasional "fits" which would require him locking me in my cabin on some nights, and that it would please me if he and his crew paid no heed to the sounds made at these times, as I was most embarass'd by the state to which these "fits" reduced me. While he thought this odd he did not question it.

The same day I went on board, we set sail with design to stretch over for the Africkan coast. Keeping farther off at sea we lost sight of land and steered as if we were bound for the isle Fernando de Noronha, holding our course. In this course we passed the line in about twelve days' time, and were in northern latitude when a violent tornado took us quite out of our knowledge. It blew in such a terrible manner that for twelve days together we could do nothing but drive and let it carry us whither ever fate and the fury of the winds directed. During these twelve days, I need not say I expected every day to be swallowed up.

In this distress we had, besides the terror of the storm, one of our men died of the calenture and one man and the boy washed overboard. About the twelfth day, the weather abating a little, the master made an observation as well as he could and found he was in about 11 degrees north latitude, but he was 22 degrees of longitude difference, west from Cape St. Augustino. He was got upon the north part of Brasil, beyond the river Amazons, toward that of the river Oroonoque, commonly called the Great River. He consult'd with me what course he should take, for the ship was leaky and very much disabled, and he was going back to the coast of Brasil.

I was positively against that. Looking over the charts of the seacoast of America with him, we concluded there was no inhabited country for us to have recourse to till we came within the circle of the Caribbee islands, and therefore resolv'd to stand away for Barbadoes. We could not make our voyage to the coast of Africa without some assistance, both to our ship and ourselves.

With this design, we chang'd our course, and steer'd away in order to reach some of our English islands, where I hoped for relief. But our voyage was otherwise determined, for a second storm came upon us, which carry'd us away with the same impetuosity westward and drove us so out of the very way of all human commerce. Had all our lives been saved, we were rather in danger of being devoured by savages than ever returning to our own country.

In this distress, the wind still blowing very hard, one of our men late in the day cried out, "Land!" We had no sooner run out of the cabin in hopes of seeing whereabouts in the world we were, but the ship struck upon a sand. In a moment, her motion being so stopped, the sea broke over her in such a manner we expected we should all have perish'd. We were driven into our close quarters to shelter us from the very foam and sprye of the sea.

It is not easy for any one who has not been in the like condition to describe or conceive the consternation of men in such circumstances. In a word, we sat looking upon one another and expecting death every moment, and every man acting accordingly, as preparing for another world. There was little or nothing more for us to do in this. Our present comfort, and all the comfort we had, was that, contrary to our expectation, the ship did not break, and the master said the wind began to abate.

Now, tho' we thought the wind did a little abate, the ship having thus struck upon the sand, and sticking too fast for us to expect her getting off, we were in a dreadful condition and had nothing to do but to think of saving our lives as well as we could. We had a boat at our stern just before the storm, but she was staved by dashing against the ship's rudder and she broke away, and either sunk or was driven off to sea. We had another boat on board, but how to get her off into the sea was a doubtful thing as the sun was all but gone.

Alas, amidst these many words and crises, I was suddenly aware of the beast straining for freedom, so quiet had it slipped upon me on this first night of the moon, and was bid to ask the captain to lock me in my cabin before the "fits" came onto me again. The captain ask'd if I was madden'd, for we fancied the ship would break in pieces every minute, and some told us she was broken already. To lock me away thus would condemn me to death, or so he believ'd. However, there was no room to debate, thus he order'd the mate of our vessel to imprison me as I requested and such was our fate seal'd, for the kind hearted captain planned in secret with the mate to rescue me against my wishes. The mate was not to lock the door, for once the other long-boat was in the sea they would rush upon me, bind me against the violence of my "fits," and carry me to salvation.

I knew none of this, but only that the beast was mere moments from rising up. I pull'd off my own shoes and coats before I observ'd to my horror the door was as yet still unlock'd. I cried out for the mate to fasten the hasp, but he had gone and laid hold of the boat, and with the help of the rest of the men, they got her flung over the ship's side and prepared to get in her.

With my final clarity I bethought myself that perhaps I should hurl my body from the rail, to God's mercy and the wild sea, rather than let the beast free among good men, and so I fled from my cabin into the light of the moon. My vision grew dark and my flesh hot as the mantle of the beast fell upon me, and I felt my hands upon the rail and then no more. Merciful God has spared my mind from much of what transpired after this, but as always I glimps'd and heard meer moments of what my beast experienc'd.

It was much anger'd at finding itself cloath'd and it howled and roared and tore at the rail. The mate and another man ran to the beast, thinking it was I in my "fit" and try'd to calm it with words afore they saw its face. The terror of *den wild zee*, as the Dutch call the sea in a storm, was naught compar'd to the beast.

They fled in fear, and the beast kill'd the mate in a moment, falling on him as wolves do to lambs, tearing at his flesh until his blood flowed cross the deck. And now the crew's case was very dismal indeed, for they all saw plainly they must face the beast or risk the high sea and the dark and distant shore they had glimps'd. Being wise men all, they chose the distant shore and threw themselves into the boat.

A raging wave, mountain-like, came rolling astern and broke over the deck and the beast was driven from its kill. It slid cross the tilted deck, into the air, and was all swallow'd up in a moment, tho' I can recall a sight of the wave falling upon the long-boat much as the beast had fallen upon the mate.

Nothing can describe the confusion of thought which the beast felt, when it sunk into the water, nor is it easy to make sense from the many images my intoxicated mind saw through the smok'd lens of the beast. It swam well, yet disliked water and could not deliver itself from the waves so as to draw breath. It could not drown, for the beast is immortal yet for purest silver, yet it could be thrash'd and batter'd by the waves, as it was. At one point it felt land under its paws, yet the sea came back as a great hill of water which buried the beast deep in its body and carry'd it back away from shore.

There was much time as the beast fought with the sea. It would struggle to the shore and then be either dragged back with a howl or pounded against the land, and this did happen countless times. One time would have been well nigh fatal to me, for the sea, having hurry'd the beast along, dashed it against a piece of rock with such force as to leave it senseless. But it recover'd a little before the return of the waves and held fast to the rock till the wave abated. Then the beast struck out again and fetch'd another run up the shore and the next wave went over it yet did not carry it away.

The beast collaps'd on the grass, free from danger, and quite out of the reach of the water. Its heart raced and it panted for breath in the manner of a dog, with its tongue hung out. And then, for the first time in my life, the beast fell asleep beneath the moon and spent its time in a deep, exhausted slumber and I knew no more.

My island, the ship,
useful things

The next morning I walked about on the shore, lifting up my hands, and my whole being, as I may say, wrapt up in the contemplation of my deliverance. I reflected upon my comrades that were drowned, and that there should not be one soul saved but myself. As for them, I never saw them afterwards, or any sign of them, except three of their hats, one cap, and two shoes that were not fellows.

I cast my eyes to the stranded vessel. The breach and froth of the sea being so big I could hardly see it, it lay so far off, and considered, Lord! how was it possible even the beast could get on shore?

After I had solaced my mind with the comfortable part of my condition, I began to look round me, to see what kind of a place I was in, and what was next to be done. I was wet, had no cloathes to shift me, nor any thing either to eat or drink to comfort me. Neither did I see any prospect before me but perishing with hunger. I had no weapon, either to hunt and kill any creature for my sustenance, or to defend myself against any other creature that might desire to kill me for theirs, though I hoped the creatures of this land would avoid me for the beast within my skin, as most animals of England do. In a word, I had nothing about me but a knife, a tobacco-pipe, and a little tobacco in a box. This was all my provision, and this threw me into such terrible agonies of mind that for a good while I ran about like a madman. Night coming upon me again, I began, with a heavy heart, to consider what would be my lot if there were naught to eat in this country.

All the remedy that offered to my thoughts at that time was to get what cloathes I was left with into a thick bushy tree, like a fir but thorny, which grew near me, and consider the next day what death I should die, for as yet I saw no prospect of life. I walked about a furlong from the shore to see if I could find any fresh water to drink, which I did, to my great joy. Having drank, I went to the tree and put my cloathes up in it, and presently the beast did come upon me again for the second night, that of the true full moon. While my own unwell state of thought made it most difficult to focus thru the smok'd lens, I was aware that the beast did feed, and if it could find food, there was hope I could as well.

When I waked it was broad day, the weather clear and the storm abated, so the sea did not rage and swell as before. What surprised me most was the ship was lifted off in the night from the sand where she lay by the swelling of the tyde, and was driven up almost as far as the rock which I at first mention'd, where the beast had been so bruised by the wave dashing it against it. This being within about a mile from the shore where I was, and the ship seeming to stand upright still, I wish'd myself on board that at least I might save some necessary things for my use.

The first thing I found was the long-boat, which lay as the wind and the sea had toss'd her upon the land, about two miles on my right hand. I walked as far as I could upon the shore to have got to her, but found an inlet of water between me and the boat, which was about half a mile broad. I came back for the present, being more intent upon getting at the ship, where I hoped to find something for my present subsistence. While the beast had fed the night before on one or two creatures, I could not count on it again after tonight.

A little after noon, I found the sea very calm, and the tyde ebb'd so far out I could come within a quarter of a mile of the ship, and here I found a fresh renewing of my grief. I saw if the beast had not forced the crew to flee in terror and all had kept on board, we had all got safe on shore and I had not been so miserable as to be left destitute of all comfort and company, as I now was. This forced tears from my eyes again, but as there was little relief in that, I resolv'd to get to the ship. I pull'd off my cloathes, for the weather was hot to extremity, and took the water.

When I came to the ship, my difficulty was still greater to know how to get on board. As she lay aground and high out of the water, there was nothing within my reach to lay hold of. I swam round her twice, and the second time I spy'd a small piece of a rope, which I wonder'd I did not see at first, hanging down by the fore-chains. With great difficulty I got hold of it, and by the help of that rope got into the forecastle of the ship. Here I found the ship was bulg'd and had a great deal of water in her hold. She lay so on the side of a bank of hard sand, or rather earth; her stern lay lifted up upon the bank and her head low, almost to the water. By this means all her quarter was free and all that was in that part was dry. You may be sure my first work was to search and to see what was spoiled and what was free.

First, I found all the ship's provisions were dry and untouched by the water. Being very well disposed to eat, I went to the bread-room and fill'd my pockets with bisket, and ate it as I went about other things, for I had no time to lose. I also found some rum in the great cabin, of which I took a large dram, and which I had indeed need enough of to spirit me for what was before me. Now I wanted nothing but a boat to furnish myself with many things which I foresaw would be very necessary to me.

It was in vain to sit still and wish for what was not to be had, and this extremity roused my application. We had several spare yards, and two or three large sparrs of wood, and a spare top-mast or two in the ship. I resolv'd to fall to work with these, and flung as many overboard as I could manage for their weight, tying every one with a rope that they might not drive away. When this was done I went down the ship's side and, pulling them to me, I tied four of them fast together at both ends, as well as I could, in the form of a raft. Laying two or three short pieces of plank upon them, crossways, I found I could walk upon it very well but it was not able to bear any great weight, the pieces being too light. I went to work, and with the carpenter's saw I cut a spare top-mast into three lengths and added them to my raft with a great deal of labour and pains. But the hope of furnishing myself with necessaries encouraged me to go beyond what I should have been able to have done upon another occasion.

My raft was now strong enough to bear any reasonable weight. My next care was what to load it with and how to preserve what I laid upon it from the surf of the sea, but I was not long considering this. I first laid all the planks or boards upon it I could get, and having considered well what I most wanted, I got three of the seamen's chests, which I had broken open and empty'd, and lowered them down upon my raft; these I fill'd with provisions. There had been some barley and wheat together, but, to my great disappointment I found the rats had eaten or spoiled it all. As for liquors, I found several cases of bottles belonging to our skipper in which were some cordial waters. These I stowed by themselves, there being no need to put them into the chests, nor any room for them.

While I was doing this, I found the tyde began to flow and I had the mortification to see my coat, shirt, and waistcoat, which I had left upon the sand, swim away. My breeches, which were only linen and open-knee'd, I swam on board in them and my stockings. This put me upon rummaging for cloathes, of which I found enough but took no more than I wanted for present use, for I had other things which my eye was more upon. It was after long searching I found the carpenter's chest, which was indeed a very useful prize to me, and much more valuable than a ship-lading of gold would have been at that time. I got it down to my raft, even whole as it was, without losing time to look into it for I knew in general what it contained.

My next care was for some ammunition and arms. There were two good fowling-pieces in the great cabin and two pistols. These I secured first with some powder-horns, and a small bag of shot, and two old rusty swords. I knew there were three barrels of powder in the ship but knew not where our gunner had stowed them. With much search I found them, two of them dry and good, the third had taken water. Those two I got to my raft. And now I thought myself pretty well freighted and began to think how I should get to shore with them, having neither sail, oar, nor rudder. The least cap-full of wind would have overset all my navigation.

I had three encouragements; 1, a smooth, calm sea; 2, the tide rising, and setting in to the shore; 3, what little wind there was blew me towards the land. And thus, having found two or three broken oars belonging to the long-boat, with this cargo I put to sea. For a mile, or thereabouts, my raft went very well, only I found it drive a little distant from the place where I had landed before. I perceived there was some indraft of the water, and consequently I hoped to find some creek or river there which I might make use of as a port to get to land with my cargo.

As I imagined, so it was, there appear'd before me a little opening of the land, and I found a strong current of the tyde set into it. I guided my raft as well as I could to get into the middle of the stream. But here I had like to have suffer'd a second shipwreck, for knowing nothing of the coast my raft ran aground at one end of it upon a shoal. Not being aground at the other end, it wanted but a little that all my cargo had slipped off towards that end that was afloat. I did my utmost, by setting my back against the chests to keep them in their places, but could not thrust off the raft with all my strength. Neither durst I stir from the posture I was in. Holding up the chests with all my might, I stood in that manner near half an hour, in which time the rising of the water brought me a little more upon a level. A little after, the water still rising, my raft floated again and I thrust her off with the oar I had into the channel. Driving up higher, I at length found myself in the mouth of a little river, with land on both sides and a strong current or tyde running up. I looked on both sides for a proper place to get to shore, for I was not willing to be driven too high up the river, hoping, in time, to see some ship at sea, and therefore resolv'd to place myself as near the coast as I could.

At length I spy'd a little cove on the right shore of the creek, to which, with great pain and difficulty, I guided my raft, and at last got so near as that, reaching ground with my oar, I could thrust her directly in. All I could do was to wait 'till the tide was at the highest, keeping the raft with my oar like an anchor, to hold the side of it fast to the shore near a flat piece of ground. As soon as I found water enough, for my raft drew about a foot of water, I thrust her upon that flat piece of ground and there fastened or moored her by sticking my two broken oars into the ground, one on one side near one end, and one on the other side near the other end. Thus I lay 'till the water ebb'd away, and left my raft and all my cargo safe on shore.

My next work was to view the country. Where I was, I yet knew not, whether on the continent or on an island, whether inhabited or not inhabited. There was a hill not above a mile from me which rose up very steep and high and which seemed to overtop some other hills northward. I took out one of the fowling-pieces, one of the pistols, and a horn of powder. Thus arm'd, I travel'd for discovery up to the top of that hill, where, after I had with great labour and difficulty got up to the top, I saw my fate.

I was on an island, environed every way with the sea. No land to be seen except some jagged black rocks, like cathedral spires 'neath the waves, which lay a way off, and two small islands, less than this, which lay about three leagues to the west.

I found also the island I was on was barren and, as I saw good reason to believe, uninhabited except by wild creatures. I saw abundance of fowls, but knew not their kinds. Neither when I killed them could I tell what was fit for food and what not. At my coming back, I shot at a great bird which I saw sitting upon a tree on the side of a great wood. I believe it was the first gun that had been fired there since the creation of the world. I had no sooner fired but from all the parts of the wood there arose an innumerable number of fowls, of many sorts, making a confused screaming and crying, every one according to his usual note. As for the creature I killed, I took it to be a kind of a hawk, its colour and beak resembling it, but had no talons or claws more than common. Its flesh was carrion and fit for nothing.

Contented with this discovery, I came back to my raft, and fell to work to bring my cargo on shore, which took me up the rest of that day. What to do with it for this last night of the moon I knew not, nor indeed where to rest it. I was afraid to leave my cargo too reveal'd, for the beast had in the past committed wanton destruction of the things of men for no discernable reason.

As well I could, I made a solid form with the chests and boards I had brought on shore, and made a kind of a wall for that night. As for food, I yet saw not which way to supply myself, except I had seen two or three creatures, like hares, run out of the wood where I shot the fowl. I knew for a certainty if there were food on this island, the beast would find more of it.

I remov'd my cloathes as the sun dropped and stowed them within one of the seamen's chests. As the beast came upon me, I could not help but sense its pleasure to still be unchayn'd and free in its new home. That night it kill'd two of the hares and feasted well on something larger, tho' I could not tell what.

On the morrow, I now began to consider I might yet get a great many things out of the ship which would be useful to me, and particularly some of the rigging and sails, and such other things as might come to land. I resolv'd to make another voyage on board the vessel, if possible. And as I knew the first storm that blew must break her all in pieces, I resolv'd to set all other things apart 'till I got every thing out of the ship I could get. Then I called a council in my thoughts as to whether I should take back the raft, but this appeared impracticable. I resolv'd to go as before, when the tyde was down, and I did so, having nothing on but a chequered shirt, a pair of linen drawers, and a pair of pumps on my feet.

I got on board the ship as before, and prepared a second raft. Having had experience of the first, I neither made this so unwieldy nor loaded it so hard, but yet I brought away several things very useful to me. First, in the carpenter's stores, I found two or three bags of nails and spikes, a dozen or two of hatchets, and above all, that most useful thing called a grind-stone. All these I secured together, with several things belonging to the gunner, particularly two or three iron crows, two barrels of musket bullets, seven muskets, and a large bag-full of small shot.

Besides these things, I took all the men's cloathes I could find, and a spare fore-top sail, a hammock, and some bedding. With this I loaded my second raft and brought them all safe on shore, to my very great comfort.

Having got my second cargo on shore I went to work to make me a little tent with the sail, and some poles which I cut for that purpose. Into this tent I brought every thing I knew would spoil either with rain or sun. I piled all the empty chests and casks up in a circle round the tent, to fortify it from any sudden attempt either from man or animal.

When I had done this, I blocked up the door of the tent with some boards within and an empty chest set up on end without. Spreading one of the beds upon the ground, laying my two pistols just at my head, and my gun at length by me, I went to bed for the first time since the shipwreck and slept very quietly all night, for I was very weary and heavy. The night before the beast had run long and hard, and I had laboured very hard all day, as well, to fetch all those things from the ship and to get them on shore.

I had the biggest magazine of all kinds now that ever was laid up, I believe, for one man. But I was not satisfied, still. While the ship sat upright in that posture, I thought I ought to get every thing out of her I could. So every day, at low water, I went on board, and brought away something or other. The third time I went, I brought away as much of the rigging as I could, as also all the small ropes and rope-twine I could get, along with a piece of spare canvas which was to mend the sails upon occasion, and the barrel of wet gunpowder. In a word, I brought away all the sails first and last, only I was fain to cut them in pieces and bring as much at a time as I could. They were no more useful to be sails but as mere canvas only.

But that which comforted me still more was that, last of all, after I had made five or six such voyages as these, and thought I had nothing more to expect from the ship that was worth my meddling with, I found a great hogshead of bread, three large runlets of rum or spirits, a box of sugar, and a barrel of fine flour. This was surprising to me because I had given over expecting any more provisions, except what was spoiled by the water. I soon emptied the hogshead of that bread and wrapt it up, parcel by parcel, in pieces of the sails which I cut out, and got all this safe on shore also.

The next day I made another voyage, and now having plundered the ship of what was portable and fit to hand out, I began cutting the great cable into pieces, such as I could move. This was most unpleasant, for on deck was the dark stain where the mate had fallen to the beast, which had not been entirely washed away by the sea, and now lay in my sight all the time while I worked. I got two cables and a hawser on shore, with all the iron-work I could get, including a set of manakles from the brig were it ever needed to contain the beast on this island. Having cut down the spritsail-yard and the mizen-yard and every thing I could to make a large raft, I loaded it with all those heavy goods and came away. But my good luck began now to leave me. This raft was so unwieldy and so over-laden, after I entered the little cove where I had landed the rest of my goods, not being able to guide it so handily as I did the other, it overset and threw me and all my cargo into the water. For myself, it was no great harm, for I was near the shore, but as to my cargo, it was a great part of it lost, especially the iron, which I expected would have been of great use to me. However, when the tyde was out, I got most of the pieces of cable ashore and some of the iron, tho' with infinite labour for I was fain to dip for it into the water, a work which fatigued me very much. After this I went every day on board, and brought away whatever was left I could get.

My new home, goats,
my calendar

I had been now thirteen days ashore and had been eleven times on board the ship, in which time I had brought away all one pair of hands could well be supposed capable to bring. I believe, had the calm weather held, I should have brought away the whole ship piece by piece. Tho' I thought I had rummaged the cabin so as nothing could be found, on my twelfth visit I discovered a locker with drawers in it, in one of which I found two or three razors, and one pair of large scissars with some dozen of good knives and forks. In another I found about thirty-six pounds value in money, some European coin, some Brasil, some pieces of eight, some gold, and some silver.

I smil'd to myself at the sight of this money: "O drug!" said I aloud, "what art thou good for? E'en remain where thou art, and go to the bottom, as a creature whose life is not worth saving." However, upon second thoughts, I took it away. Wrapping all this in a piece of canvas, I began to think of making another raft. But while I was preparing this, I found the sky over-cast, and the wind began to rise. In a quarter of an hour it blew a fresh gale from the shore. It occur'd to me it was in vain to pretend to make a raft with the wind off shore. It was my business to be gone before the tyde of flood began, or otherwise I might not be able to reach the shore at all. Accordingly, I let myself down into the water and swam across the channel which lay between the ship and the sands, and even that with difficulty enough, with the weight of the things I had about me and the roughness of the water. The wind rose and, before it was quite high water, it blew a storm.

But I got home to my little tent, where I lay with all my wealth about me very secure. It blew very hard all night. In the morning, when I looked out, behold, no more ship was to be seen! I was a little surprised, but recovered myself with this satisfactory reflection. I had lost no time, nor abated no diligence, to get every thing out of her that could be useful to me, and, indeed, there was little left in her I was able to bring away if I had had more time. I now gave over any more thoughts of the ship, or of any thing out of her, except what might drive on shore from her wreck.

My thoughts were now employ'd about securing myself against savages, if any should appear, and also against the wild acts of the beast, for if it were to destroy any of the many treasures I had saved from the ship, my life would become the harsher for it. I had many thoughts of the method how to do this and what kind of dwelling to make, whether I should make me a cave in the earth or a tent upon the earth. In short, I resolv'd upon both, the manner and description of which it may not be improper to give an account of.

I soon found the place I was in was not for my settlement because it was upon a low, moorish ground, near the sea. I believed it would not be wholesome because there was no fresh water near it. So I resolv'd to find a more healthy and more convenient spot of ground.

I consulted several things in my situation, which I found would be proper for me: 1st, health and fresh water, I just now mentioned: 2dly, shelter from the heat of the sun: 3dly, security from ravenous creatures, whether men or the beast: 4thly, a view to the sea, that if God sent any ship in sight, I might not lose any advantage for my deliverance, of which I was not willing to banish all my expectation yet.

In search for a place proper for this, I found a little plat of land on the side of a rising hill, whose front, towards this plain, was steep as a house-side, so nothing could come down upon me from the top. On the side of this rock there was a hollow place, worn a little way in, like the entrance of a cave, but there was not really any cave at all.

On the flat of the green, just before this hollow place, I resolv'd to pitch my tent. Before I set it up, I drew a half-circle before the hollow place which took in about ten yards in its semi-diameter from the rock, and twenty yards in its diameter from its beginning and ending.

In this half-circle I pitched two rows of strong stakes, driving them into the ground till they stood very firm like piles, the biggest end being out of the ground about five feet and a half and sharpened on the top. The two rows did not stand above six inches from one another, and this fence was so strong neither man nor the beast could get into it or over it. This cost me a great deal of time and labour, to cut the piles in the woods, bring them to the place, and drive them into the earth, but I thought it time well spent to know my livelihood would not be endangered by the beast.

The entrance into this place I made to be not by a door, but by a short ladder to go over the top, which, when I was in, I lifted over after me. I was fenced in and fortified from all the world and consequently slept secure in the night, which otherwise I could not have done.

Into this fence, or fortress, with infinite labour, I carry'd all my riches, all my provisions, ammunition, and stores, of which you have the account above. The last three days of this activity were the nights of the moon, and it did increase the time of moving, as I could not risk assuming the mantle of the beast either within my fence or whilst moving my treasures.

I made a large tent which, to preserve me from the rains, I made double, viz. one smaller tent within, and one larger tent above it, and covered the uppermost with a large tarpaulin, which I had saved among the sails. And now I lay no more for a while in the bed which I had brought on shore, but in a hammock, which was indeed a very good one and belonged to the mate of the ship. For many years, while I lay in it on nights not of the moon, I would recall his face as the beast pounced upon him. It is an awful thing to allow the beast to kill a man, and often my father told me such things would torment one's thoughts and meditations for life.

I began to work my way into the rock, bringing all the earth and stones I dug down out through my tent. I laid them up within my fence in the nature of a terrace so it raised the ground within about a foot and an half. Thus I made me a cave just behind my tent, which served me like a cellar to my house. It cost me much labour and many days before all these things were brought to perfection. Therefore I must go back to some other things which took up some of my thoughts.

It happen'd, after I had laid my scheme for setting up my tent and making the cave, that a storm of rain falling from a thick, dark cloud, a sudden flash of lightning came, and after that, a great clap of thunder, as is naturally the effect of it. I was not so much surpris'd with the lightning as I was with a thought, one which darted into my mind as swift as the lightning itself: O my powder! My very heart sunk within me when I thought at one blast all my powder might be destroyed. Tho' had the powder took fire, I would have never known who had hurt me.

Such impression did this make upon me, after the storm was over, I laid aside all my works and applied myself to make bags and boxes to separate the powder, in hope whatever might come it might not all take fire at once, and to keep it so apart that it should not be possible to make one part fire another. I finished this work in about a fortnight. I think my powder, which in all was about 240 lb. weight, was divided in not less than a hundred parcels. As to the barrel that had been wet, I did not apprehend any danger from that, so I placed it in my new cave, which, in my fancy, I called my kitchen. The rest I hid up and down in holes among the rocks so no wet might come to it, marking where I laid it.

In the interval of time while this was doing, I went out at least once every day with my gun, as well to divert myself as to see if I could kill any thing fit for food, and to acquaint myself with what the island produced. The first time I went out, I presently discovered there were goats upon the island, which was a great satisfaction to me, and I observ'd this was the creature the beast had fed upon during those first nights on the island. Then it was attended with this misfortune to me. They were so shy, so subtle, and so swift of foot, it was the most difficult thing in the world to come at them. I was not discouraged at this, not doubting but I might now and then shoot one, as it soon happened. The first shot I made among these creatures, I killed a she-goat, which had a little kid by her which she gave suck to, which grieved me heartily. But when the old one fell, the kid stood stock still by her, 'till I came and took her up. Not only so, but when I carried the old one with me upon my shoulders, the kid followed me quite to my enclosure. I laid down the dam and took the kid in my arms and carried it over my pale, in hopes to have bred it up tame. But it would not eat, and stood in terror of the beast's scent. So I was forced to kill it and eat it myself. These two supplied me with flesh a great while, for I ate sparingly and preserved my provisions (my bread especially) as much as I could.

This was also of great relief, for my father had always taught me that the beast must hunt and it must feed, for these things are in its nature. While all of our family are wont to chayn our beasts at some time or another, if it is not allow'd to follow its nature it becomes more angry and vengeful towards those it lives within. I had wor-ry'd with nothing to hunt and eat, the beast would destroy all that I laboured to build up here on this island.

Having now fixed my habitation, I found it necessary to provide a place to make a fire in and fuel to burn. What I did for that, as also how I enlarged my cave and what conveniences I made, I shall give a full account of in its proper place. I must first give some little ac-count of myself and of my thoughts about living, which, it may well be supposed, were not a few.

I had a dismal prospect of my condition. As I was not cast away upon that island without being driven, as is said, by a violent storm, quite out of the course of our intended voyage and some hundreds of leagues out of the ordinary course of the trade of mankind, I had great reason to consider it as a determination of Heaven that in this desolate place I should end my life. The tears would run plentifully down my face when I made these reflections. Sometimes I would expostulate with myself why Providence should thus completely ruin its creatures and render them so miserable, so abandoned without help, so entirely depressed, that it could hardly be rational to be thankful for such a life.

But something always returned swift upon me to check these thoughts, and to reprove me. Particularly, one day, walking with my gun in my hand by the sea side, I was very pensive upon the subject of my present condition, when reason, as it were, expostulated with me t'other way.

"Well, you are in a desolate condition, 'tis true. But, pray re-member, where are the rest of you? Were there not eleven on the ship? Did not nine of them escape into the boat? Where are the nine? Why were not they sav'd and you lost? Why were you singled out? Is it better to be here or there?" And then I pointed to the sea. All evils are to be considered with the good that is in them, and with what worse attends them.

Then it occurr'd to me again how well I was furnished for my subsistence, and what would have been my case if it had not happened (which was a hundred thousand to one) that the ship floated from the place where she first struck, and was driven so near to the shore I had time to get all these things out of her? What would have been my case if I had to have lived in the condition in which I at first came on shore, without necessaries of life, or necessaries to supply and procure them?

"Particularly," said I aloud, tho' to myself, "what should I have done without a gun, without ammunition, without any tools to make any thing or to work with? Without cloathes, bedding, a tent, or any manner of covering?" And now I had all these to a sufficient quantity, and was in a fair way to provide myself in such a manner as to live without my gun, when my ammunition was spent. I had a tolerable view of subsisting without any want as long as I lived. I considered from the beginning how I should provide for the accidents that might happen, and for the time that was to come, not only after my ammunition should be spent, but even after my health or strength should decay.

And now entering into a melancholy relation of a scene of silent life, such, perhaps, as was never heard of in the world before, I shall take it from its beginning and continue it in its order. It was, by my account, the 30th of September, when, in the manner as above said, the beast first set foot upon this horrid island. The sun being to us in its autumnal equinox, was almost just over my head. I reckoned myself, by observation, to be in the latitude of 9 degrees 22 minutes north of the line.

After I had been there about ten or twelve days, it came into my thoughts that I should lose my reckoning of time for want of books, and pen and ink, and should even forget the Sabbath days from the working days. To prevent this, I cut it with my knife upon a large post in capital letters. Making it into a great cross, I set it up on the shore where I first landed, viz. *'I came on shore here on the 30th of*

September, 1659.' Upon the sides of this square post I cut every day a notch with my knife, and every seventh notch was as long again as the rest, and every first day of the month as long again as that long, and every full moon marked by a second notch across that one for the day. Thus I kept my kalendar, or weekly, monthly, and yearly reckoning of time.

My papers and books, my account,
my chair and table

B ut it happened among the many things which I brought out of the ship in the several voyages I made to it, I got several things of less value, but not at all less useful to me, which I found some time after rummaging in the chests. In particular, pens, ink, and paper. Several parcels in the captain's, mate's, gunner's, and carpenter's keeping. Three or four compasses (which point'd in many directions, but ne'er north in the many years on this island), some mathematical instruments, perspective glasses , charts, and books of navigation, all which I huddled together, whether I might want them or no. Also I found three very good bibles, which came to me in my cargo from England and which I had packed up among my things. Some Portugueze books also, and, among them, two or three popish prayer books, and several other books, all which I secured.

As I observ'd before, I found pens, ink, and paper, and I husbanded them to the utmost. I shall show, while my ink lasted, I kept things very exact, but after that was gone I could not, for I could not make any ink by any means I could devise.

And this put me in mind that I wanted many things, notwithstanding all I had amassed together. Of these, this of ink was one. Also a spade, pick-axe, and shovel, to dig or remove the earth. Needles, pins, and thread. As for linen, I soon learned to want that without much difficulty.

This want of tools made every work I did go on heavily. It was near a whole year before I had finished my little pale and surrounded my habitation. The stakes, which were as heavy as I could well lift, were a long time in cutting and preparing in the woods, and more by far in bringing home. I spent sometimes two days in cutting and bringing home one of those posts, and a third day in driving it into the ground. But what need I have been concerned at the tediousness of any thing I had to do, seeing I had time enough to do it in? Nor had I any other employment if that had been over, at least I could foresee, except the ranging the island to seek for food, which I did, more or less, every day.

I now began to consider my condition, and the circumstance I was reduced to. I drew up the state of my affairs in writing, not so much to leave them to any that were to come after me as to deliver my thoughts from daily poring upon them and afflicting my mind. As my reason began now to master my despondency, I began to comfort myself as well as I could, and to set the good against the evil, that I might have something to distinguish my case from worse. I stated very impartially, like debtor and creditor, the comforts I enjoyed against the miseries I suffered, thus:

Evil	*Good*
I am cast upon a horrible, desolate island, void of all hope of recovery.	*But I am alive and not drowned, as all my ship's company were.*
I am singled out and separated, as it were, from all the world to be miserable.	*But I am singled out too from all the ship's crew to be spared from death. He that miraculously saved me from death can deliver me from this condition.*

I am divided from mankind, a solitaire, one banished from human society.	*But was I not divided such before by the beast? I am not starved and perishing in a barren place, affording no sustenance.*
I am without any defence, or means to resist any violence.	*But I am cast on an island where the beast can inflict violence on no others.*
I have no soul to speak to, or relieve me.	*But I have got out so many necessary things from the wreck as will either supply my wants, or enable me to supply myself, even as long as I live.*
I am afflicted with the memories of what the beast has done.	*But I have been given time to reflect and repent, in a place where the beast can hurt no other.*

Upon the whole, here was an undoubted testimony that there was scarce any condition in the world so miserable but there was something positive to be thankful for in it.

Having now brought my mind a little to relish my condition, and given over looking out to sea to see if I could spy a ship, I began to apply myself to accommodate my way of living, and to make things as easy to me as I could.

I have already describ'd my habitation, which was a tent under the side of a rock, surrounded with a strong pale of posts and cables. I might now rather call it a wall, for I raised a kind of wall against it of turfs, about two feet thick on the outside. After some time (I think it was a year and a half) I raised rafters from it, leaning to the rock, and thatched or covered it with boughs of trees and such things as I could get to keep out the rain, which I found at some times of the year very violent.

I have already observ'd how I brought all my goods into this pale, and into the cave which I had made behind me. But I must observe, too, at first this was a confused heap of goods which, as they lay in no order, so they took up all my place. I had no room to turn myself. So I set myself to enlarge my cave and work farther into the earth. It was a loose, sandy rock which yielded to the labour I bestowed on it. I worked sideways, to the right hand, into the rock, and then turning to the right again worked quite out, and made me a door to the outside of my fortification.

This gave me not only egress and regress, as it were, a back-way to my tent and to my storehouse, but gave me room to stow my goods.

And now I began to apply myself to make such necessary things as I found I most wanted, particularly a chair and a table. Without these I was not able to enjoy the few comforts I had in the world. I could not write, or eat, or do several things with so much pleasure without a table, so I went to work.

And here I must needs observe, that every man may be, in time, master of every mechanic art. I had never handled a tool in my life. Yet, in time, by labour, application, and contrivance, I found, at last, I wanted nothing but I could have made, especially if I had had tools. However, I made abundance of things even without tools, and some with no more tools than an adze and a hatchet, which perhaps were never made that way before and that with infinite labour.

For example, if I wanted a board, I had no other way but to cut down a tree, set it on an edge before me, and hew it flat on either side with my axe till I had brought it to be as thin as a plank, and then dub it smooth with my adze. It is true, by this method I could make but one board of a whole tree, but this I had no remedy for but patience, any more than I had for a prodigious deal of time and labour which it took me up to make a plank or board. But my time or labour was little worth, and so it was as well employed one way as another.

However, I made me a table and a chair, as I observ'd above, in the first place. This I did out of the short pieces of boards I brought on my raft from the ship. But when I wrought out some boards, as above, I made large shelves of the breadth of a foot and a half, one over another, all along one side of my cave to lay all my tools, nails, and iron-work on. In a word, to separate every thing at large in their places that I might easily come at them. I knocked pieces into the wall of the rock to hang my guns and all things that would hang up. Had my cave been seen, it looked like a general magazine of all necessary things. I had every thing so ready at my hand, it was a great pleasure to me to see all my goods in such order and to find my stock of all necessaries so great.

And now it was I began to keep a journal of every day's employment. Indeed, at first, I was in too much hurry, and not only hurry as to labour, but in much discomposure of mind. My journal would have been full of many awful things. For example, I must have said thus—"Sept. 30th. After I had allow'd the beast free reign to cause the death of a good man, and to drive many others to their dooms, it was set loose upon the sea and suffered only a little afore it escap'd drowning and then did lie down on the grass for the most peaceful sleep it e'er have."

Some days after this, and after I had been on board the ship and got all I could out of her, I could not forbear getting up to the top of a little mountain and looking out to sea in hopes of seeing a ship. Then fancy that, at a vast distance, I spied a sail, please myself with the hopes of it, and after looking 'till I was almost blind, lose it quite and sit down to weep like a child, and thus increase my misery by my folly.

But, having gotten over these things in some measure, and having settled my household-stuff and habitation, made me a table and a chair, and all as handsome about me as I could, I began to keep my journal. I shall here give you the copy as long as it lasted, for, having no more ink, I was forced to leave it off.

My journal, my adventure recounted, a miracle

September 30th, 1659.
I, poor miserable Robinson Crusoe, child of the moon, being ship-wrecked during a dreadful storm, came on shore on this dismal unfortunate island, which I called the ISLAND OF DESPAIR, the ship's mate being killed by the beast and all the rest of the ship's company being drowned, and even the beast almost drowned in the violent sea.

October 1.
In the morning I saw, to my great surprise, the ship had floated with the high tyde, and was driven on shore again much nearer the island. At length, seeing the ship almost dry, I went upon the sand as near as I could, and then swam on board. This day also it continued raining, tho' with no wind at all. The beast did run free again tonight, and took much pleasure in this place.

From the 1st of October to the 24th.

All these days entirely spent in many several voyages to get all I could out of the ship, which I brought on shore, every tyde of flood, upon rafts. Much rain also in these days, tho' with some intervals of fair weather. It seems this was the rainy season.

Oct. 20.

I overset my raft, and all the goods I had got upon it; but being in shoal water, and the things being chiefly heavy, I recovered many of them when the tyde was out.

Oct. 25.

It rain'd all night and all day, with some gusts of wind, during which time the ship broke in pieces (the wind blowing a little harder than before) and was no more to be seen, except the wreck of her, and that only at low water. I spent this day in covering and securing the goods which I had saved, that the rain might not spoil them.

Oct. 26.

I walked about the shore almost all day, to find out a place to fix my habitation. Greatly concerned to secure myself from any attack in the night, either from wild beasts or men.

From the 26th to the 30th,

I work'd very hard in carrying all my goods to my new habitation, tho' some part of the time it rain'd exceedingly hard. The mantle of the beast was on me for these last nights, which did slow the work.

Nov. 6.

After my morning walk, I went to work with my table again, and finished it, tho' not to my liking. Nor was it long before I learned to mend it.

Nov. 7.

Now it began to be settled fair weather. The 7th, 8th, 9th, 10th, and part of the 12th (for the 11th was Sunday, according to my reckoning) I took wholly up to make me a chair, and with much ado, brought it to a tolerable shape, but never to please me. Even in the making, I pulled it in pieces several times.

Note. I soon neglected my keeping Sundays, for, omitting my mark for them on my post, I forgot which was which.

Nov. 13.

This day it rained, which refreshed me exceedingly and cooled the earth. But it was accompanied with terrible thunder and lightning, which frightened me dreadfully, for fear of my powder. As soon as it was over, I resolv'd to separate my stock of powder into as many little parcels as possible, that it might not be in danger.

Nov. 14, 15, 16.

These three days I spent in making little square chests or boxes, which might hold about a pound, or two pounds at most, of powder. Putting the powder in, I stowed it in places as secure and as remote from one another as possible. On one of these three days I killed a large bird that was good to eat, but I knew not what to call it.

Nov. 17.

This day I began to dig behind my tent, into the rock, to make room for my farther convenience.

Note. Three things I wanted exceedingly for this work, viz. a pick-axe, a shovel, and a wheel-barrow, or basket; so I desisted from my work, and began to consider how to supply these wants, and make me some tools. As for a pick-axe, I made use of the iron crows, which were proper enough, tho' heavy. The next thing was a shovel or spade. This was so necessary I could do nothing effectually without it, but what kind of one to make I knew not.

Nov. 18.

The next day, in searching the woods, I found a tree of that wood, or like it, which, in the Brasils, they call the iron tree, from its exceeding hardness. Of this, with great labour and almost spoiling my axe, I cut a piece and brought it home, too, with difficulty enough, for it was exceeding heavy. The excessive hardness of the wood, and my having no other way, made me a long while upon this machine. I worked it by little and little into the form of a spade, the handle shaped like ours in England. Only the broad part having no iron shod upon it at bottom, it would not last me so long. However, it served well enough for the uses which I had occasion to put it to. Never was a shovel, I believe, made after that fashion, or so long a-making.

I was still deficient, for I wanted a basket or a wheel-barrow. A basket I could not make by any means, having no such things as twigs that would bend to make wicker-ware, at least, none yet found out. As to the wheel-barrow, I fancied I could make all but the wheel, but that I had no notion of, neither did I know how to go about it. Besides, I had no possible way to make iron gudgeons for the spindle or axis of the wheel to run in. So I gave it over. For carrying away the earth which I dug out of the cave, I made me a thing like a hod, which the labourers carry mortar in for the brick-layers. This was not so difficult to me as making the shovel. Yet this and the shovel, and the attempt which I made in vain to make a wheel-barrow, took me up no less than four days. I mean, always excepting my morning walk with my gun, which I seldom omitted, and very seldom failed also bringing home something fit to eat.

Nov. 23.

My other work having now stood still, because of my making these tools, when they were finished I went on. Working every day, as my strength and time allowed, I spent eighteen days in widening and deepening my cave, that it might hold my goods commodiously.

Note. During all this time, I worked to make this room, or cave, spacious enough to accommodate me as a warehouse or magazine, a kitchen, a dining-room, and a cellar. As for a lodging, I kept to the tent. Except sometimes in the wet season of the year it rained so hard I could not keep myself dry, which caused me afterwards to cover all my place within my pale with long poles, in the form of rafters, leaning against the rock, and load them with flags and large leaves of trees like a thatch.

Nov. 27.

Being the first night of the moon, I did let the beast wander free outside the pale. It has taken to running the forest and hunting the small things like hares I did see upon my arrival. This first night it kill'd three of them and ate them entirely.

Nov. 29.

Was not able to work this day, as the beast left me so far from my new home in the morning it took much of the day to return. Was badly burn'd by the sun in the hours I spent walking.

December 10.

I began now to think my cave or vault finished, when on a sudden (it seems I had made it too large) a great quantity of earth fell down from the top and one side. So much it frightened me, and not without reason too. If I had been under it, I should never have wanted a grave-digger. Upon this disaster, I had a great deal of work to do over again, for I had the loose earth to carry out and, which was of more importance, I had the ceiling to prop up so I might be sure no more would come down.

Dec. 11.

This day I went to work with it and got two shores or posts pitched upright to the top, with two pieces of board across over each post. This I finished the next day. Setting more posts up with boards, in about a week more I had the roof secured. The posts, standing in rows, served me for partitions to part off my house.

Dec. 17.

From this day to the 30th, I placed shelves and knocked up nails on the posts to hang every thing up that could be hung up. Now I began to be in some order within doors.

Dec. 20.

I carried every thing into the cave and began to furnish my house, and set up some pieces of boards, like a dresser, to order my victuals upon, but boards began to be very scarce with me. Also I made me another table.

Dec. 24.

Much rain all night and all day. No stirring out. Had an awful dream of the mate and the beast, wherein the beast did attack again and again and the mate was kill'd many times over.

Dec. 25.

Rain all day.

Dec. 26.

No rain, and the earth much cooler than before, and pleasanter.

Dec. 27.

Killed a young goat and lamed another, so I catched it and led it home in a string. When I had it home, I bound and splintered up its leg, which was broke. *N.B.* I took such care of it that it lived. The leg grew well and as strong as ever. By nursing it so long, it grew almost tame and fed upon the little green at my door and would not go away, e'en though it still was wary of me by nature of the beast. This was the first time I entertained a thought of breeding up some tame creatures, that I might have food when my powder and shot was all spent.

Dec. 28, 29, 30, 31.
Great heats, and no breeze so there was no stirring abroad, except in the evening, for food. This time I spent in putting all my things in order within doors.

On the first morning I woke up not far from my pale. The many footprints, or paw prints as they may be call'd, show'd me the beast had spent much of the night pacing before my wall. Perhaps it smelt the young goat and wish'd to eat it.

January 1.
Very hot still, but I went abroad early and late with my gun, and lay still in the middle of the day. This evening, going farther into the vallies which lay towards the centre of the island, I found there was plenty of goats, tho' exceeding shy because of the scent of the beast, and hard to come at. I wonder'd if the beast would find them and slaughter the herd afore I could make use of them, or if it would kill and eat only what was needed to slake its hunger?

Jan. 3.
I began my fence or wall. Being still jealous of my being attacked by somebody, I resolv'd to make very thick and strong.

N.B. This wall being described before, I purposely omit what was said in the journal. It is sufficient to observe, I was no less time than from the 3d of January to the 14th of April, working, finishing, and perfecting this wall, tho' it was no more than about 25 yards in length, being a half-circle from one

place in the rock to another place, about twelve yards from it, the door of the
cave being in the centre behind it.

All this time I work'd very hard. The rains hindering me many
days, nay, sometimes weeks together. But I thought I should never
be secure 'till this wall was finished. It is scarce credible what inexpressible labour every thing was done with, especially the bringing
piles out of the woods, and driving them into the ground. I made
them much bigger than I needed to have done.

When this wall was finished, and the outside double-fenced, with
a turf-wall raised up close to it, I persuaded myself if any people
were to come on shore there they would not perceive any thing like
a habitation. It was very well I did so, as may be observ'd hereafter,
upon a very remarkable occasion.

During this time, I made my rounds in the woods for game every
day, when the rain permitted me, and made frequent discoveries,
in these walks, of something or other to my advantage. I found a
kind of wild pigeons, who built, not as wood-pigeons, in a tree,
but rather as house-pigeons, in the holes of the rocks. Taking some
young ones I endeavoured to breed them up tame, but when they
grew older they flew all away. Which, more likely than not, was in
terror of the beast, for all creatures but man can smell it within my
skin. However, I frequently found their nests and got their young
ones, which were very good meat.

And now, in managing my household affairs, I found myself
wanting in many things, which I thought at first it was impossible
for me to make. I was at a great loss for candle. As soon as it was
dark, which was generally by seven o'clock, I was obliged to go to
bed. I remember the lump of bees-wax with which I made can-
dles in my African adventure, but I had none of that now. The only
remedy I had was when I had killed a goat I saved the tallow. With a
little dish made of clay, which I baked in the sun, to which I added

a wick of some oakum, I made me a lamp. This gave me light, tho' not a clear steady light like a candle.

In the middle of all my labours it happened that, in rummaging my things, I found a little bag which had been fill'd with corn for the feeding of poultry. What little remainder of corn had been in the bag was all devoured with the rats, and I saw nothing in the bag but husks and dust. Being willing to have the bag for some other use (I think, it was to put powder in, when I divided it for fear of the lightning, or some such use), I shook the husks of corn out of it on one side of my fortification, under the rock.

It was a little before the great rain just now mentioned I threw this stuff away, taking no notice of any thing, and not so much as remembering I had thrown any thing there. About a month after I saw some few stalks of something green shooting out of the ground, which I fancied might be some plant I had not seen. I was surprised and perfectly astonished when, after a little longer time, I saw about ten or twelve ears come out which were perfect green barley of the same kind as our European, nay, as our English barley.

It is impossible to express the astonishment and confusion of my thoughts on this occasion. I had hitherto acted upon no religious foundation at all. Indeed, I had very few notions of religion in my head, as my father did speak often against those who would prejudge us for the blood we carried. But after I saw barley grow there in a climate which I knew was not proper for corn, and as I knew not how it came there, it startled me strangely. I began to suggest God had caused this grain to grow without any help of seed sown, and it was so directed purely for my sustenance on that wild miserable place.

I began to bless myself that such a prodigy of nature should happen upon my account. And this was the more strange to me, because I saw near it still some other straggling stalks which proved to be stalks of rice, which I knew because I had seen it grow in Africa when I was ashore there.

At last it occurred to my thoughts I had shook out a bag in that place and then the wonder began to cease. I must confess, my religious thankfulness to God's providence began to abate too upon the discovering all this was nothing but what was common. Tho' I ought to have been as thankful for so strange and unforeseen a providence, as if it had been miraculous.

Laying up every corn, I resolv'd to sow them all again, hoping, in time, to have some quantity sufficient to supply me with bread. Besides this barley, there were, as above, 20 or 30 stalks of rice, which I preserv'd with the same care, and whose use was of the same kind or to the same purpose, viz. to make me bread, or rather food. I found ways to cook it up without baking, tho' I did that also after some time.

My island moves, the ship returns,
my illness

But to return to my journal.

I work'd excessively hard these three or four months to get my wall done, and the 14th of April I closed it up, contriving to get into it not by a door, but over the wall, by a ladder, that there might be no sign on the outside of my habitation.

April 16.

I finished the ladder. I went up with the ladder to the top and then pulled it up after me and let it down in the inside. This was a complete enclosure to me. Within I had room enough, and nothing could come at me from without unless it could first mount my wall.

The very next day after this wall was finished, I had almost all my labour overthrown at once, and myself killed.

As I was busy in the inside of it, just at the entrance into my cave, I was terribly frightened with a most dreadful surprising thing indeed. All on a sudden I found the earth come crumbling down from the roof of my cave and from the edge of the hill over my head. Two of the posts I had set up in the cave cracked in a frightful manner. I was scared, but thought nothing of what was the cause, only thinking that the top of my cave was falling in as some of it had done before. For fear I should be buried in it, I ran forward to my ladder, and not thinking myself safe there neither, I got over my wall for fear of the pieces of the hill which I expected might roll down upon me.

I had no sooner stepped down upon the firm ground than I saw it was a terrible earthquake. The ground I stood on shook three times at about eight minutes' distance, with three such shocks as would have overturned the strongest building that could be supposed to have stood on the earth. A great piece of the top of a rock, which stood about half a mile from me, fell down, with such a terrible noise as I never heard in all my life. I perceived also the very sea was put into a violent motion by it. I believe the shocks were stronger 'neath the water than on the island, and for reasons I could not give a name to, I was struck with the thought of some great creature turning and stretching in its sleep, as does a man or e'en a dog.

I was so much amaz'd with the thing itself (having never felt the like, nor discours'd with any one that had) I was like one dead or stupify'd. The motion of the earth made my stomach sick, like one that was toss'd at sea, or so I first thought. I did soon recognize this as the beast, growling and snarling within me tho' it was still more than a week from the first night of the moon, for some element of this earthquake disturbed it greatly, and I did try to examine the beast within my skin to learn why. But the noise of the falling of the rock awak'd me, as it were, and rousing me from the stupify'd condition I was in, fill'd me with horror. I thought of nothing but the hill falling upon my tent and my household goods, and burying all at once. This sunk my very soul within me a second time.

After the third shock was over and I felt no more for some time, I began to take courage and the beast grew quiet within me. Yet I had not heart enough to go over my wall again for fear of being buried alive, but sat still upon the ground cast down and disconsolate, not knowing what to do. All this while, I had not the least serious religious thought. Nothing but the very common *Lord, have mercy upon me!* and when it was over, that went away too.

While I sat thus I found the air overcast, and grow cloudy, as if it would rain. Soon after the wind rose by little and little, so in less than half an hour it blew a most dreadful hurricane. The sea 'round the black rocks was, all on a sudden, covered with foam and froth. The shore was covered with a breach of the water, the trees were torn up by the roots, and a terrible storm it was. This held about three hours, and then began to abate. In two hours more it was quite calm, and began to rain very hard.

All this while I sat upon the ground, very much terrify'd and dejected, when on a sudden it came into my thoughts that these winds and rain being the consequence of the earthquake, the earthquake itself was spent and over. I might venture into my cave again. With this thought my spirits began to revive, and the rain also helping to persuade me, I went in and sat down in my tent. But the rain was so violent my tent was ready to be beaten down with it. I was forced to get into my cave, tho' very much afraid and uneasy for fear it should fall on my head.

This violent rain forced me to a new work, viz. to cut a hole through my new fortification like a sink, to let the water go out, which would else have drown'd my cave. After I had been in my cave for some time and found no more shocks of the earthquake follow, I began to be more composed. And now to support my spirits, which indeed wanted it very much, I went to my little store and took a small sup of rum, which I did then, and always, very sparingly, knowing I could have no more when that was gone.

It continued raining all night, and a great part of the next day, so I could not stir abroad. My mind being more composed, I began to think of what I had best do, concluding if the island was subject to these earthquakes, there would be no living for me in a cave. I must consider of building me some little hut in an open place which I might surround with a wall, as I had done here. If I staid where I was I should be buried alive.

With these thoughts, I resolv'd to remove my tent from the place where it now stood, being just under the hanging precipice of the hill, and which if it should be shaken again would certainly fall upon my tent. I spent the two next days, being the 19th and 20th of April, in contriving where and how to remove my habitation.

The fear of being swallowed alive affected me so that I never slept in quiet. Yet the apprehension of lying abroad, without any fence, was almost equal to it. Still, when I looked about, and saw how every thing was put in order, how I was concealed, and how safe from danger, it made me very loth to remove.

In the mean time, it occurred to me it would require a vast deal of time for me to do this. I must be contented to run the risk where I was till I had formed a convenient camp and secured it so as to remove to it. With this conclusion I composed myself for a time, and resolv'd I would go to work with all speed to build me a wall with piles and cables, &c. in a circle as before, and set up my tent in it when it was finished. I would venture to stay where I was till it was ready and fit to remove to. This was the 21st.

April 22.

The next morning I began to consider of means to put this measure into execution. I was at a great loss about the tools. I had three large axes and abundance of hatchets (for we carried the hatchets for traffic with the Indians), but with much chopping and cutting knotty hard wood, they were all full of notches and dull. Tho' I had a grind-stone, I could not turn it and grind my tools too. This caused me as much thought as a statesman would have bestowed upon a grand point of politics or a judge upon the life and death of a man. At length I contrived a wheel with a string to turn it with my foot, that I might have both my hands at liberty.

Note. I had never seen any such thing in England, or at least not to take notice how it was done, tho' since I have observ'd it is very common there. Besides, my grind-stone was very large and heavy. This machine cost me a full week's work to bring it to perfection.

April 24, 25, 26.
The beast was most unhappy and bothered still by the earthquake. It would not run or hunt or feed, but only pace in the area it awoke in. All three mornings I would find myself just a few yards from where the mantle of the beast had fallen upon me, the ground covered with its many footprints, or paw prints as they may be called. It was very hungry, and thus I awoke each day finding myself ravenous and desiring for much food.

April 28, 29.
These two whole days I took up in grinding my tools, my machine for turning my grind-stone performing very well.

April 30.
Having perceived my bread had been low a great while, I now took a survey of it, and reduced myself to one bisket-cake a day, which made my heart very heavy.

May 1.
In the morning, looking toward the sea-side, the tyde being low, I saw something lie on the shore bigger than ordinary, and it looked like a cask. When I came to it, I found a small barrel and two or three pieces of the wreck of the ship which were driven on shore by the late hurricane. Looking towards the wreck itself, I thought it seemed to lie higher out of the water than it used to do. I examined the barrel that was driven on shore and soon found it was a barrel of gunpowder. It had taken water, and the powder was caked as hard as a stone. However, I rolled it farther on the shore for the present

and went on upon the sands, as near as I could to the wreck of the ship, to look for more.

When I came down to the ship, I found it strangely remov'd. The forecastle, which lay before buried in sand, was heaved up at least six feet. The stern (which was broke to pieces and parted from the rest by the force of the sea soon after I had left rummaging of her) was tossed up, as it were, and cast on one side. The sand was thrown so high on that side next her stern I could now walk quite up to her when the tyde was out, whereas there was a great piece of water before, so I could not come within a quarter of a mile of the wreck without swimming. I was surprised with this at first, but soon concluded it must be done by the earthquake. As by this violence the ship was more broke open than formerly, so many things came daily on shore which the sea had loosened and which the winds and water rolled by degrees to the land.

This diverted my thoughts from the design of removing my habitation. I busied myself, that day especially, in searching whether I could make any way into the ship, but I found nothing was to be expected of that kind, for all the inside of the ship was choked up with sand. However, as I had learned not to despair of any thing, I resolv'd to pull every thing to pieces I could of the ship, concluding every thing I could get from her would be of some use or other to me.

I could not help but see that prominent on the broken part of the stern was the dark stain where the mate had been kill'd.

May 3.

I began with my saw and cut a piece of a beam through which I thought held some of the upper part or quarter deck together. When I had cut it through, I clear'd away the sand as well as I could from the side which lay highest. The tyde coming in, I was oblig'd to give over for that time.

May 4.

I went a-fishing, but caught not one fish I durst eat of till I was weary of my sport. I had made me a long line of some rope-yarn, but I had no hooks. Yet I frequently caught fish enough, as much as I cared to eat, all which I dried in the sun and ate them dry.

May 5.

Worked on the wreck. Cut another beam asunder, and brought three great fir-planks off from the decks, which I tied together, and made swim on shore when the tyde of flood came on.

May 6.

Worked on the wreck. Got several iron bolts out of her and other pieces of iron-work. Worked very hard and came home very much tired and had thoughts of giving it over.

May 7.

Went to the wreck again, but not with an intent to work. Found the weight of the wreck had broke itself down, the beams being cut. Several pieces of the ship seemed to lie loose, and the inside of the hold lay so open I could see into it; but almost full of water and sand.

May 8.

Went to the wreck and carried an iron crow to wrench up the deck, which lay now quite clear of the water and sand. I wrenched up two planks and brought them on shore also with the tyde. I left the iron crow in the wreck for next day.

May 9.

Went to the wreck, and with the crow made way into the body of the wreck. Felt several casks, and loosened them with the crow, but could not break them up. I felt also a roll of English lead, and could stir it but it was too heavy to remove.

May 10—14.
Went every day to the wreck. Got a great many pieces of timber, and boards, or plank, and two or three hundred weight of iron. Six of these planks did carry the dark stain of the mate's death.

May 15.
I carried two hatchets to try if I could not cut a piece off the roll of lead by placing the edge of one hatchet and driving it with the other. As it lay about a foot and a half in the water, I could not make any blow to drive the hatchet.

May 16.
It had blow'd hard in the night and the wreck appear'd more broken by the force of the water. I staid so long in the woods, to get pigeons for food, the tyde prevented my going to the wreck that day.

May 17.
I saw some pieces of the wreck blown on shore at a great distance, two miles off me, but resolv'd to see what they were and found it was a piece of the head, but too heavy for me to bring away.

May 24.
Every day, to this day, I worked on the wreck. With hard labour I loosened some things so much with the crow that the first blowing tyde several casks floated out, and two of the seamen's chests. The wind blowing from the shore, nothing came to land that day but pieces of timber and a hogshead which had some Brasil pork in it. The salt-water and the sand had spoil'd it.

I continued this work every day to the 15th of June, except the time necessary to get food, which I always appointed, during this part of my employment, to be when the tyde was up that I might be ready when it was ebb'd out. And also to prepare for the moon, of which this was the second day. By its foot or paw prints, I saw that the beast had inspect'd the wreck which I had spent so much time at, which made me wonder if this were animal curiosity, or if it had a smok'd lens of its own which it saw thru my eyes with. There were many things my father had never instruct'd me about our family blood, for he said there were some things a man must learn on his own and not thru lessons given by other men.

By this time I had gotten timber, and plank, and iron-work. I also got, at several times, and in several pieces, near 100 weight of the sheat-lead.

June 16.
Going down to the sea-side I found a large tortoise, or turtle. This was the first I had seen, which, it seems, was only my misfortune, not any defect of the place or scarcity. Had I happened to be on the other side of the island I might have had hundreds of them every day, as I found afterwards, but perhaps had paid dear enough for them.

June 17.
I spent in cooking the turtle. I found in her threescore eggs. Her flesh was to me, at that time, the most savoury and pleasant I ever tasted in my life, having had no flesh but of goats and fowls since I landed in this horrid place.

June 18.
Rain'd all day, and I staid within. I thought, at this time, the rain felt cold and I was somewhat chilly, which I knew was not usual in that latitude.

June 19.
Very ill, and shivering, as if the weather had been cold.

June 20.
No rest all night. Violent pains in my head, and feverish.

June 21.
Very ill. Frightened almost to death with the apprehensions of my sad condition; to be sick, and no help. Pray'd to God for the first time since the storm off Hull. Scarce knew what I said or why, my thoughts being all confused.

June 22.
A little better, but under dreadful apprehensions of sickness. Crawled outside my pale for the first night of the moon, leaving my cloathes in a pile at the foot of my wall.

June 23.
Very bad again. Cold and shivering, and then a violent head-ache. The beast is upset by my illness, which would seem to take effect upon it as well, tho' not as bad as it does to me. This night it did little but howl at the moon, which frighten'd my young goat very much so.

June 24.
Much better. The beast did run and hunt this night, and kill'd one of the small hares and a goat. In my youthful experience, it had oft seem'd to me that the mantle of the beast could clear away many such illnesses and injuries, or lessen them at best. I bethought myself that I may have help for my sickness after all.

June 25.
An ague. The fit held me seven hours. Cold fit, and hot, with faint sweats after it. It would seem my help, that is to say, the beast, has left and my health is taken with it.

The dream lord, my revelation,
my protections

June 26.
Better. Having no victuals to eat, took my gun, but found myself very weak. However, I kill'd a she-goat and, with much difficulty, got it home and broiled some of it and ate. I would fain have stewed it and made some broth, but had no pot.

June 27.
The ague again, so violent I lay a-bed all day and neither ate nor drank. I was ready to perish for thirst, so weak I had not strength to stand up or to get myself any water to drink. Prayed to God again, but was light-headed. When I was not, I was so ignorant I knew not what to say. I suppose I did nothing else for two or three hours till, the fit wearing off, I fell asleep and did not wake till far in the night. When I awoke, I found myself much refreshed but weak and exceeding thirsty. However, as I had no water in my whole habitation, I was forced to lie till morning, and went to sleep again. In this second sleep I had this terrible dream.

I thought I was sitting on the ground on the outside of my wall, where I sat when the storm blew after the earthquake, and I saw a thing rise from the sea beneath a great black cloud and light upon the shore. He, for I somehow knew it to be male, was all over as dark as pitch and projected from him a terrible wrongness, so I could but just bear to look towards him. His countenance was most inexpressibly dreadful, impossible for words to describe, with a beard of thick ropes of flesh, like those of a cuttel fish, and cold eyes that bit at the skin like winter wind. When he stepped upon the shore with his broad feet the island trembled, just as it had done before in the earthquake, and all the air looked, to my apprehension, as if it had been fill'd with flashes of fire.

He had no sooner lighted upon the shore but his wrongness spread out across the island as ripples spread across a pool of water, and every hill became changed and every stone black and unnatural. He moved forward towards me, and he did tower so high he looked down upon me and seem'd to cover leagues with each step. When he came to a rising ground, still enormous at some distance, he spoke to me, or I heard a voice so terrible it is impossible to express the terror of it. All I can say I understood, was this:

"Robinson Crusoe. There you are. Seeing all these things have not brought thee to my service, now thou shalt die."

At which words he lifted up his great and terrible hand to kill me. A terrible howl filled the air, and it was somehow made known to me, as is the way of dreams, that this was the beast, which also fear'd this great dark lord, but rally'd against him as well. At this point I start'd awake, though my heart did race in terror, and for some time I could not believe the dream was not a true thing I had remembered.

No one that shall ever read this account will expect I should be able to describe the horrors of my soul at this terrible vision. I mean, even while it was a dream, I even dreamed of those horrors. Nor is it any more possible to describe the impression that remained upon my mind when I awaked and found it was but a dream.

I had, alas! no divine knowledge. What I had received by the good instruction of my father was then worn out by an uninterrupted series of seafaring wickedness and a constant conversation with none but such as were, like myself, wicked and profane to the last degree. I do not remember I had, in all that time, one thought that so much as tended either to looking upward towards God or inward towards a reflection upon my own ways. A certain stupidity of soul, without desire of good, or consciousness of evil, had overwhelmed me. I was all the most hardened, unthinking, wicked creature among our common sailors can be supposed to be, not having the least sense either of the fear of God in danger or of thankfulness to him in deliverances.

Even when I was, on due consideration, made sensible of my condition, how I was cast on this dreadful place, out of the reach of human kind, out of all prospect of redemption, as soon as I saw but a prospect of living, and that I should not starve and perish for hunger, all the sense of my affliction wore off. These were thoughts which very seldom entered into my head.

But now, when I began to be sick, and a leisure view of the miseries of death came to place itself before me, when my spirits began to sink under the burden of a strong distemper, and nature was exhausted with the violence of the fever, conscience, that had slept so long, began to awake. I reproached myself with my past life, in which I had, by uncommon wickedness, invited dark creatures unto my soul which God in his vindictiveness did allow.

It is good that I mention some may find the beast to be a dark creature, and it is a wild and vicious one, but in truth it is a part of nature, as has my father often taught all his sons, and as his father taught him.

These reflections oppressed me for the second or third day of my distemper. In the violence, as well of the fever as of the dreadful terror of my dream, extorted from me some words like praying to God. Tho' I cannot say it was a prayer attended either with desires or with hopes. It was rather the voice of mere fright and distress. It was exclamation, such as, "Lord, what a miserable creature am I! What will become of me?" Then the tears burst out of my eyes, and I could say no more for a good while.

In this interval, the good advice of my father came to my mind, and his prediction which I mentioned at the beginning of this story. "Now," said I, aloud, "my dear father's words are come to pass. God's justice has overtaken me, and I have none to help or hear me. I rejected the voice of Providence, which had mercifully put me in a station of life wherein I might have been happy and easy. I would neither see it myself, nor learn from my parents to know the blessing of it. I left them to mourn over my folly, and now I am left to mourn under the consequences of it."

This was the first prayer, if I may call it so, I had made for many years.

But I return to my Journal.

June 28.

Having been somewhat refreshed with the sleep I had had, and the fit being entirely off, I got up. Tho' the fright and terror of my dream was very great, yet I considered the fit of the ague would return again the next day, and now was my time to get something to refresh and support myself when I should be ill. The first thing I did was to fill a large square case-bottle with water and set it upon my table in reach of my bed. To take off the chill or aguish disposition of the water, I put about a quarter of a pint of rum into it and mixed them together, which the sailors call grog. Then I got me a piece of goat's flesh, and broiled it on the coals, but could eat very little. I walked about but was very weak and withal very sad and heavy-hearted under a sense of my miserable condition, dreading the return of my distemper the next day and a return of the dream if I slept. At night, I made my supper of three of the turtle's eggs, which I roasted in the ashes and ate in the shell.

After I had eaten, I tried to walk, but found myself so weak I could hardly carry the gun, for I never went out without that. So I went but a little way and sat down upon the ground, looking out upon the sea, which was just before me, and very calm and smooth. It did appear in my thoughts that this was the same place I had sat for the earthquake and the same place I also sat during my most horrible dream.

As I sat here, some such thoughts as these occurred to me. What was the awful dream lord which still darken'd my mood so? Whence did such a vision produce from? Did the beast truly see this dark lord, or was that meerly part of the dream as well? Surely some secret power was having influence over me. And who is that?

It did come to my mind that this power was guilt, or riding upon my guilt the way one would ride a horse. The death of the mate still hung heavy in my thoughts, and as guilty as his death made me was that I, who considered myself good among men, had not even made clear to learn or remember his name, a point I had not put to words before. Truly was I a wretch, and the beast as thrice-damned as the church did teach. Could there be another reason God had seen fit to have this banishment befall me?

However, I then bethought myself that if God guides and governs all his creations, and all things that concern them, for the power that could make all things must have power to guide and direct them, nothing can happen in the great circuit of his works either without his knowledge or appointment. How, then, did this come to pass? If I was a wretch and the beast thrice-damned, why were we not long ago destroyed? Why was I not drown'd in Yarmouth Roads, kill'd in the fight when the ship was taken by the Sallee pirates, or devoured by the wild creatures of Africk? Why was I not allowed to throw myself from the rail *here* when all the crew perish'd but myself?

I was struck dumb with these reflections, as one astonished, and had not a word to say. Rising up pensive, I walked back to my retreat and went over my wall, as if I had been going to bed. But my thoughts were many, and I had no inclination to sleep. So I sat down in the chair and lighted my lamp, for it began to be dark.

Now, as the apprehension of the return of my distemper and the dreams it brought terrified me very much, it occurred to my thought that the Brasilians took no physic but their tobacco for almost all distempers. I had a piece of a roll of tobacco in one of the chests, which was quite cured, and some also that was green and not quite cured.

I went directed by Heaven no doubt, for in this chest I found a cure both for soul and body. I opened the chest and found what I looked for, viz. the tobacco. As the few books I had saved lay there too, I took out one of the Bibles which I mentioned before and which to this time I had not found leisure, or so much as inclination, to look into. I took it out and brought both that and the tobacco with me to the table.

What use to make of the tobacco I knew not, as to my distemper, nor whether it was good for it or not. I try'd several experiments with it, as if I was resolv'd it should hit one way or other.

In the interval of this operation I took up the Bible and began to read, but my head was too much disturbed with the tobacco to bear reading, at least at that time. Having opened the book, the first words that occurred to me were these:

Call on me in the day of trouble, and I will deliver thee,
and thou shalt glorify me.

These words were very apt to my case and made some impression upon my thoughts at the time of reading them, tho' not so much as they did afterwards. It now grew late and the tobacco had dozed my head so much I inclined to sleep. So I left my lamp burning in the cave, lest I should want any thing in the night, and went to bed.

I fell into a sound sleep and waked no more till, by the sun, it must necessarily be near three o'clock in the afternoon the next day.

Nay, to this hour I am partly of opinion I slept all the next day and night and till almost three the day after. Otherwise, I know not how I should lose a day out of my reckoning in the days of the week, as it appeared some years after I had done. If I had lost it by crossing and re-crossing the Line, I should have lost more than one day, but certainly I lost a day or more in my account and never knew which way.

Be that, however, one way or the other, when I awaked I found myself refreshed, and my spirits lively and cheerful. When I got up, I was stronger than I was the day before, and my stomach better, for I was hungry. In short, I had no fit the next day, but continued much altered for the better. This was the 29th.

The 30th was my well day, of course. I went abroad with my gun, but did not care to travel too far. I killed a sea-fowl or two, something like a brand goose, and brought them home, but was not very forward to eat them. I ate some more of the turtle's eggs, which were very good. However, I was not so well the next day, which was the 1st of July, as I hoped I should have been. I had a little of the cold fit, but it was not much.

July 2.

I renewed the tobacco medicine in many ways. Dosed myself with it as at first, and doubled the quantity which I drank steeped in rum.

July 3.

I miss'd the fit for good and all, tho' I did not recover my full strength for some weeks after. While I was thus gathering strength, my thoughts ran upon this scripture, *I will deliver thee.* As I was discouraging myself with such thoughts, it occurred to my mind that I pored so much upon my deliverance from the main affliction, I disregarded the deliverance I had receiv'd. It was then that my soul did see the light even as my eyes saw the truth of this place. This island was not to be my banishment, but my refuge, for here the beast could run free and harm no other man. Here I could meditate on the crime for which I could not be punish'd in society without bringing shame and danger to my family. Here on this island, through the grace of God, the beast and I could be free. This touched my heart very much, and immediately I gave God thanks aloud.

July 4.

In the morning I took the Bible and, beginning at the New Testament, I began to read it and imposed upon myself to read awhile every morning and every night, as long as my thoughts should engage me. It was not long after I set seriously to this work that I found my heart more deeply and sincerely affected with the wickedness of my past life.

Now I began to construe the words mentioned above, *Call on me, and I will deliver thee*, in a different sense from what I had ever done before. Then I had no notion of any thing being called deliverance, but my being delivered from the captivity I first saw myself in. But now I learned to take it in another sense. Now I looked back upon my past life and my sins appeared so dreadful, my soul sought nothing of God but deliverance from the load of guilt that bore down all my comfort.

But, leaving this part, I return to my Journal.

My condition began now to be much easier to my mind. My thoughts being directed to things of a higher nature I had a great deal of comfort within, which till now I knew nothing of. Also, as my health and strength returned, I bestirred me to furnish myself with every thing I wanted and make my way of living as regular as I could.

From the 4th of July to the 14th, I was chiefly employed in walking about with my gun in my hand, a little and a little at a time, as a man that was gathering up his strength after a fit of sickness. It is hardly to be imagined how low I was and to what weakness I was reduced. The application which I made use of was new and perhaps what had never cured an ague before. Neither can I recommend it to any one to practise, by this experiment. Tho' it did carry off the fit it rather contributed to weakening me, for I had frequent convulsions in my nerves and limbs for some time.

I learned from it also this, in particular. Being abroad in the rainy season was the most pernicious thing to my health that could be, especially in those rains which came attended with storms and hurricanes of wind. As the rain which came in the dry season was almost always accompanied with such storms, so I found this rain was much more dangerous than the rain which fell in September and October.

I had now been on this unhappy island above 10 months. All possibility of rescue or escape from this condition seemed to be taken from me. I firmly believed no human shape had ever set foot upon that place, and yet I was lighter of heart and spirit than ever in my memory. Having secured my habitation fully to my mind, I had a great desire to make a more perfect discovery of the island and to see what other productions I might find which I yet knew nothing of.

The fruitful valley, strange behaviors,
my anniversary

It was on the 15th of July I began to take a more particular survey of the island itself. I went up the creek first, where, as I hinted, I brought my rafts on shore. I found, after I came about two miles up, the tyde did not flow any higher. It was no more than a little brook of running water, very fresh and good. This being the dry season, there was hardly any water in some parts of it.

On the banks of this brook I found many pleasant savannahs or meadows, plain, smooth, and covered with grass. On the rising parts of them, next to the higher grounds where the water never overflowed, I found a great deal of tobacco growing to a very great and strong stalk. There were diverse other plants which I had no knowledge of, or understanding about, and might, perhaps, have virtues of their own, which I could not find out.

I searched for the cassava root, which the Indians in all that climate make their bread of, but I could find none. I saw large plants of aloes but did not understand them. I saw several sugar-canes, but wild and, for want of cultivation, imperfect. I contented myself with these discoveries for this time and came back, musing with myself what course I might take to know the virtue of any of the fruits or plants which I should discover, but could bring it to no conclusion. For, in short, I had made so little observation while I was in the Brasils that I knew little of the plants in the field. At least, very little that might serve me to any purpose now.

The next day, the 16th, I went up the same way again. After going something farther than I had gone the day before, I found the brook and the savannahs began to cease, and the country became more woody than before. In this part I found different fruits. I found melons upon the ground, in great abundance, and grapes upon the trees. The vines, indeed, had spread over the trees and the clusters of grapes were now just in their prime, very ripe and rich. This was a surprising discovery and I was exceedingly glad of them, but I was warned by my experience to eat sparingly of them. When I was ashore in Barbary, the eating of grapes killed several of our Englishmen who were slaves there, throwing them into fluxes and fevers. I found, however, an excellent use for these grapes, and that was to cure or dry them in the sun and keep them as dried grapes or raisins are kept.

I spent all evening there and went not back to my habitation, which, by the way, was the first night I had lain from home, as I might say, discounting those nights when the beast ran free. At night I got up into a tree, where I slept well, and the next morning proceeded on my discovery, traveling near four miles, as I might judge by the length of the valley, keeping still due north, with a ridge of hills on the south and north sides of me.

At the end of this march, I came to an opening where the country seemed to descend to the west. A little spring of fresh water, which issued out of the side of the hill by me, ran the other way, due east. The country appeared so fresh, so green, so flourishing, every thing being in a constant verdure, or flourish of spring, that it looked like a planted garden.

I descended a little on the side of that delicious vale, surveying it with a secret kind of pleasure to think this was all my own. I was king and lord of all this country indefeasibly, and had a right of possession. If I could convey it, I might have it in inheritance as completely as any lord of a manor in England. I saw here abundance of cocoa trees, and orange, lemon, and citron trees, but all wild and very few bearing any fruit, at least not then. However, the green limes I gathered were not only pleasant to eat but very wholesome. I mixed their juice afterwards with water, which made it very cool and refreshing.

I found now I had business enough to gather and carry home. I resolv'd to lay up a store of grapes and limes and lemons to furnish myself for the wet season, which I knew was approaching. In order to this, I gathered a great heap of grapes in one place, a lesser heap in another place, and a great parcel of limes and melons in another place. Taking a few of each with me, I traveled homeward and re-solv'd to come again and bring a bag or sack or what I could make to carry the rest home.

Having spent three days in this journey, I came home, so I must now call my tent and my cave. But before I got thither, the grapes were spoiled, the richness of the fruits and the weight of the juice having broken and bruised them. They were good for little or nothing. As to the limes, they were good, but I could bring only a few.

The next day, being the 19th, I went back, having made me two small bags to bring home my harvest. I was surprised when, coming to my heap of grapes, which were so rich and fine when I gathered them, I found them all spread about, trod to pieces, and dragged about, some here, some there, and abundance eaten and devoured. By this I concluded there were some wild creatures thereabouts which had done this, but what they were I knew not.

However, as I found there was no laying them up in heaps, and no carrying them away in a sack I took another course. I then gathered a large quantity of the grapes, and hung them upon the out-branches of the trees, that they might cure and dry in the sun. As for the limes and lemons, I carried as many back as I could well stand under.

When I came home from this journey, I contemplated with great pleasure the fruitfulness of that valley and the pleasantness of the situation, and concluded I had pitched upon a place to fix my abode which was by far the worst part of the country. Upon the whole, I began to consider of removing my habitation and to look out for a place equally safe as where I was now situate, if possible, in that pleasant fruitful part of the island.

This thought ran long in my head, and I was exceeding fond of it for some time, the pleasantness of the place tempting me. I was so enamoured of this place I spent much of my time there for the whole remaining part of the month of July. Tho', upon second thoughts, I resolv'd not to remove, yet I built me a little kind of a bower, and surrounded it at a distance with a strong fence, being a double hedge as high as I could reach, well staked, and fill'd between with brush-wood. Here I lay very secure, sometimes two or three nights together. So I fancied now I had my country and my sea-coast house, and always one would be close no matter where I awaken'd after the full moon. This work took me up till the beginning of August.

It is worth recalling an oddity of behavior, though not one of my own. The beast had been strangely control'd since the fever vision of last month, as if the sight of the dark dream lord had made it more wary than vicious. On these three nights of late July, viz. 21-23, it did not hunt the island so much as stalk it, as an animal does patrol and mark its territory. This had ne'er happen'd afore, yet this was the first time the beast had found itself with such a territory of its own, so I pay'd it not too much mind.

I had but finish'd my fence and began to enjoy my labour when the rains came on and made me stick close to my first habitation. For tho' I had made a tent like the other, with a piece of sail, and spread it very well, yet I had not the shelter of a hill to keep me from storms, nor a cave behind me to retreat into when the rains were extraordinary.

About the beginning of August, as I said, I had finished my bower and began to enjoy myself. The 3d of August, I found the grapes I had hung up were perfectly dried, and indeed were excellent good raisins of the sun. I began to take them down from the trees, and it was very happy I did so, as the rains which followed would have spoiled them and I should have lost the best part of my winter food. No sooner had I taken them all down, and carried most of them home to my cave, but it began to rain, and from hence, which was the 14th of August, it rained, more or less, every day till the middle of October.

From the 14th of August to the 26th, incessant rain, so I could not stir, and was now very careful not to be much wet. Still I was for three nights forced out to let the mantle of the beast come upon me, and was much pleased that it did not wander far. For these three nights it still act'd much more like a wary animal, and thru the smok'd lens I did see that it would often focus out to sea, its sight much sharper than my own, but saw nothing. In the mornings I did realize it was focus'd on that view of the waters that had appear'd in my fever vision, 'round the black rocks, and I did bethought myself that the mind of the beast might still perceive it had been a true vision, and the dark dream lord did indeed hide beneath the waves. At this I felt some humor, as a man may feel at the foolish antics of a dog.

During this confinement in my cover by the rain, I worked daily two or three hours at enlarging my cave, and by degrees worked it on towards one side till I came to the outside of the hill and made a door which came beyond my fence or wall. I came in and out this way, but I was not easy at lying so open. As I had managed myself before, I was in a perfect enclosure, whereas now, I thought I lay exposed. Yet I could not perceive there was any living thing to fear, the biggest creature I had yet seen upon the island being a goat.

September 18.

The first night of the full moon. The beast began to act in its usual manner once again, and kill'd two hares.

September the thirtieth, 1660.

I was now come to the unhappy anniversary of my landing. I cast up the notches on my post, and found I had been on shore three hundred and sixty-five days since the shipwreck and the death of the mate. I kept this day as a solemn fast, having not tasted the least refreshment for twelve hours, even till the going down of the sun. I then ate a bisket and a bunch of grapes, and went to bed, finishing the day as I began it.

A little after this, my ink beginning to fail me, I contented myself to use it more sparingly and to write down only the most remarkable events of my life without continuing a daily memorandum of other things.

My first crops, my strange discoveries, my second anniversary

The rainy season and the dry season began now to appear regular to me, and I learned to divide them so as to provide for them accordingly. I have mentioned I had saved the few ears of barley and rice which I had so surprisingly found sprung up. I believe there were about thirty stalks of rice, and about twenty of barley. Now I thought it a proper time to sow it after the rains, the sun being in its southern position, going from me.

I dug a piece of ground with my wooden spade. As I was sowing, it occurred to my thoughts I should not sow it all at first because I did not know when was the proper time for it. It was a great comfort to me afterwards that I did so, for not one grain of what I sowed this time came to any thing.

Finding my first seed did not grow, which I imagined was from the drought, I sought for a moister piece of ground to make another trial in. I dug up a piece of ground near my new bower and sowed the rest of my seed in February, a little before the vernal equinox. This, having the rainy month of March and April to water it, sprung up and yielded a very good crop. But having only part of the seed left, and not daring to sow all I had, I got but a small quantity at last, my whole crop not amounting to above half a peck of each kind.

But by this experiment I was made master of my business and knew when was the proper time to sow. I might expect two seed-times, and two harvests, every year.

I found now the seasons of the year might generally be divided, not into summer and winter, as in Europe, but into the rainy seasons and the dry seasons, which were thus:

From the middle of February to the middle of April rainy; *the sun being then on or near the equinox.*

From the middle of April till the middle of August dry; *the sun being then north of the line.*

From the middle of August till the middle of October rainy; *the sun being then come back to the line.*

From the middle of October till the middle of February dry; *the sun being then to the south of the line.*

The rainy seasons held sometimes longer and sometimes shorter, as the winds happen'd to blow, but this was the general observation I made. After I had found the ill consequences of being abroad in the rain, I took care to furnish myself with provisions beforehand, that I might not be obliged to go out.

In this time I found much employment, and very suitable also to the time. I found great occasion for many things which I had no way to furnish myself with but by hard labour and constant application. During the next season, I employed myself in making, as well as I could, several baskets to carry earth or lay up any thing as I had occasion for. Tho' I did not finish them very handsomely, yet I made them serviceable for my purpose.

At this point another business took me up more time than it could be imagined I could spare. I mention'd before I had a great mind to see the whole island. I had traveled up the brook and so on to where I had built my bower, and where I had an opening quite to the sea on the other side of the island. I now resolv'd to travel quite across to the sea-shore on that side.

When I had passed the vale where my bower stood, I came within view of the sea to the west. It being a very clear day, I fairly descried land, whether an island or continent I could not tell. It lay very high. By my guess it could not be less than fifteen or twenty leagues off.

I could not tell what part of the world this might be. I knew it must be part of America and, as I concluded by all my observations, must be near the Spanish dominions and perhaps was all inhabited by savages. If I should have landed there, I had been in a worse condition than I was now. I quieted my mind with this.

Besides, after some pause upon this affair, I considered if this land was the Spanish coast, I should, one time or other, see some vessel pass or repass one way or other. If not, then it was the savage coast between the Spanish country and the Brasils, whose inhabitants are indeed the worst of savages. They are cannibals, or men-eaters, and fail not to murder and devour all human beings that fall into their hands.

With these considerations, I walk'd very leisurely forward. I found this side of the island where I now was much pleasanter than mine, the open or savannah fields adorned with flowers and grass and full of very fine woods. I saw abundance of parrots and fain would have caught one, if possible, to have kept it to be tame and taught it to speak to me. I did, after taking some pains, catch a young parrot. I knock'd it down with a stick and, having recover'd it, I brought it home. It was some years before I could make him speak, as the scent of the beast would oft send him into a flurry, and e'en then he spoke at length but once, which was a terrible thing I shall recount in time.

I was amused with this journey. I found in the low grounds hares, as I had seen oft thru the beast's eyes, and foxes, but they differed from all the other kinds I had met with. But I had no need to be venturous, for I had no want of food and of that which was very good too.

I never travel'd on this journey above two miles outright in a day, or thereabouts. Yet I took so many turns and returns to see what discoveries I could make that I came weary enough to the place where I resolv'd to sit down for the night. Then I either reposed myself in a tree or surround'd myself with a row of stakes, set upright in the ground, either from one tree to another, or so as no wild creature could come at me without waking me.

As soon as I came to the sea-shore, I was surpriz'd to see I had taken up my lot on the worst side of the island. Here indeed the shore was covered with innumerable turtles, whereas on the other side I had found but three in a year and a half. Here was also an infinite number of fowls of many kinds, some of which I had seen and some of which I had not seen before and many of them very good meat.

I confess this side of the country was much pleasanter than mine, yet I had not the least inclination to remove. As I was fixed in my habitation it became natural to me, and I seem'd all the while I was here to be as it were upon a journey and from home. Still, this was a pleasing divershin, and for three nights the beast did run gleefully on the shore as it had not done in many moons.

I travel'd along the sea-shore towards the east, I suppose about twelve miles. Then setting up a great pole upon the shore for a mark, I concluded I would go home again. The next journey I took should be on the other side of the island, east from my dwelling, and so round till I came to my post again.

I took another way to come back than I went, thinking I could easily keep so much of the island in my view I could not miss my first dwelling by viewing the country, but I found myself mistaken. Come about two or three miles, I found myself descended into a very large valley, but so surrounded with hills, and those hills covered with wood, I could not see which was my way by any direction. Indeed, this valley lay deep in shadows, and all the trees and plants were twisted and wither'd with their great desire for sun. And it happened to my farther misfortune the weather proved foggy for all the four or five days while I was in this valley.

Not being able to see the sun, I wandered about very uncomfortable and chill'd, and all this time I sensed a deep discomfort within my skin from the beast, such as I had only e'er felt before during the earthquake of the year previous. I could not help but feel if these nights were of the moon that the beast would have fled this valley at once, even though it has no sense of fear as men know it. Indeed, in a like manner, I bethought myself often that were it not for the beast which lurk'd within me, this valley would be a far worse place for me, tho' I could not say how I knew this. Much as the lesser creatures are afraid of the beast, so did I know something in this valley also did stay clear of me though by not as much, and for not the same reason.

At last I was obliged to find out the sea-side, look for my post, and come back the same way I went. Then by easy journies I turned homeward, the weather being exceeding hot, and my gun, ammunition, hatchet, and other things very heavy.

In this journey, I surprised a young kid and seized upon it. I had a great mind to bring it home if I could. I had often been musing whether it might not be possible to get a kid or two, and so raise a breed of tame goats which might supply me when my powder and shot should be all spent. I made a collar for this little creature with a string which I had made of some rope-yarn, which I always carried about me. I led him along, tho' with some difficulty for he did pull away from the beast he smelt upon me, till I came to my bower. There I enclosed him and left him, for I was very impatient to be at home, from whence I had been absent above a month.

I cannot express what a satisfaction it was to me to come into my old hutch and lie down in the hammock-bed of the mate, for so I still thought of it. This little wandering journey without a settl'd place of abode had been so unpleasant to me, most pointedly the days in the shadow'd and strange valley, that my own house was a perfect settlement to me. It rendered every thing about me so comfortable I resolv'd I would never go a great way from it again while it should be my lot to stay on the island.

I reposed myself here a week to rest and regale myself after my long journey, during which, most of the time was taken up in the weighty affair of making a cage for my Poll, who still spent much time scared of the beast within me. Then I began to think of the poor kid which I had penn'd within my little circle, and resolv'd to fetch it home or give it some food. I went and found it where I left it, for indeed it could not get out, but was almost starv'd for want of food. I went and cut boughs of trees and branches of such shrubs as I could find and threw it over.

The rainy season of the autumnal equinox was now come, and I kept the 30th of September in the same solemn manner as before, being the anniversary of my landing on the island, having now been there two years. I spent the whole day in humble and thankful acknowledgments for the many wonderful mercies which my solitary condition was attended with, and without which it might have been infinitely more miserable. I gave humble and hearty thanks to God for having been pleased to discover to me, that it was possible the beast and I might be more happy even in this solitary condition than we should have been in the enjoyment of society.

My scare-crows, first words,
my third year inventions

It was now I began sensibly to feel how much more happy the life I now led was than the wicked, cursed life I led all the past part of my days. From this moment I began to conclude in my mind it was possible for me to be more happy in this forsaken, solitary condition, than it was probable I should ever have been in any other particular state in the world.

Thus, and in this disposition of mind, I began my third year. Tho' I have not given the reader the trouble of so particular an account of my works this year as the first, yet in general it may be observ'd, I was very seldom idle, having divided my time according to the several daily employments that were before me.

To this short time allowed for labour, I desire may be added the exceeding laboriousness of my work. For want of tools, want of help, and want of skill, every thing I did took up out of my time. But notwithstanding this, with patience and labour I went through many things, indeed, every thing my circumstances made necessary for me to do, as will appear by what follows.

I was now in the months of November and December, expecting my crop of barley and rice. The ground I had manured or dug up for them was not great, but now my crop promised very well. When, on a sudden, I found I was in danger of losing it all again by enemies of several sorts, which it was scarce possible to keep from it. First, the goats, and wild creatures which I called hares, who, tasting the sweetness of the blade, lay in it night and day as soon as it came up and ate it so close it could get no time to shoot up into stalk.

I saw no remedy for this but by making an enclosure about it with a hedge, which I did with a great deal of toil, and the more because it required speed. However, as my arable land was but small and suited to my crop, I got it tolerably well fenced in about three weeks' time. Shooting some of the creatures in the day-time, in a little time the enemies forsook the place and the corn grew very strong and well and began to ripen apace.

But as the goats and hares ruin'd me before, while my corn was in the blade, so the birds were as likely to ruin me now when it was in the ear. Going along by the place to see how it throve I saw my little crop surrounded with fowls who stood, as it were, watching till I should be gone. I immediately let fly among them, for I always had my gun with me. I had no sooner shot but there rose up a little cloud of fowls which I had not seen at all from among the corn itself.

This touched me sensibly, for I foresaw in a few days they would devour all my hopes. I should be starved and never be able to raise a crop at all. What to do I could not tell. However, I resolv'd not to lose my corn if possible, tho' I should watch it night and day. In the first place, I went among it to see what damage was already done and found they had spoiled a good deal of it. But as it was yet too green for them the loss was not so great. The remainder was likely to be a good crop if it could be saved.

I staid by it to load my gun, and then coming away, I could see the thieves sitting upon all the trees about me, as if they only waited till

I was gone away, and the event proved it to be so. As I walked off, as if gone, I was no sooner out of their sight than they dropt down one by one into the corn again. I was so provoked I could not have patience to stay till more came on, knowing every grain they eat now was, as it might be said, a peck-loaf to me in the consequence. I rush'd on them and my cries with the scent of the beast did make them run off again, this time all the farther, tho' I did suspect they would return for the sweet corn, a feast they had never tasted afore.

As it would be, however, this was the first night of the November moon. I did stay by my crops until the mantle of the beast did come upon me, and peer'd with great intent thru the smok'd lens, or as best could be done through the intoxicated muddle the beast made of my mind.

In the morn I did follow the tracks and spoor of the beast and located some of its prey. Half of a hare, and another all but whole the beast had kill'd just for the joy of the hunt, and a she-goat which had been gutt'd and eaten out. This was what I wished for. I took them up and served them as we serve notorious thieves in England, viz. hanged them in chayns, for a terror to others. It is impossible to imagine this should have such an effect as it had. The fowls not only never came to the corn, but, in short, they forsook all that part of the island and I could never see a bird near the place as long as my scare-crows hung there.

This I was very glad of, you may be sure, and about the latter end of December, which was our second harvest of the year, I reaped my corn. At the end of all my harvesting, I found that out of my half peck of seed I had near two bushels of rice, and above two bushels and a half of barley, by my guess, for I had no measure.

However, this was great encouragement to me. I foresaw that, in time, it would please God to supply me with bread. Yet here I was perplexed again. I neither knew how to grind, or make meal of my corn, or indeed how to clean it and part it. Nor if made into meal, how to make bread of it, and if how to make it, yet I knew not how to bake it. These things being added to my desire of having a good quantity for store, and to secure a constant supply, I resolv'd not to taste any of this crop, but to preserve it all for seed against the next season, and in the mean time to employ all my study and hours of working to accomplish this great work of providing myself with corn and bread.

It might be truly said, now I worked for my bread. It is a little wonderful, and what I believe few people have thought much upon, viz. the strange multitude of little things necessary in the providing, producing, curing, dressing, making, and finishing this one article of bread.

But now I was to prepare more land, for I had seed enough to sow above an acre of ground. Before I did this, I had a week's work at least to make me a spade. When it was done it was but a sorry one indeed, and very heavy, and requir'd double labour to work with it. However, I went through and sowed my seed in two large flat pieces of ground, as near my house as I could find them to my mind, and fenced them in with a good hedge. This work took me up full three months because a great part of the time was in the wet season when I could not go abroad.

Within doors when it rained and I could not go out, I diverted myself with talking to my parrot and teaching him to speak. I slowly learned him to know his own name and at last to speak it out pretty loud, "Poll," which was the first word I ever heard spoken in the island by any mouth but my own.

It also happened some time after, making a pretty large fire for cooking my meat, when I went to put it out after I had done with it I found a broken piece of one of my earthen-ware vessels in the fire, burnt as hard as a stone and red as a tile. I was surpris'd to see it, and said to myself, "Certainly they might be made to burn whole if they would burn broken."

This set me to study how to order my fire, so as to make it burn some pots. No joy at a thing of so mean a nature was ever equal to mine when I found I had made an earthen pot that would bear the fire. I had hardly patience to stay till they were cold before I set one on the fire again with some water in it to boil me some meat. With a piece of a kid I made some very good broth, tho' I wanted oatmeal and several other ingredients requisite to make it so good as I would have had it been.

My next concern was to get a stone mortar to stamp or beat some corn in. After a great deal of time lost in searching for a stone, I gave it over, and resolv'd to look out a great block of hard wood, which I found indeed much easier. My next difficulty was to make a sieve to dress my meal, and to part it from the bran and the husk, without which I did not see it possible I could have any bread. The remedy I found for this was, at last recollecting I had among the seamen's cloathes, some neckcloths of calico or muslin. With some pieces of these I made three small sieves, proper enough for the work, and thus I made shift for some years.

The baking part was the next thing to be considered, and how I should make bread when I came to have corn. For an oven I was indeed puzzled. At length I found out an expedient for that also, and thus I baked my barley-loaves and became, in a little time, a good pastry-cook into the bargain. I made myself several cakes and puddings of the rice, but made no pies as I had nothing to put into them except the flesh of fowls or goats.

It need not be wondered at, if all these things took me up most part of the third year of my abode here. It is to be observ'd, in the intervals of these things, I had my new harvest and husbandry to manage. I reaped my corn in its season, and carried it home as well as I could, and laid it up in the ear till I had time to rub it out, for I had no floor to thrash it on, or instrument to thrash it with.

And now, indeed, my stock of corn increasing, I wanted to build my barns bigger. I wanted a place to lay it up in, for the increase of the corn now yielded me so much I had of the barley about twenty bushels and of rice as much, or more. I resolv'd to begin to use it freely, for my bread had been quite gone a great while. I resolv'd also to see what quantity would be sufficient for me a whole year and to sow but once a year.

Upon the whole, I found the forty bushels of barley and rice were much more than I could consume in a year. I resolv'd to sow just the same quantity every year that I sowed the last, in hopes such a quantity would provide me with bread, etc.

Years go by, my sea voyage, the ominous voice

I finish'd my fourth year in this place and kept my anniversary with the same devotion and with as much comfort as before. By a constant study and serious application to the word of God, I gained a different knowledge from what I had before. I entertained different notions of things. I look'd now upon the world as a thing remote, which I had nothing to do with, no expectation from, and, indeed, no desires about. In a word, I had nothing to do with it, nor was ever likely to have. I thought it looked, as we may perhaps look upon it hereafter, viz. as a place I had lived in, but was come out of it.

In the first place, I was here removed from all the risk of the world. I had neither the danger of the beast, the need of concealment, nor the pride of life. I had nothing to covet, for I had all I was now capable of enjoying. I was lord of the whole manor. If I pleased, I might call myself king or emperor over the whole country which I had possession of. I might have raised ship-loadings of corn, but I had no use for it. I had tortoise or turtle enough, but now and then one was as much as I could put to any use. I had timber enough to have built a fleet of ships, and I had grapes enough to have made wine, or to have cured into raisins, to have loaded that fleet when it had been built.

I had now brought my state of life to be much more comfortable in itself than it was at first, and much easier to my mind, as well as to my body. I often sat down to meat with thankfulness, and admired the hand of providence which had thus spread my table in the wilderness. I learned to look more upon the bright side of my condition and less upon the dark side, and to consider what I enjoy'd rather than what I wanted. This gave me sometimes such secret comforts that I cannot express them. All our discontents about what we want appear'd to me to spring from the want of thankfulness for what we have.

The beast, too, had come to accept the island as its home and territory. The change was a thing of gentleness, as neither of us fought to hold back the other a whit when either the moon or the dawn came. It had outgrown its moody reticence and once again ran and howl'd and kill'd, some time for sport and other time for food. It did not leave my side of the island, and rare was it that I awoke less than a half hour's walk from either my cave or my country home, as I called it.

I had now been here so long that many things which I brought on shore for my help were either quite gone or very much wasted and near spent.

My ink, as I observ'd, had been gone for some time, all but a very little, which I eek'd out with water till it was so pale it scarce left any appearance of black upon the paper. As long as it lasted, I made use of it to minute down the days of the month on which any remarkable thing happen'd to me.

My cloathes, too, began to decay. As to linen, I had none for a great while except some chequer'd shirts which I found in the chests of the other seamen and which I preserved, because many times I could bear no cloathes on but a shirt. It was a very great help to me I had, among all the men's cloathes of the ship, almost three dozen of shirts. There were also several thick watch-coats of the seamen's which were left, but they were too hot to wear. Tho' it is true the weather was so hot there was no need of cloathes, yet I could not go quite naked, no, tho' I had been inclined to it, which I was not. Nor could I abide the thought of it, tho' I was all alone.

The reason why I could not go quite naked was I could not bear the heat of the sun. The very heat blistered my skin, whereas with a shirt on the air itself made some motion, and whistling under the shirt, was twofold cooler than without it. No more could I ever bring myself to go out in the heat of the sun without a cap or hat. The heat of the sun, beating with such violence as it does in that place, would give me the head-ache by darting so directly upon my head so I could not bear it. Whereas if I put on my hat it would go away.

Upon these views, I began to consider about putting the few rags I had, which I call'd cloathes, into some order. I had worn out all the waistcoats I had, and my business was now to try if I could not make jackets out of the great watch-coats I had by me, and with such other materials as I had. So I set to work a taylering, or rather a botching, for I made most piteous work of it. However, I made shift to make two or three new waistcoats, which I hoped would serve me a great while. As for breeches or drawers, I made but a very sorry shift indeed till afterwards.

I have mentioned I saved the skins of all the creatures I kill'd. The first thing I made of these was a great cap for my head, with the hair on the outside, to shoot off the rain. This I performed so well, after this I made me a suit of cloathes of the skins, that is to say, a waist-coat, and breeches open at the knees, and both loose. They were rather wanting to keep me cool than warm. I must not omit to ac-knowledge they were wretchedly made, for if I was a bad carpenter I was a worse taylor. However, when I was abroad if it happened to rain, the hair of my waistcoat and cap being uppermost, I was kept very dry.

As I had a raft, my next design was to make a cruise round the island. As I had been on the other side in one place, crossing, as I have already described it, over the land, so the discoveries I made in that little journey made me very eager to see other parts of the coast.

And thus I every now and then took a little voyage upon the sea, but never went far out, nor far from the little creek. At last, being eager to view the circumference of my little kingdom, I resolv'd upon my cruise. It was the sixth of November, in the sixth year of my reign, that I set out on this voyage, and I found it much longer than I expected. For tho' the island it self was not very large, yet when I came to the east side of it, I found a great ledge of black rocks lye out about two leagues into the sea, some above water, some under it, which I could not recall having seen there before. Like great teeth they did rise from the sea, some pointed and some angled and some flat, and but for their senseless angles and shapes some of these black rocks would seem carv'd. Beyond that ledge was a shoal of sand, lying dry half a league more, so I was obliged to go a great way out to sea to double the point.

But I am a warning piece again to all rash and ignorant pilots. No sooner was I come to the point, when I was not even my raft's length from the shore, but I found myself in a great depth of water and a current like the sluice of a mill. It carried my raft along with it with such violence all I could do could not keep her so much as on the edge of it. I found it hurried me farther and farther out, and all I could do with my paddles for more than a day signify'd nothing. Now I began to give myself over for lost. I had no prospect before me but of perishing, not by the sea, for that was calm enough, but of starving for hunger. I had my victuals, but what was all this to being driven into the vast ocean where there was no shore, no main land, or island for a thousand leagues at least?

However, I found being between two great currents, viz. that on the south side, which had hurried me away, and that on the north, which lay about a league on the other side in the wake of the island, I found the water at least still and running no way. Having still a breeze of wind fair for me, I kept on paddling for the island, tho' not making such fresh way as I did heading out away from it.

About four o'clock in the evening on the fourth day, being then within a league of the island, I found the point of the rocks which occasioned this disaster, stretching out, as is described before, to the southward, and casting off the current more southerly, had, of course, made another eddy to the north. I stretched across this eddy, slanting north-west and, in about an hour, came within about a mile of the shore, where, it being smooth water, I soon got to land.

When I was on shore, I fell on my knees, and gave God thanks for my deliverance. Refreshing myself with such things as I had, I brought my raft close to the shore, in a little cove I had spied under some trees, and laid me down to sleep, being quite spent with the labour and fatigue of the voyage.

I was now at a great loss which way to get home with my raft. I had run so much hazard, and knew too much of the case to think of attempting it by the way I went out. What might be at the other side (I mean the west side) I knew not, nor had I any mind to run any more ventures. So I only resolv'd in the morning to make my way westward along the shore and to see if there was no creek where I might lay up my raft in safety, so as to have her again if I wanted her. In about three miles or thereabouts, coasting the shore, I came to a very good inlet about a mile over where I found a very convenient harbour for my boat and where she lay as if she had been in a little dock made on purpose for her. Here I put in, and having stowed my raft very safe I went on shore to look about me and see where I was.

I soon found I had but a little passed by the place where I had been before, when I travel'd on foot to that shore. So taking nothing from my raft but my gun, I began my march. The way was comfortable enough after such a voyage as I had been upon, and I reached my old bower in the evening, where I found every thing standing as I left it. I always kept it in good order, being, as I have said before, my country house.

I got over the fence and laid me down in the shade to rest my limbs, for I was very weary, and fell asleep. But judge, you that read my story, if you can, what a surprise I must be in when I was awaked out of my sleep by a voice calling me by my name several times. "Robin, Robin, Robin Crusoe. Poor Robin Crusoe! Where are you, Robin Crusoe? Where are you?"

I was so dead asleep at first, being fatigued with paddling the first part of the day and with walking the latter part, I did not wake thoroughly. But I did think I dreamt somebody spoke to me. As the voice continued to repeat "Robin Crusoe, Robin Crusoe," at last I began to wake more and was at first frightened and started up in the utmost consternation. But no sooner were my eyes open but I saw my Poll sitting on the top of the hedge and knew it was he that spoke to me. In just such bemoaning language I had used to talk to him, and teach him.

"Robin Crusoe," he repeated. "There you are." And then, quite unexpectedly, did he utter words I had not taught him, and these words did give me a chill and a shiver like the icy sea of England. "They will kill you, Robin Crusoe."

I confess, at first I was so torn tween the joy of hearing my name aloud by one other than I, and a terror at the same after six long years, that I did not think on what little Poll did say. Then the import of his words was known to me, and I wonder'd who had taught my parrot such words, and why, and when.

"Robin Crusoe! Robin Crusoe!" squawk'd he. "They come to kill you and eat your flesh. Your beast cannot save you, Robin Crusoe. Your soul shall feed the Great Dreamer! *Ia! Ia!!*"

At this did Poll fall into madness, as one who has seen awful things that cannot be unremembered, as for a while I thought I may do upon this island. The parrot shook on the hedge as if chill'd and squawk'd out many sounds and noises that had no meaning behind them. Tho' as I watched and listen'd I did hear a pattern, and knew the sounds were a language unknown to me, and Poll call'd out the same words again and again as one who chants or prays. And as I listened more, these words did began to hurt my ears and head. As the sound of a cannon at close quarters may bleed the ears, so did Poll's squawks make me recoil and cover my ears, tho' they were little louder than his usual cries. Beneath my skin, the beast growl'd, making its rage at these words known as well.

And then Poll stiffen'd and fell over dead on the floor of my bower. His blood ran from his eyes and beak, as it some times is wont to do in man or creature when death comes swift.

More time, my herd, my condition

I could not leave Poll in my summer house, nor would I bury
him within the walls of my bower. Thus I did climb over the
fence and find a spot beneath a large tree, much like the tree
I had first found Poll in many years afore this. Using one of my
hatchets and my hands, I made the dead bird a small grave fit for
any manor Lord or Lady. Yet when I climb'd back over the wall to
retrieve his little body, I discover'd I could not tolerate the thought
of touching the dead parrot. A great unease hung across my shoulders, and I bethought myself that this was the beast, still anger'd at
the little bird for reasons unknown to me. Then did I realize that
this unease was all my own. "This is," I said aloud, "what each of
God's creatures feels at the sight of me and the smell of the beast
under my skin. Is it little wonder none but my hungry goat can
abide me?" And thus did I wonder what had dwelt beneath Poll's
skin and hidden itself with his feathers as it spoke to me.

At last I pull'd off my great cap and wore it upon my hand like a
glove, and even then touching the dead bird gave me a great unease,

as if many ants were marching across my bare skin, tho' there were no such things. This feeling did not pass until dear Poll was bury'd beneath the soil of the island.

That moon, the beast was most territorial again, and stalk'd the forest for three nights as one who invites trouble into their lives. I found its tracks criss'd and cross'd by my summer house, oft approaching the grave of Poll but never going to it. Together with Poll's dark words this did worry my thoughts, and the next month was one of much apprehension and reflection for me. By the next moon, tho', the beast once again ran and hunted and kill'd, and I took this as a sign the darkness had past us by again.

In this government of my temper I remained near a year, lived a very sedate, retired life, as you may well suppose. My thoughts being very much composed as to my condition, and comforted in resigning myself to the dispositions of Providence, I thought I lived very happily in all things, except that of society.

I improved myself in this time in all the mechanic exercises which my necessities put me upon applying myself to. I believe I could, upon occasion, have made a very good carpenter, considering how few tools I had.

Besides this, I arrived at an unexpected perfection in my earthen-ware and contrived well enough to make them with a wheel, which I found easier and better. But I think I was never more vain of my own performance, or more joyful for any thing I found out, than for my being able to make a tobacco-pipe, tho' it was a very ugly clumsy thing when it was done, and only burnt red like other earthen-ware. Yet as it was hard and firm, and would draw the smoke, I was comforted with it, for I had been always used to smoke.

I began now to perceive my powder abated considerably. This was a want which it was impossible for me to supply, and I began to consider what I must do when I should have no more powder. That is to say, how I should do to kill any goats. I had, as is observ'd in the third year of my being here, kept a young kid and bred her up tame, and I was in hopes of getting a he-goat. But I could not by any means bring it to pass, as they still fled from the hidden beast, till my kid grew an old goat. As I could never find in my heart to kill her, she died at last of meer age.

But being now in the eleventh year of my residence, and, as I have said, my ammunition growing low, I set myself to study some art to trap and snare the goats, to see whether I could not catch some of them alive. Particularly, I wanted a she-goat great with young. At length I resolv'd to try a pitfall. I dug several large pits in the earth in places where I had observ'd the goats used to feed. Not to trouble you with particulars, going one morning to see my traps, I found in one of them a large old he-goat and in one of the others three kids, a male and two females. As to the old one, I knew not what to do with him. He was so fierce, I durst not go into the pit to him. I could have kill'd him, or let him for the beast, but that was not my business, nor would it answer my end. So I let him out, and he ran away, frightened out of his wits once he had smell'd the scent of the beast.

It was a good while before the kids would feed near me, but throwing them some sweet corn tempted them and they began to be tame. And now I found if I expected to supply myself with goat's flesh when I had no powder or shot left, breeding some up tame was my only way.

But then it occurred to me I must keep the tame from the wild or else they would always run wild when they grew up. And the beast must be kept out lest it see my herd as a banquet table to slake its own appetites. The only way for this was to have some enclosed piece of ground, well fenced, either with hedge or pale, to keep them in so that those within might not break out or those without break in.

This was a great undertaking for one pair of hands, yet as I saw there was an absolute necessity for doing it, my first work was to find out a proper piece of ground where there was herbage for them to eat, water for them to drink, and cover to keep them from the sun.

I was about three months hedging in the first piece. Till I had done it, I tethered the three kids in the best part of it and used them to feed as near me as possible to make them familiar. Very often I would go and carry them some ears of barley or a handful of rice, but they would shy away from the scent of the beast and press themselves against the farthest reach of the tether. After my enclosure was finish'd and I let them loose, they would huddle together in that part which was away from me.

In about a year and a half, I had a flock of about twelve goats, kids and all. In two years more I had three and forty, besides several I took and kill'd for my food. After that I enclosed five several pieces of ground to feed them in, with little pens to drive them into, to take them as I wanted, and gates out of one piece of ground into another.

But this was not all. Now I not only had goat's flesh to feed on when I pleased, but milk too, a thing which in the beginning I did not so much as think of, and which, when it came into my thoughts, was an agreeable surprise. Now I set up my dairy, and had sometimes a gallon or two of milk in a day. What a table was here spread for me in a wilderness, where I saw nothing, at first but to perish for hunger!

One morning, well within my thirteenth year upon the island, I awoke in the hills after the last night of the moon. The beast had run long and hard those past nights, and yet I had a strange uneasiness in my mind to go down to the point of the island. This inclination increased upon me every day, and at length I resolv'd to travel thither by land, following the edge of the shore. I did so, but had any one in England been to meet such a man as I was, it must either have frightened him or raised a great deal of laughter. As I frequently stood still to look at myself, I could not but smile at the notion of my traveling through Yorkshire with such an equipage and in such a dress. Be pleased to take a sketch of my figure, as follows:

I had a great high shapeless cap, made of a goat's skin, with a flap hanging down behind as well, to keep the sun from me as to shoot the rain off from running into my neck.

I had a short jacket of goat's skin, the skirts coming down to about the middle of the thighs, and a pair of open-kneed breeches of the same. The breeches were made of the skin of an old he-goat, whose hair hung down such a length on either side, that, like panta-loons, it reached to the middle of my legs. Stockings and shoes I had none, but had made me a pair of somethings, I scarce know what to call them, like buskins, to flap over my legs and lace on either side like spatterdashes.

I had on a broad belt of goat's skin dried, which I drew together with two thongs of the same instead of buckles. In a kind of a frog on either side of this, instead of a sword and dagger, hung a little saw and a hatchet. I had another belt, not so broad and fastened in the same manner, which hung over my shoulder. At the end of it, under my left arm, hung two pouches, in one of which hung my powder, in the other my shot. At my back I carried my basket, and on my shoulder my gun.

As for my face, the colour of it was not so mulatto-like as one might expect from a man not at all careful and living within nine or ten degrees of the equinox. My beard I had once suffered to grow till it was about a quarter of a yard long. As I had both scissars and razors sufficient, I had cut it pretty short, except what grew on my upper lip, which I had trimmed into a large pair of Mahometan whiskers, such as I had seen worn by some Turks at Sallee. The Moors did not wear such, tho' the Turks did. Of these mustachios or whiskers, I will not say they were long enough to hang my hat upon them, but they were of a length and shape monstrous enough, and in England, would have passed for frightful.

But all this is by the by. As to my figure, I had so few to observe me that it was of no manner of consequence, so I say no more to that part. In this kind of figure I went on my new journey, and was out five or six days. I traveled first along the sea-shore. I went over the land, a nearer way, to the same height I was upon before. When looking forward to the point which lay out, I was surprised to see the sea all smooth and quiet. No rippling, no motion, no current, any more there than in any other places. Indeed, even the black rocks could not be seen. For reasons I could not name, I bethought myself that this was why the beast had run with such glee for its three nights, viz. that nothing moved in the sea. While rarely I felt anxious, at this time a sense of great peace did come upon me, nay, upon my entire island. Two years more past, and the beast and I were most pleas'd with our lives here.

But now I come to a new scene of my life.

The foot print, my terrors,
my decisions

❀

It happened one day, about a week after the last night of the moon, I was surprised with the print of a man's naked foot on the shore, which was very plain to be seen in the sand.

I stood like one thunder-struck, or as if I had seen an apparition. I listened, I looked round me, but I could hear nothing, nor see any thing. I went up the shore and down the shore, but it was all one. I went to it again to see if there were any more, and to observe if it might not be my fancy. But there was no room for that, for there was the print of a foot, toes, heel, and every part of a foot, splayed wide upon the sand. After innumerable fluttering thoughts, like a man confused and out of myself, I came home to my fortification terrified to the last degree, looking behind me at every two or three steps, mistaking every bush and tree and stump at a distance to be a man. Nor is it possible to describe how many wild ideas were found every moment in my fancy, and what strange unaccountable whimsies came into my thoughts by the way.

When I came to my castle (for so I think I called it ever after this) I fled into it like one pursued. Whether I went over by the ladder or went in at the hole in the rock, which I had called a door, I cannot remember. Nor could I remember the next morning. Never frightened hare fled to cover, or fox to earth, with more terror of mind than I to this retreat.

I slept none that night. The farther I was from the occasion of my fright the greater my apprehensions were. I was so embarrassed with my own frightful ideas of the thing I formed nothing but dismal imaginations to myself, even tho' I was now a great way off it. Sometimes I fancied it must be the Devil and reason joined in with me upon this supposition. How should any other thing in human shape come into the place? Where was the vessel that brought them? What marks were there of any other footsteps?

But then to think Satan should take human shape upon him, in such a place, to leave the print of his foot behind him. I considered the Devil might have found out abundance of other ways to have terrified me than this of the single print of a foot. As I lived quite on the other side of the island, it was ten thousand to one whether I should ever see it or not. And in the sand, too, which the first surge of the sea upon a high wind would have defaced entirely. All this seemed inconsistent with the notions we entertain of the subtilty of the Devil.

Abundance of such things as these assisted to argue me out of all apprehensions of its being the Devil.

I presently concluded it must be some of the dangerous savages of the main land who had wandered out to sea in their canoes and, either driven by the currents or by contrary winds, had made the island. They had been on shore but were gone away again to sea, being as loth, perhaps, to have stayed on my desolate island as I would have been to have had them.

Thus my fear banished all former confidence in God. I reproached myself with my laziness, that would not sow any more corn one year than would just serve me till the next season, as if no accident would intervene to prevent my enjoying the crop that was upon the ground. This I thought so just a reproof, I resolv'd for the future to have two or three years' corn beforehand, so whatever might come, I might not perish for want of bread.

How strange a chequer-work of providence is the life of man! That I should now tremble at the very apprehensions of seeing a man, and was ready to sink into the ground at but the shadow or silent appearance of a man's having set his foot in the island.

One morning, lying in my bed and fill'd with thoughts about my danger from the appearances of savages, I found it discomposed me very much. Upon which these words of the Scripture came into my thoughts, *Call upon me in the day of trouble, and I will deliver thee, and thou shalt glorify me.*

Upon this, rising out of my bed, my heart was not only comforted but I was guided and encouraged to pray. When I had done praying, I took up my Bible, and, opening it to read, the first words presented to me were, *Wait on the Lord, and be of good cheer, and he shall strengthen thy heart; wait, I say, on the Lord.* It is impossible to express the comfort this gave me. In answer, I thankfully laid down the book and was no more sad, at least on that occasion.

In the middle of these cogitations, apprehensions, and reflections, it came into my thoughts all this might be a mere chimera of my own. This might be the print of my own foot, or e'en that of the beast, since distorted by the tydes. This cheered me up a little too, and I began to persuade myself it was all a delusion, that it was nothing else but my own foot.

Now I began to take courage and to peep abroad again, for I had not stirred out of my castle for three days and nights, so I began to starve for provisions. I had little or nothing within doors but some barley-cakes and water. I knew my goats wanted to be milked too, which was my evening diversion, and the poor creatures were in great pain and inconvenience for want of it. Indeed, it almost spoiled some of them and dried up their milk.

As I went down thus two or three days, and having seen nothing, I began to be a little bolder and to think there was nothing in it but my own imagination. But I could not persuade myself fully of this till I should go down to the shore again and see this print of a foot and measure it by my own and see if there was any similitude or fitness. The wind had dull'd it somewhat, but still it was there in the damp sand.

First, it appeared to me I could not possibly be on shore any where thereabouts. Secondly, when I came to measure the mark with my own foot, I found my foot not so large and not as broad by a great deal. Also, there were peculiarities of the mark, such as the small holes by each toe, as those left by the beast's claws, tho' this was most assuredly not a track of the beast. There also was an odd-ness I could not put a name to, as if the foot print-maker had worn fine stockings stretched between each splayed toe.

All these things fill'd my head with new imaginations and gave me the vapours again to the highest degree, so I shook with cold like one in an ague. I went home again fill'd with the belief some man or men had been on shore there, or the island was inhabited and I might be surprised before I was aware. What course to take for my security I knew not.

O what ridiculous resolutions men take when possessed with fear! It deprives them of the use of those means which reason offers for their relief. The first thing I proposed to myself was to throw down my enclosures and turn all my tame cattle wild into the woods, lest the enemy should find them and then frequent the island in prospect of the same or the like booty. Then to the simple thing of digging up my two corn fields lest they should find such a grain there and still be prompted to frequent the island. Then to demolish my bower and tent, that they might not see any vestiges of habitation and be prompted to look farther, in order to find out the persons inhabiting.

These were the subjects of the first night's cogitations after I was come home again, while the apprehensions which had so over-run my mind were fresh upon me and my head was full of vapours, as above. Thus fear of danger is ten thousand times more terrifying than danger itself, when apparent to the eyes.

This confusion of my thoughts kept me awake all night, but in the morning I fell asleep. Having been, by the amusement of my mind, tired and my spirits exhausted, I slept and waked much better composed than I had ever been before. And now I began to think. Upon the utmost debate with myself I concluded this island, which was so exceeding pleasant, fruitful, and no farther from the main land than as I had seen, was not so abandoned as I might imagine. Altho' there were no stated inhabitants who lived on the spot, yet that there might sometimes come boats off from the shore who might come to this place.

I had lived here fifteen years now and had not met with the least shadow or figure of any people yet. If at any time they should be driven here, it was probable they went away again as soon as ever they could, seeing they had never thought fit to fix here upon any occasion.

The most I could suggest any danger from was from any casual accidental landing of straggling people from the main, who went off again with all possible speed, seldom staying one night on shore lest they should not have the help of the tydes and daylight back again. Therefore I had nothing to do but to consider of some safe retreat in case I should see any savages land upon the spot.

Now I began to repent I had dug my cave so large as to bring a door through again which, as I said, came out beyond where my fortification joined to the rock. Upon considering this, therefore, I resolv'd to draw me a second fortification in the same manner of a semi-circle at a distance from my wall, just where I had planted a double row of stakes about twelve years before, of which I made mention. These having been planted so thick before, they wanted but few piles to be driven between them that they might be thicker and stronger, and my wall would be soon finished.

I had now a double wall. My outer wall was thickened with pieces of timber, old cables, and every thing I could think of, to make it strong, and having in it seven little holes about as big as I might put my arm out at. In the inside of this, I thickened my wall to about ten feet thick, with continually bringing earth out of my cave and laying it at the foot of the wall and walking upon it. Through the seven holes I contrived to plant the muskets like my cannon and fitted them into frames that held them like a carriage, so I could fire all the seven guns in two minutes' time. This wall I was many a weary month in finishing, and yet never thought myself safe till it was done.

When this was done, I stuck all the ground without my wall, for a great length every way, as full with stakes, or sticks, of the osier-like wood as they could well stand. Insomuch, I believe I might set in near twenty thousand of them, leaving a pretty large space between them and my wall. I might have room to see an enemy and they might have no shelter from the young trees if they attempted to approach my outer wall.

Over these months, I am ashamed to say, I did give the beast excessive freedom and not attempt to watch through the smok'd lens or to exert any influence over its nature. It was my belief that the howls and cries of the beast might be heard for many miles, and perhaps the savages, upon hearing such sounds, would be less de-siring to land on my island. Indeed, perhaps such a thing had already happen'd many times in my long years here.

I was at the expense of all this labour purely from my apprehen-sions on the account of the print of a man's foot which I had seen. For, as yet, I never saw any human creature come near the island. I had now lived two years under this uneasiness, which, indeed, made my life much less comfortable than it was before, as may be well imagined by any who know what it is to live in the constant snare of fear. And this I must observe, with grief too, that the discomposure of my mind had too great impressions also upon the religious part of my thoughts. The dread of falling into the hands of savages and cannibals lay so upon my spirits that I seldom found myself in a due temper for application to my Maker, at least not with the sedate calmness and resignation of soul which I was wont to do. I rather prayed to God as under great affliction and pressure of mind, surrounded with danger, and in expectation every night of being murdered and devoured before morning.

The dark church, my plans,
my rational mind

But to go on.

I went about the whole island, searching for another private place, when, wandering more to the west point of the island than I had ever done yet and looking out to sea, I thought I saw a boat upon the sea at a great distance. I had found a perspective-glass or two in one of the seamen's chests, which I saved out of our ship, but I had it not about me. This was so remote I could not tell what to make of it, tho' I looked at it till my eyes were not able to hold to look any longer. Whether it was a boat or not, I do not know, but as I descended from the hill I could see no more of it. I resolv'd to go no more out without a perspective-glass in my pocket.

When I was come down the hill to the end of the island, where, indeed, I had never been before, I was presently convinced that seeing the print of a man's foot was not such a strange thing in the island as I imagined. It was a special providence I was cast upon the side of the island where the savages never came. I should easily have known nothing was more frequent than for the canoes from the main, when they happened to be a little too far out at sea, to shoot over to that side of the island for harbour.

When I was come down the hill to the shore, as I said above, being the south west point of the island, I was confounded and amazed. Nor is it possible for me to express the horror of my mind at seeing the shore spread with skulls, hands, feet, and other bones of human bodies. I observ'd a place where there had been a fire made and a circle dug in the earth, where I supposed the savage wretches, according to their dreadful customs, had sat down to their inhuman feastings upon the bodies of their fellow creatures.

I further observ'd this whole corner of the island had been shaped and arrang'd to serve their needs, and just as I had made a homestead on my side of the island, the savages had made a church for their awful beliefs. Many trees had strange symbols and shapes cut within their bark, and these symbols were also painted large on many stones, altho' the growls of the beast told me what the paint most certainly was. I stepp'd over the bones and skulls to closer examine a tree, and saw the cuts and carving were very old. The sand itself, indeed, was all red with long use. This savage church had been here on my island long before the fateful night that brought the beast and I to the shores here. Tho' now I wonder'd the wisdom of calling it my island, and if it ever had been.

Twelve great strides from the fire-circle was a large iron-wood tree, one which dwarft all I had ever seen, and all things had been clear'd away from it. Were four men to stretch their arms only then might they just encircle the base of such a giant, and it took another twelve steps to walk about and examine it. To the height of two men had the living tree been shaped and cut to make a living totem or statue from the wood, which continued to grow as its roots and leaves attested. It was the shape of a great man, one who crouch'd like a child at play, or an animal, I could not say which. Upon his carv'd feet and hands were great claws, like those of the beast, which made these appendages even longer and more disturbing.

His head was large and his eyes long and wide. A beard of thick, fat hairs trail'd down his face, and crouched as he was the hairs all but reached his ancles. And then a cold chill did creep through my limbs, for I knew this figure and had seen it before. This was the same cuttel fish dream lord who had appear'd to me in a fever-vision some seventeen years before, when I was only ten months onto the island. How was such a thing possible, for it to be a ne'er before seen creation wholly of my mind, and yet a figure of worship to the savages?

I durst not approach too close to this thing, but the cuts and carving did appear even older than those on the other trees, and I did bethought myself that I could only guess how long this totem had stood on the island. A hundred-year? Three? Was it carv'd when Rome still ruled England, or when Moses toiled in Aegypt? My mind said such was impossible, yet my heart felt some truth in such thoughts.

Within me the beast made many growls. The smell of flesh and blood excited it, as such things do, but it was also cow'd by the sight of this large totem. It did react to this place much as it had to the shadow'd valley I had found many years before and ne'er visited again.

I was so astonished with the sight of these things and the reactions of the beast, I entertain'd no notions of any danger to myself from it for a long while. All my apprehensions were buried in the thoughts of such a fearsome creature of the totem, the awful rituals perform'd before it, and the horror of the degeneracy of human nature, which, tho' I had heard of it often, yet I never had so near a view of before. In short, I turned away my face from the horrid spectacle. My stomach grew sick, and I was just at the point of fainting when nature discharged the disorder from my stomach. Having vomited with uncommon violence, I was a little relieved, but could not bear to stay in the place a moment. I got me up the hill again with all the speed I could and walked on towards my own habitation.

When I came a little out of that part of the island, I stood still awhile, as amazed, and then recovering myself, I looked up with the utmost affection of my soul and gave God thanks that had cast my first lot in a part of the world where I was distinguished from such dreadful creatures as these. In this frame of thankfulness, I went home to my castle and began to be easier now as to the safety of my circumstances than ever I was before. I observ'd these wretches never came to this island in search of what they could get. Perhaps not seeking, not wanting, or not expecting any thing here aside from the performance of their awful customs and feast within their church, as I must think of it. I knew I had been here now almost eighteen years and never saw the least footsteps of human creature there before. I might be eighteen years more as concealed as I was now if I did not discover myself to them, which I had no manner of occasion to do.

Yet I entertain'd such an abhorrence of the savage wretches I have been speaking of, and of the wretched inhuman custom of their devouring and eating one another up, I continued pensive and sad and kept close within my own circle for almost two years after this. When I say my own circle, I mean by it my three plantations, viz. my castle, my country-seat, which I called my bower, and my enclosure in the woods. Nor did I look after this for any other use than as an enclosure for my goats. The aversion which nature gave me to these hellish wretches was such that I was as fearful of seeing them as of seeing the Devil himself. If I had happened to have fallen into their hands, I knew what would have been my lot.

Also within this time did my memories go back to little Poll, who died speaking awful words. The parrot did tell of a great dreamer who would feed upon my soul. And yet here had I not found a graven image of a thing from my dreams, the bearded dream lord, a thing which those who eat the bodies of men did worship as a saint or icon? Were the awful, unknowable words Poll spoke at his end the words of savages? The two things, viz. the dream lord and Poll's dire profesy, did seem surely link'd.

Time, however, and the satisfaction I was in no danger of being discovered by these people, began to wear off my uneasiness. I began to live just in the same composed manner as before, with this difference. I used more caution, and kept my eyes more about me than I did before, lest I should happen to be seen by any of them. Particularly I was more cautious of firing my gun, lest any of them being on the island should happen to hear it. It was therefore a very good providence to me I had furnished myself with a tame breed of goats, and I had no need to hunt any more about the woods. If I did catch any of them after this, it was by traps and snares, as I had done before. So for two years after this I believe I never fired my gun once off, tho' I never went out without it. Which was more, as I had saved three pistols out of the ship, I always carried at least two of them out with me, sticking them in my goat-skin belt. I also furbish'd up one of the great cutlasses I had out of the ship, and made me a belt to hang it on. I was now a most formidable fellow to look at when I went abroad, if you add to the former description of myself the particular of two pistols, and a great broad-sword hanging at my side.

Things going on thus for some time, I seemed, excepting these cautions, to be reduced to my former calm sedate way of living. Even the beast still ran across the island, tho' now I was keenly aware that it never ran or hunt'd in the south-west point or in the shadow'd valley. All these things tended to show me, more and more, how far my condition was from being miserable compared to some others, even if it were not perfect.

As in my present condition there were not many things which I wanted, so, indeed, I thought the frights I had been in about these savage wretches, and the concern I had been in for my own preservation, had taken off the edge of my invention for my own conveniences. But my invention now ran quite another way. Night and day I could think of nothing but how I might destroy some of these monsters in their cruel, bloody ritual, and, if possible, save the victim they should bring hither to destroy. It would take up a larger volume than this whole work to set down all the contrivances I brooded upon for destroying these creatures, or at least frightening them so as to prevent their coming hither any more. But all this was abortive. Nothing could be possible to take effect unless I was to be there to do it myself. And what could one man do among them, when perhaps there might be twenty or thirty of them together, with their darts or their bows and arrows, with which they could shoot as true to a mark as I could with my gun? Even the beast would be hard press'd against such numbers, tho' their weapons could do naught to kill it.

Sometimes I thought of digging a hole under the place where they made their fire, and putting in five or six pounds of gunpowder, which, when they kindled their fire, would take fire and blow up all that was near it. But as, in the first place, I should be unwilling to waste so much powder upon them, my store being now within the quantity of one barrel, so neither could I be sure of its going off at any certain time when it might surprise them. At best it would do little more than just blow the fire about their ears and fright them, but not sufficient to make them forsake the place.

So I laid it aside and then proposed I would place myself in ambush in some convenient place, with my three guns all double-loaded, and in the middle of their bloody ceremony let fly at them, when I should be sure to kill or wound perhaps two or three at every shot. Then falling in upon them with my three pistols and my sword, I made no doubt but if there were twenty I should kill them all. This fancy pleased my thoughts for some weeks.

I went so far with it in my imagination, I employed myself several days to find out proper places to put myself in ambuscade, as I said, to watch for them. I went to the dark church itself, which was now grown more familiar to me. But while my mind was thus fill'd with thoughts of revenge, and a bloody putting twenty or thirty of them to the sword, as I may call it, the unease I had at the place abetted my malice.

Well, at length I found a place in the side of the hill where I was satisfied I might wait till I saw any of their boats coming. There was a hollow large enough to conceal me. There I might sit and observe all their bloody doings and take my full aim at their heads when they were so close together as it would be next to impossible I should miss my shot, or that I could fail wounding three or four of them at the first shot.

After I had thus laid the scheme of my design, and, in my imagination put it in practice, I made my tour every morning up to the top of the hill, which was from my castle about three miles, to see if I could observe any boats upon the sea coming near the island or standing over towards it. But I began to tire of this hard duty after I had, for two or three months, constantly kept my watch but came always back without any discovery. There was not, in all that time, the least appearance, not only on or near the shore but on the whole ocean, so far as my eyes or glasses could reach every way.

As long as I kept my daily tour to the hill to look out, my spirits seemed to be all the while in a suitable form for so outrageous an execution as the killing of twenty or thirty naked savages. But now, when I began to be weary of the fruitless excursion which I had made so far every morning in vain, so my opinion of the action itself began to alter. I began, with cooler and calmer thoughts which enter'd my mind, to consider what I was going to engage in.

What authority or call had I to pretend to be judge and executioner upon these men as criminals, whom Heaven had thought fit, for so many ages, to suffer to go on unpunished? I debated this very often with myself thus: How do I know what God himself judges in this particular case? It is certain these people do not commit this as a crime. They do not know it to be an offence and then commit it in defiance of divine justice, as we do in almost all the sins we commit. They think it no more a crime to kill a captive taken in war than we do to kill an ox, nor to eat human flesh than we do to eat mutton. Indeed, they were much as the beast in this manner.

When I considered this a little, it followed that I was certainly in the wrong in it. These people were not murderers in the sense I had before condemned them in my thoughts, any more than the beast was a murderer for what it had done. It had a fine animal mind, but still animal, with no understanding of sin or crime or justice. That it kill'd the mate was indeed an awful thing, but it was not an evil thing. As I have oft said before, the beast is not evil. Indeed, if it were, should I have not put myself, and it, to death to punish it? No! I had been satisfied to leave it here, where it enjoyed freedom with no danger to others.

These considerations put me to a pause. I began, by little and little, to be off my design, and to conclude I had taken wrong measures in my resolution to attack the savages. It was not my business to meddle with them unless they first attacked me, and this it was my business, if possible, to prevent. If I were discovered and attacked by them I knew my duty.

On the other hand, I argued with myself, this was the way to ruin and destroy myself. Unless I was sure to kill every one that not only should be on shore at that time, but that should ever come on shore afterwards, if but one of them escaped to tell their country-people what had happened, they would come over again by thousands to revenge the death of their fellow.

Upon the whole, I concluded, that neither in principle nor in policy I ought to concern myself in this affair. My business was, by all possible means, to conceal myself from them and not to leave the least signal to them to guess by that there were any living creatures upon the island of human shape.

My new cave, dark symbols,
my resolution

I n this disposition I continued for near a year after this. So far was I from desiring an occasion for falling upon these wretches in all that time, I never once went up the hill to see whether there were any of them in sight, or to know whether any of them had been on shore there or not, that I might not be tempted to renew any of my contrivances against them. I kept myself more retired than ever and seldom went from my cell. Certain it is these savage people who sometimes haunted this island never came with any thoughts of finding any thing here aside from their great totem, and consequently never wandered off from the coast. I doubt not but they might have been several times on shore after my apprehensions of them had made me cautious, as well as before. Indeed, I looked back with some horror upon the thoughts of what my condition would have been if I had chopped upon them and been discovered before that, when, naked and unarmed, except with one gun, and that loaded often only with small shot, I walked every where, peering about the island to see what I could get. What a surprise should I have been in if, when I discovered the print of a man's foot, I had instead seen fifteen or twenty cannibals and found them pursuing me!

I believe the reader of this will not think it strange if I confess these anxieties, these constant dangers I lived in, and the concern that was now upon me, put an end to all invention and to all the contrivances I had laid for my future accommodations and conveniences. I had the care of my safety more now upon my hands than that of my food. I cared not to drive a nail or chop a stick of wood for fear the noise I might make should be heard. Much less would I fire a gun. Above all, I was uneasy at making any fire, lest the smoke, which is visible at a great distance in the day, should betray me. For this reason I removed that part of my business which required fire into my new apartment in the woods. After some time I found, to my unspeakable consolation, a meer natural cave in the earth which went in a vast way and where, I dare say, no savage, had he been at the mouth of it, would be so hardy as to venture in. Nor would any man else, but one who, like me, wanted nothing so much as a safe retreat.

The place was a most delightful cavity or grotto of its kind, as could be expected, tho' perfectly dark. The floor was dry and level and had a sort of a small loose gravel upon it, so there was no nauseous or venomous creature to be seen, neither was there any damp or wet on the sides or roof. The only difficulty in it was the entrance. However, as it was a place of security, and such a retreat as I wanted, I thought that was a convenience. I was rejoiced at the discovery and resolv'd, without any delay, to bring some of those things which I was most anxious about to this place. Particularly, I resolv'd to bring hither my magazine of powder and all my spare arms. I kept at my castle only seven, which stood ready-mounted, like pieces of cannon, on my outmost fence, and were ready also to take out upon any expedition. I carried all away thither, never keeping above two or three pounds of powder with me in my castle, for fear of a surprise of any kind. I also carried thither all the lead I had left for bullets.

I fancy'd myself now like one of the ancient giants which were said to live in caves in the rocks where none could come at them. For I persuaded myself, while I was here, if five hundred savages were to hunt me, they could never find me out. If they did, they would not venture to attack me here.

The beast and I were now in the twenty-second year of our residence in this island and were so naturalized to the place, and the manner of living, that could I have but enjoyed the certainty no savages would come to the place to disturb me, we could have been content to have capitulated for spending the rest of our time there. Even to the last moment, till I had laid me down and died.

But it was otherwise directed. It may not be amiss for all people who shall meet with my story to make this just observation from it, viz. how frequently in the course of our lives the evil which in itself we seek most to shun, and which is the most dreadful to us, is oftentimes the very means or door of our deliverance, by which alone we can be raised again from the affliction we are fallen into. I could give many examples of this in the course of my unaccountable life. But in nothing was it more remarkable than in the circumstances of my last years of solitary residence in this island.

It was now the month of December, as I said above, in my twenty-second year. This, being the southern solstice (for winter I cannot call it), was the particular time of my harvest and required my being pretty much abroad in the fields. When going out pretty early in the morning, even before it was thorough daylight, I was surprised with seeing a light of some fire upon the shore, at a distance from me of about two miles, towards the end of the island where I had observ'd some savages had been, as before. And not on the other side, but, to my great affliction, it was on my side of the island.

I was indeed terribly surprised at the sight, and stopped short within my grove, not daring to go out, lest I might be surprised.

Yet I had no more peace within from the apprehensions I had that if these savages, in rambling over the island, should find my corn standing or cut, or any of my works and improvements, they would conclude there were people in the place and would then never give over till they had found me out. In this extremity, I went back to my castle, pulled up the ladder after me, and made all things without look as wild and natural as I could.

Then I prepared myself within, putting myself in a posture of defence. I loaded all my cannon, as I called them, that is to say, my muskets, which were mounted upon my new fortification, and all my pistols, and resolv'd to defend myself to the last gasp. I continued in this posture about two hours, and began to be mighty impatient for intelligence abroad, for I had no spies to send out.

After sitting awhile longer and musing what I should do in this, I was not able to bear sitting in ignorance any longer. Setting up my ladder to the side of the hill where there was a flat place, and then pulling the ladder up after me, I set it up again and mounted to the top of the hill. Pulling out my perspective-glass, which I had taken on purpose, I laid me down flat on my belly on the ground and began to look for the place.

I found there were no less than nine naked savages, with dark eyes and skin the color of wetted clay, sitting round a small fire they had made. Not to warm them, for they had no need of that, the weather being extremely hot, but, as I supposed, to dress some of their barbarous diet of human flesh, which they had brought with them. Whether alive or dead, I could not tell.

They had two canoes with them, which they had haul'd up upon the shore, and as it was then tyde of ebb, they seemed to me to wait for the return of the flood to go away again. It is not easy to imagine what confusion this sight put me into, especially seeing them come on my side of the island, and so near me too. But when I considered their coming must be always with the current of the ebb, I began, afterwards, to be more sedate in my mind, being satisfied I might go abroad with safety all the time of the tyde of flood, if they were not on shore before. Having made this observation, I went abroad about my harvest-work with the more composure.

As I expected, so it proved. As soon as the tyde made to the westward, I saw them all take boat and paddle away. I should have observ'd for an hour or more before they went off they went a dancing, and I could discern their hunch'd postures and gestures by my glass, altho' something unnamable in their writhing motions did bother my thoughts. I could not perceive, by my nicest observation, but they were stark naked and had not the least covering upon them.

As soon as I saw them shipped and gone, I took two guns upon my shoulders, and two pistols in my girdle, and my great sword by my side, and with all the speed I was able to make went away to the hill where I had discovered the first appearance of all. As soon as I got thither, which was not in less than an hour (for I could not go apace, being so loaden with arms as I was), I perceived there had been three canoes more of savages at that place. Looking out farther, I saw they were all at sea together, making over for the main.

This was a dreadful sight to me, especially as, going down to the shore, I could see the marks of horror which the dismal work they had been about had left behind it, viz. the blood, the bones, and part of the flesh of human bodies, all eaten and devoured by those wretches with merriment and sport. Even my trees and stones had been mark'd with their strange symbols.

I was so fill'd with indignation at the sight, I now began to premeditate the destruction of the next I saw there, let them be whom or how many soever. I took my hatchet to the trees to gouge the marks from their bark, and I could sense a great satisfaction in the spirit of the beast when this was done. When the tyde came it took the bits of flesh, and I scrub'd the stones as a sailor scrubs his deck until the dark symbols vanish'd and the stones were cleansed.

It seemed evident to me the visits which they made thus to this island were not very frequent, for it was above fifteen months before any more of them came on shore there again. I neither saw them nor any footsteps or signals of them in all that time. As to the rainy seasons, then they are sure not to come abroad, at least not so far. Yet all this while I lived uncomfortably, by reason of the constant apprehensions of their coming upon me by surprise. I observe the expectation of evil is more bitter than the suffering, especially if there is no room to shake off that expectation or those apprehensions.

During all this time I was in the murdering humour, and took up most of my hours in contriving how to fall upon them the very next time I should see them, especially if they should be divided into two parties, as they were the last time.

I spent my days now in great perplexity and anxiety of mind, expecting I should, one day or other, fall into the hands of these merciless creatures. If I did at any time venture abroad, it was not without looking round me with the greatest care and caution imaginable. And now I found, to my great comfort, how happy it was I had provided a tame flock or herd of goats. I durst not, upon any account, fire my gun, especially near that side of the island where they usually came, lest I should alarm the savages. If they had fled from me now, I was sure to have them come again, with perhaps two or three hundred canoes with them, and then I knew what to expect.

However, I wore out a year and three months more before I ever saw any more of the savages, and then I found them again. It is true, they might have been there once or twice, but either they made no stay or at least I did not see them. Nor did any memories of them come from the beast, which had once again reach'd one of its territorial phases and stalked our shores and savannahs and woods each night of the moon. The perturbation of my mind, and its mind, during this fifteen or sixteen months' interval, was very great. In the day great troubles overwhelmed my mind, and in the night I dreamed often of killing the savages, and of the reasons why I might justify the doing of it.

But in the month of May, as near as I could calculate, and in my four and twentieth year, I had a very strange encounter.

A new shipwreck, useless wealth,
my decision

It was in the middle of May, on the sixteenth day, I think, as
well as my poor wooden calendar would reckon, for I marked
all upon the post still, and four nights had past since the beast
last ran free. It blew a very great storm of wind all day with a great
deal of lightning and thunder, and a very foul night it was after it. In
many ways it did remind me of that night on the Yarmouth Roads,
when white worms did rise from the sea, *shoggoths* as the crew
called them, to ravage our ship and scuttle it faster than e'en two
dozen sailors could. The sea threw itself at the shore in great, loud
hills of water, in a word as loud as the wind and the thunder. I knew
not what was the particular occasion of it, but as I was reading and
taken up with very serious thoughts about my present condition, I
was surprised with the noise of a gun fired at sea.

This was, to be sure, a surprise quite of a different nature from
any I had met with before, for the notions this put into my thoughts
were quite of another kind. I started up in the greatest haste imaginable, clapped my ladder to the middle place of the rock, and pulled

it after me. Mounting it the second time, I got to the top of the hill the very moment a flash of fire bid me listen for a second gun, which, in about half a minute, I heard.

I considered this must be some ship in distress and they had some comrade, or some other ship in company, and fired these guns for signals to obtain help. I had the presence of mind at that minute to think tho' I could not accept help from them, it might be I might help them. So I brought together all the dry wood I could get at hand, and making a good handsome pile, I set it on fire upon the hill. The wood was dry and blazed, and tho' the wind blew very hard, yet it burnt fairly out, so I was certain if there was any such thing as a ship they must needs see it, and no doubt they did. As soon as ever my fire blazed up I heard another gun, and after that several others, all from the same quarter.

I plied my fire all night long. When it was broad day and the air cleared up, I saw something at a great distance at sea, full east of the island, whether a sail or a hull I could not distinguish, no, not with my glass. The distance was so great, and the weather still something hazy also.

I looked at it all day, and soon perceived it did not move, so I concluded it was a ship at anchor. Being eager, you may be sure, to be satisfied, I took my gun in my hand, and ran towards the south side of the island. Getting up there, the weather by this time being perfectly clear, I could see, to my great sorrow, the wreck of a ship, cast away in the night upon those jagged black rocks which I found when I was out in my raft.

It seemed these men, whoever they were, being out of their knowledge, and the black rocks being under water at this time, had been driven upon them in the night, the wind blowing hard. Had they seen the island, as I must suppose they did not, they must have endeavour'd to have saved themselves on shore by the help of their boat. But their firing off guns for help when they saw, as I imagined, my fire, fill'd me with many thoughts. In the condition I was in, I could do no more than look on upon the misery of the poor men and pity them.

I cannot explain, by any possible energy of words, what a strange longing of desires I felt in my soul upon this sight. In all the time of my solitary life, I never felt so earnest a desire after the society of my fellow-creatures, or so deep a regret at the want of it. Let the naturalists explain these things and the reason and manner of them. It was doubtless the effect of ardent wishes and of strong ideas formed in my mind, realizing the comfort which the conversation of one of my fellow-Englishmen would have been to me.

But it was not to be. Till the last year of my being on this island, I never knew whether any were saved out of that ship or no. I had only the affliction, some days after, to see the corpse of a drown'd boy come on shore at the end of the island which was next the shipwreck, only a mile from the heathen church of the savages. He had no cloathes on but a seaman's waistcoat, a pair of open-kneed linen drawers, and a blue linen shirt. Nothing to direct me so much as to guess what nation he was of. He had nothing in his pockets but two pieces-of-eight and a tobacco-pipe.

The last was to me of ten times more value than the first.

It was now calm and I had a great mind to venture out on my raft to this wreck, not doubting but I might find something on board that might be useful to me. But that did not altogether press me so much as the possibility there might be yet some living creature on board whose life I might not only save, but might, by saving that life, comfort my own to the last degree and perhaps balance the scales for the lost mate of my own voyage. Committing the rest to Providence, I thought the impression was so strong upon my mind it could not be resisted, it must come from some invisible direction, and I should be wanting to myself if I did not go.

Under the power of this impression, I hastened back to my castle, prepared every thing for my voyage, and thus, loading myself with every thing necessary, I went down to my raft, put her afloat, and loaded all my cargo on her. Praying to God to direct my voyage, I resolv'd the next morning to set out with the first of the tyde.

I first made a little out to sea, full north, till I began to feel the benefit of the current which carried me at a great rate and yet did not so hurry me as the current on the south side had done before, so as to take from me all government of the raft. Having a strong steerage with my paddle, I went at a great rate for the wreck, and in less than two hours I came up to it.

It was a dismal sight to look at. The ship, which, by its building, was Spanish, stuck fast, jammed in between two of the black spires. All the stern and quarter of her were beaten to pieces with the sea. As her forecastle, which stuck in the rocks, had run on with great violence, her mainmast and foremast were broken short off. But her bowsprit was sound, and the head and bow appeared firm. When I came close a dog appeared upon her, who, seeing me coming, yelped and cried as soon as I called him. I took him onto the raft, but found him almost dead with hunger and thirst, so weak he could not flee from me, tho' it was plain in his eyes he desired to do so. I gave him a cake of my bread and he devour'd it like a ravenous wolf. I then gave the poor creature some fresh water, with which, if I would have let him, he would have burst himself.

After this, I went on board. The first sight I met with was two men drown'd in the cook-room, or forecastle of the ship. I con-cluded when the ship struck the men were not able to bear it and were strangled with the constant rushing in of the water as much as if they had been under water. Besides the dog there was nothing left in the ship that had life, nor any goods I could see but what were spoiled by the water. There were some casks of liquor, whether wine or brandy I knew not, which lay lower in the hold and which I could see, but they were too big to meddle with. I saw several chests which I believed belonged to some of the seamen and I got two of them onto the raft without examining what was in them. I saw at this point the dog had fled from me, as most animals tended to do, and was swimming for the island with its head pok'd above the waves. I do not know if it made the shore, and one way or another I never laid eyes on it again.

Had the stern of the ship been fixed, and the fore-part broken off, I am persuaded I might have made a good voyage. By what I found in these two chests, I had room to suppose the ship had a great deal of wealth on board, but of no use, at that time, to any body.

I found besides these chests a little cask full of liquor, which I got into my raft with much difficulty. There were several muskets in the cabin, and a great powder-horn, with about four pounds of powder in it. I took a fire shovel and tongs, which I wanted extremely. Also two little brass kettles, a copper pot to make chocolate, and a grid-iron. With this cargo I came away, the tyde beginning to make home again. The same evening, about an hour within night, I reached the island again, weary and fatigued to the last degree.

I reposed that night on the raft. In the morning I resolv'd to harbour what I had got in my new cave and not carry it home to my castle. After refreshing myself, I got all my cargo on shore, and began to examine the particulars. The cask of liquor I found to be a kind of rum, but not such as we had at the Brasils and not at all good. When I came to open the chests, I found several things of great use to me. I found in one a fine case of bottles fill'd with cordial waters, fine and very good. I found two pots of very good succades, or sweetmeats, so fastened on the top the salt water had not hurt them. I found some very good shirts, which were very welcome to me, and about a dozen and a half of white linen handkerchiefs and coloured neck-cloths. When I came to the till in the chest, I found there three great bags of pieces-of-eight, which held about eleven hundred pieces in all. In one of them, wrapped up in a paper, six doubloons of gold, and some small bars or wedges of gold. I suppose they might all weigh near a pound.

In the other chest were some cloathes, but of little value. By the circumstances, it must have belonged to the gunner's mate, tho' there was no powder in it, except two pounds of fine glazed powder in three small flasks. Upon the whole, I got very little by this voyage that was of any use to me. As to the money, I had no manner of occasion for it. It was to me as the dirt under my feet. I would have given it all for three or four pair of English shoes and stockings. I had indeed got two pair of shoes now, which I took off the feet of the two drowned men, and I found two pair more in one of the chests, which were very welcome to me. But they were not like our English shoes, either for ease or service, being rather what we call pumps than shoes. I found in this seaman's chest about fifty pieces-of-eight in rials, but no gold. I suppose this belonged to a poorer man than the other, which seemed to belong to some officer.

However, I lugged this money home to my cave, and laid it up, as I had done that before which I brought from our own ship. It was a great pity, as I said, the other part of this ship had not come to my share. I am satisfied I might have loaded my raft several times over with money, and thought if I ever return to England it might lie here safe enough till I may come again and fetch it.

Having now brought all my things on shore and secured them, I went back to my raft and rowed or paddled her along the shore to her old harbour, where I laid her up and made the best of my way to my old habitation, where I found every thing safe and quiet. I began now to repose myself, live after my old fashion, and take care of my affairs. If at any time I did stir with any freedom, it was always to the east part of the island where I was pretty well satisfied the savages never came, and where I could go without so many precautions and such a load of arms and ammunition as I always carried with me if I went the other way. I had more wealth, indeed, than I had before, but was not at all the richer. I had no more use for it than the Indians of Peru had before the Spaniards came there.

I lived in this condition near two years more. Sometimes I was for making another voyage to the wreck, tho' my reason told me there was nothing left there worth the hazard of my voyage.

It was one of the nights in the rainy season in March, I was lying in the mate's hammock, awake. Very well in health, had no pain, no uneasiness of body, nor any uneasiness of mind, more than ordinary, but could by no means close my eyes. No, not a wink all night long, otherwise than as follows.

It is impossible to set down the innumerable crowd of thoughts that whirled through that great thoroughfare of the brain in this night's time. In my reflections, I was comparing the happy posture of my affairs in the first years of my habitation here on this land, compared to the life of anxiety, fear, and care, which I had liv'd ever since I had seen the print of a foot in the sand and further found the dark church that had been profesy'd by my parrot, Poll. I did believe the savages had frequented the island even all the while, and might have been several hundreds of them at times on shore. But I had never known it, and was incapable of any apprehensions about it. My satisfaction was perfect, tho' my danger was the same.

After these thoughts had for some time entertain'd me, I came to reflect upon the real danger I had been in for so many years in this very island and how I had walked about in the greatest security and with all possible tranquility, even when perhaps nothing but the brow of a hill, a great tree, or the casual approach of night, had been between me and the worst kind of destruction.

When these thoughts were over, my head was for some time taken up in considering the nature of these twist'd creatures, I mean the cannibals. How had it come to pass in the world that the wise Governor of all things should give up any of his creatures to such in-humanity? As this ended in some fruitless speculations, it occurred to me to inquire what part of the world these wretches lived in? How far off the coast was from whence they came? What they ventured over so far from home for? Had they come all this way to build their dark church, or had they discover'd it here in waiting for them? What kind of boats had the savages? By what means did they travel the high seas? And why might I not order myself and my business so that I might be as able to go over thither as they were to come to me?

This was key in my thoughts. I did reflect that this island, which I would often think of as mine alone, was perhaps never a safe place. I was neither alone here nor safe, and most evidence would say at the least my life and immortal soul may be at great risk. Indeed, upon further reflection, it seem'd the beast had oft times tried to warn me of the wrongness here, as a loyal dog does warn its master from danger.

As such, there was little doubt what my course must be now. The time of penance had come to an end. The beast and I must, at first chance, escape this accursed island.

My dream companion, the savages,
the prisoner

W hen this had agitated my thoughts for two hours or
more, and my pulse beat as if I had been in a fever
meerly with the extraordinary fervour of my mind
about it, nature threw me into a sound sleep. One would have
thought I should have dream'd of it, but I did not, nor of any thing
relating to it.

No, I dreamed as I was going out in the morning, as usual, from my
castle I saw upon the shore two canoes and eleven savages coming to
land. In my vision they were the same creatures I had seen through
my perspective-glass, with glossy gray skin most unlike the flesh of
Negroes, yet also had they wide eyes that recall'd to me the eyes of
the lowest of creatures, viz. frogs and fish.

They brought with them another savage, whom they were going
to kill in order to eat him. The savage they were going to kill jumped
away and ran for his life. I thought, in my sleep, he came running
into my little thick grove before my fortification to hide himself.
I, seeing him alone and not perceiving the others sought him that

{ 153 }

way, showed myself to him, and smiling upon him, encouraged him. He kneeled down to me, seeming to pray me to assist him. Upon which I showed him my ladder and carried him into my cave and he became my servant. As soon as I had got this man, I said to myself, "Now I may venture to the main land. This fellow will serve me as a pilot, and will tell me what to do, and whither to go for provisions, and whither not to go for fear of being devoured."

I waked with this thought, and was under such inexpressible impressions of joy at the prospect of my escape in my dream that the disappointments which I felt upon coming to myself, and finding it was no more than a dream, were equally extravagant the other way and threw me into a very great dejection of spirits.

Upon this, however, I made this conclusion. My only way to go about an escape was to get a savage into my possession. If possible, it should be one of their prisoners whom they had condemned to be eaten and should bring hither to kill.

But these thoughts still were attended with this difficulty. It was impossible to effect this without attacking a whole caravan of them and killing them all. This was not only a very desperate attempt, and might miscarry, but I had scrupled the lawfulness of it to myself. My heart trembled at the thoughts of shedding so much blood, tho' it was for my deliverance from this island. I need not repeat the arguments which occurred to me against this, they being the same mentioned before. I had other reasons to offer now, viz. that those men were enemies to my life and would devour me if they could. It was self-preservation, in the highest degree, to deliver myself from this death of a life, and I was acting in my own defence as much as if they were assaulting me. These things argued for it, yet the thoughts of shedding human blood for my deliverance were very terrible to me, and such as I could by no means reconcile myself to for a great while.

However, at last, after many secret disputes with myself, and after great perplexities about it (for all these arguments, one way and another, struggled in my head a long time), the eager prevailing desire of escape at length mastered all the rest. I resolv'd, if possible, to get one of those savages into my hands, cost what it would. My next thing was to contrive how to do it, and this indeed was very difficult to resolve on. As I could pitch upon no probable means for it, so I resolv'd to put myself upon the watch, to see them when they came on shore, and leave the rest to the event, taking such measures as the opportunity should present.

With these resolutions in my thoughts, I set myself upon the scout as often as possible, and indeed so often I was heartily tired of it. It was above a year and a half I waited. For great part of that time I went out to the west end, and to the awful church of the south-west corner of the island, almost every day to look for canoes, but none appeared. This was very discouraging and began to trouble me much. Tho' I cannot say that it did in this case (as it had done some time before) wear off the edge of my desire to the thing. The longer it seemed to be delayed, the more eager I was for it. In a word, I was not at first so careful to shun the sight of these savages and avoid being seen by them as I was now eager to be upon them.

About a year and a half after I entertained these notions, as I have said, I was surprised one morning with seeing no less than five canoes all on shore together on my side of the island, and the people who belonged to them all landed and out of my sight. The number of them broke all my measures. Seeing so many, and knowing they always came four or six or sometimes more in a boat, I could not tell what to think of it, or how to take my measures to attack twenty or thirty men single-handed. However, I put myself into all the same postures for an attack that I had formerly provided and was just ready for action if any thing had presented. Having waited a good while, listening to hear if they made any noise, at length, being very impatient, I set my guns at the foot of my ladder, and clambered up to the top of the hill.

Here I observ'd, by the help of my perspective-glass, which was this time by selection the better of the two I had, they were no less than thirty in number. They had a fire kindled and they had meat dressed. How they had cooked it I knew not, or what it was. They were all dancing and writhing in their own way, round the fire, bellowing and braying words that were but sounds to distant me, but awful none the less for it. Their naked skin, I could see, was slick and grey, like that of an eel, and with their hunch'd backs and wide eyes they made for a most monstrous crowd of figures. Also I observ'd, as their hands would be thrown up, that each man and woman among them had very long fingers, enough so that it could be observ'd thru the glass. In a like manner were their feet long and broad, as each would kick up their legs in the wild dancing. I bethought myself that there was little doubt such a foot had left the long-ago print which had shap'd my life on the island since and up till this moment.

It did also occur to me that the full moon had been only one night earlier, and had the savages arriv'd the day before a most unpleasant surprise would have met them upon the shore. Even now, I could sense the beast's great dislike of these beings, and had little doubt it would have hunt'd many of them for the meer pleasure of the kill.

While I was thus looking on them, I perceived, by my perspective, two miserable wretches dragged from the boats, where, it seemed they were laid by, and were now brought out for the slaughter. I observ'd one of them fall, being knocked down, I suppose, with a club or wooden sword, for that was their way, and two or three others were at work, cutting him open for their cookery, while the other victim was left standing by himself till they should be ready for him. In that very moment, this poor wretch, seeing himself a little at liberty and unbound, started away from them and ran with incredible swiftness along the sands towards me. I mean, towards that part of the coast where my habitation was.

I was frighten'd, I must acknowledge, when I perceived him run my way and when, as I thought, I saw him pursued by the whole body. Now I expected that part of my dream was coming to pass, and that he would certainly take shelter in my grove. But I could not depend upon my dream for the rest of it, viz. that the other savages would not pursue him thither and find him there. However, I kept my station, and my spirits began to recover when I found there was not above three men that followed him. Still more was I encouraged when I found he outstript them in running and gained ground of them. If he could but hold it for half an hour, I saw he would fairly get away from them all, for he ran true and the three ran in a shambling manner, not true running but a manner of throwing one leg before the other, as a man who has not yet found his "sea legs," as sailors call them, sometimes will walk on deck.

There was between them and my castle the creek, which I mentioned often in the first part of my story, where I landed my cargoes out of the ship. This I saw the poor wretch must swim over or he would be taken there. When the escaping savage came thither, he made nothing of it, tho' the tyde was then up. Plunging in, he swam through in about thirty strokes, landed, and ran on with exceeding strength and swiftness.

When the three persons came to the creek, I found two of them could swim, but the third would not. Standing on the other side, he looked at the others, but went no farther, and soon after went back again, which, as it happened, was very well for him in the end. I observ'd the two who swam, tho' clumsy apace, were yet more than twice as fast swimming over the creek as the fellow was that fled from them. It came now upon my thoughts, and indeed irresistibly, that now was the time to get me a servant and perhaps a companion or assistant, and I was called plainly by Providence to save this poor creature's life. I ran down the ladders with all possible expedition, fetched my two guns, and getting up again to the top of the hill I crossed towards the sea. Having a very short cut, and all down hill, I placed myself in the way between the pursuers and the pursued, hallooing aloud to him that fled. Looking back, he was at first perhaps as much frightened at me as at them. I beckoned with my hand to him to come back.

In the mean time, I advanced towards the two that followed. Rushing at once upon the foremost, I knocked him down with the stock of my piece. I was loth to fire because I would not have the rest hear, tho' at that distance they would not have known what to make of it. Having knock'd this fellow down, the other who pursued him stopped as if he had been frightened and I advanced apace towards him. As I came nearer, I perceived he had a bow and arrow and was fitting it to shoot at me. I was then necessitated to shoot at him first, which I did, and killed him at the first shot.

The poor savage who fled, tho' he saw both his enemies fallen and killed, was so frightened with the fire and noise of my piece he stood stock-still and neither came forward nor went backward. He seemed rather inclined still to fly. I hallooed again to him and made signs to come forward, which he understood and came a little way. Then stopped again. And then a little farther, and stopped again. I could then perceive he stood trembling, as if he had been taken prisoner just to be killed, as his two enemies were. I beckoned to him again to come to me and gave him all the signs of encouragement I could think of. He came nearer and nearer, kneeling down every ten or twelve steps in token of acknowledgment for saving his life. I smiled at him and looked pleasantly and beckoned to him to come still nearer. At length he came close to me. He kneeled down again, kissed the ground, and laid his head upon the ground, and taking me by the foot, set my foot upon his head. This, it seems, was in token of swearing to be my slave for ever. I took him up, and made much of him, and encouraged him all I could.

But there was more work to do yet. I perceived the savage whom I knocked down was not killed but stunned with the blow, and began to come to himself. I pointed to him and showed my savage he was not dead. Upon this he spoke some words to me, and tho' I could not understand them, I thought they were pleasant to hear, for they were the first sound of a man's voice I had heard for above twenty-five years.

But there was no time for such reflections now. The savage who was knocked down recovered himself so far as to sit up upon the ground and I perceived my savage, for so I call him now, began to be afraid. When I saw that, I presented my other piece at the other man as if I would shoot him. Upon this my savage made a motion to me and took up the other savage's great wooden sword, which had fallen when I struck him. My savage no sooner had it but he ran to his enemy and, at one blow, cut off his head so cleverly no executioner in Germany could have done it sooner or better. When he had done this, he came laughing to me in triumph and brought me the sword again and, with abundance of gestures which I did not understand, laid it down just before me with the head of the savage he had killed.

I turned to go away, and beckoned him to follow me, making signs to him more might come after them. Upon this, he made signs to me he should bury the bodies with sand, that they might not be seen by the rest if they followed. I made signs to him again to do so. He fell to work and in an instant he had scraped a hole in the sand with his broad hands big enough to bury the first in, then dragged him into it and covered him, and did so by the other also. I believe he had buried them both in a quarter of an hour. Then calling him away, I carried him, not to my castle, but quite away to my cave, on the farther part of the island. So I did not let my dream come to pass in that part, viz. that he came into my grove for shelter.

Here I gave him bread and a bunch of raisins to eat and a draught of water, which I found he was indeed in great distress for, by his running. Having refreshed him, I made signs for him to go and lie down to sleep, showing him a place where I had laid some rice-straw and a blanket upon it which I used to sleep upon myself sometimes. The poor creature lay down and went to sleep.

He was a comely fellow, oddly made, with long straight limbs, not too large or tall, well shaped despite the hunch to his back, and, as I reckon, about twenty-six years of age. The smell of fish did hang about him like a cloud, as if it were his only sustenance. His hands were long and flat, with fingers as long again, and I bethought myself that he could wrap his whole head within them. Likewise were his feet and toes long, and broad, with a tiny claw on each rather than a toenail, yet as I examin'd them more I was amaz'd to see a thin web of skin twixt each splayed toe, as one would see on the feet of a duck.

He had a very good countenance, not a fierce and surly aspect, but seem'd to have something very manly in his face. Yet he had all the sweetness and softness of an European in his countenance too, especially when he smiled. His hair was long and black, not curled like wool. His forehead very high and large. A great vivacity and sparkling sharpness in his large, dark eyes, 'tho not as wide apart as those of the other savages. The colour of his skin was, again, not quite the slick grey of the other savages, but very dusky. And yet not an ugly, mottled, nauseous dusky, but of a bright kind of a polished slate colour that had in it something very agreeable, tho' not very easy to describe. His face was round and plump, his nose small and thin, not flat like the Negroes, yet with long slits. A very good mouth, thin lips, and his long, thin teeth well set, and as white as ivory.

I left him sleeping and went to tend my businesses.

My new servant, many lessons,
two monsters

After the savage had slumbered about half an hour he awoke and came out of the cave to me, for I had been milking my goats, which I had in the enclosure just by. When he espied me he came running to me, laying himself down again upon the ground with all the possible signs of an humble thankful disposition. At last, he laid his head flat upon the ground close to my foot and set my other foot upon his head as he had done before. After this, he made all the signs to me of subjection, servitude, and submission imaginable. I understood him in many things, and let him know I was very well pleased with him.

In a little time I began to speak to him, and teach him to speak to me. First, I let him know his name should be FRIDAY, which was the day I saved his life. I likewise taught him to say "Master," and then let him know that was to be my name. I likewise taught him to say "Yes" and "No" and to know the meaning of them. I gave him some milk in an earthen pot and let him see me drink it before him and sop my bread in it. I gave him a cake of bread to do the like, which he complied with and made signs it was very good for him.

I kept there with him all night. As soon as it was day, I beckoned to him to come with me and let him know I would give him some cloathes, at which he seemed very glad, for he was stark naked. As we went by the place where he had buried the two men, he showed me the marks he had made to find them again, making signs to me we should dig them up and eat them. At this I appeared very angry, expressed my abhorrence of it, made as if I would vomit at the thoughts of it, and beckoned with my hand to him to come away. He did, with great submission. I then led him up to the top of the hill to see if his enemies were gone. Pulling out my perspective glass, I looked and saw plainly the place where they had been, but no appearance of them or their canoes. It was plain they were gone and had left their two comrades behind without any search after them.

But I was not content with this discovery. Having now more courage, and consequently more curiosity, I took my man Friday with me. Away we marched to the place where these creatures had been. I had a mind now to get some fuller intelligence of them. When I came to the place, my very blood ran chill in my veins at the horror of the spectacle. Indeed, it was a dreadful sight, at least it was so to me. Friday made nothing of it. The place was covered with human bones, the ground dyed with their blood, and great pieces of flesh were left here and there, half-eaten, mangled, and scorched. I saw three skulls, five hands, and the bones of three or four legs and feet, and abundance of other parts of bodies. The trees and stones had been marked again as well.

Friday, by his signs, made me understand they brought over four prisoners to feast upon. Three of them were eaten up, and he, pointing to himself, was the fourth. There had been a great battle between them and their next king, whose subject he had been one of, and they had taken a great number of prisoners in order to feast upon them.

Whilst I took the hatchet again to the trees, I caus'd Friday to gather all the skulls, bones, flesh, and whatever remained and lay them together in a heap, and make a great fire upon it, and burn them all to ashes. I found him unnerved by my destruction of the marks, and that he had still a hankering after some of the flesh and was still a cannibal in his nature. I discovered so much abhorrence at the very thoughts of it, I had, by some means, let him know I would kill him if he offered it.

When he had done this, we came back to our castle and there I fell to work for my man Friday. First of all I gave him a pair of linen drawers, which I had out of the poor gunner's chest I found in the wreck. Then I made him a jerkin of goat's-skin, as well as my skill would allow, for I was now grown a tolerable good taylor. I gave him a cap, which I made of hare's-skin. Thus he was cloathed, for the present, tolerably well. It is true, he went awkwardly in these cloathes at first. Wearing the drawers was very awkward to him, and the sleeves of the waistcoat gall'd his shoulders and the inside of his arms, which had many thin folds of flesh much like the fins of a fish. I bethought myself wearing cloathes for him must be as it is for the beast, an unexpected and foreign experience, that is to say, one they had no call for. But after a little easing them where he complained they hurt, and using himself to them, he took to them at length very well.

The next day after I came home to my hutch with him, I began to consider where I should lodge him. That I might do well for him and yet be easy myself, I made a little tent for him in the vacant place between my two fortifications, in the inside of the last and in the outside of the first. As there was a door or entrance there into my cave, I made a formal framed door case and a door to it of boards, and set it up in the passage a little within the entrance. I bar'd it up in the night, taking in my ladders too. Friday could no way come at me in the inside of my innermost wall without making so much noise in getting over that it must needs waken me.

But I needed none of all this precaution. Never man had a more faithful, loving, sincere servant than Friday was to me. His very affections were tied to me like those of a child to a father. I dare say he would have sacrificed his life for the saving of mine. The many testimonies he gave me of this put it out of doubt and soon convinced me I needed to use no precautions as to my safety on his account.

I was delighted with Friday and made it my business to teach him every thing that was proper to make him useful, handy, and helpful, but especially to make him speak and understand me when I spoke. He was the aptest scholar that ever was and was so merry, so diligent, and so pleased when he could but understand me, or make me understand him, that it was very pleasant to me to talk to him.

After I had been two or three days returned to my castle, I thought in order to bring Friday off from his horrid way of feeding, and from the relish of a cannibal's stomach, I ought to let him taste other flesh. I took him out with me one morning to the woods. I went, indeed, intending to kill a kid out of my own flock, and bring it home and dress it, but as I was going, I saw a she-goat lying down in the shade, and two young kids sitting by her. I catched hold of Friday.

"Hold," said I. "Stand still," and made signs to him not to stir. I presented my piece, shot, and kill'd one of the kids. The poor creature, who had indeed seen me kill the savage, his enemy, but did not know how it was done, was surprised, trembled, and looked so amazed I thought he would have sunk down. He did not see the kid I shot at, or perceive I had killed it, but ripped up his waistcoat, to feel whether he was not wounded. He came and kneel'd down to me and, embracing my knees, said a great many things I did not understand. I could see the meaning was to pray me not to kill him.

I laughed at him, and pointing to the kid which I had killed, beckoned to him to run and fetch it, which he did. I brought home the kid and the same evening I took the skin off and cut it out as well as I could. Having a pot fit for that purpose, I boiled or stewed some of the flesh and made some very good broth. After I had begun to eat some, I gave some to my man, who seemed very glad of it, and liked it very well. The next day we roasted a piece of the kid. When Friday came to taste the flesh, he took so many ways to tell me how well he liked it that I could not but understand him. At last he told me, as well as he could, he would never eat man's flesh any more, which I was very glad to hear.

The next day, I set him to work to beating some corn out and sifting it in the manner I used to do, as I observ'd before. He soon understood how to do it as well as I, especially after he had seen what the meaning of it was. After that I let him see me make my bread and bake it too. In a little time Friday was able to do all the work for me as well as I could do it myself.

I began now to consider that having two mouths to feed, instead of one, I must provide more ground for my harvest, and plant a larger quantity of corn than I used to do. I marked out a larger piece of land and began the fence in the same manner as before, on which Friday work'd not only very willingly and very hard, but did it very cheerfully. I told him it was for corn to make more bread because he was now with me. He appeared very sensible of that part, and let me know he thought I had much more labour upon me on his account than I had for myself. He would work the harder for me if I would tell him what to do.

Thus three weeks pass'd and I observ'd there was a point I had not consider'd, viz. in the many years upon this island, the nature of the beast had grown to be commonplace to me. It was as much a part of my routine as making my bread or drying raisins or milking my goats. Now it was the first night of the moon, and Friday, in his cheerful way, follow'd me every where I would go in my day and would follow me out at night. Thus, it was with great difficulty I explain'd he must stay within the castle this night while I went down the hill and away. This upset him greatly, and he made it known to me that he must follow me and keep me safe. With much effort he then told me that his people were much afraid of this island at night, for their god had set a monster loose on it which kill'd all things.

At this I laughed, for it was clear to me their monster was the beast, and it seem'd I had been safer here than I had first thought. I told him his monster did not frighten me, and, in what was a small lie, that I kept the monster imprison'd and chayn'd up for many days of the month, only setting it free to run for three nights so it would stay in good spirits and behave. Altho', upon reflection, this was not a lie at all, which pleas'd me. I told him again he could not follow, and I climb'd up the ladder and over the wall. He did cry for me to return, and his laments recall'd to my mind little Xury, the boy who had escap'd with me from the Moors of Sallee. I did then observe that little Xury would be a man now, older than was I when I first awoke on this island.

I walk'd a little ways from my castle till I was well away and hidden from Friday's eyes. Then I removed my cloathes and placed them upon a tree branch, as I had on the shores of Africk and my first nights here. I resolv'd, as the moon rose and bath'd me in her light, that I should make a cabinet for my cloathes outside the castle, perhaps three or four to place across my territory, so I could always find drawers each morning at the least.

Then the mantle of the beast did fall upon me, and it howl'd long and hard. It howl'd as it did to hunt and afore the kill, and ran cross the hilltops barking, and I knew, even deep within its skin, that it want'd to put great fear into Friday. It smell'd his relation to the savages, and to the dark church, and to the great totem, and it wanted Friday to know terror and know not to take any action against me. Had I not made my castle so well, I believe the beast would have kill'd Friday that first night.

Because of this, when I awoke the next day, I did not return to the castle but instead went to my bower, or summer house as I call'd it, and spent much time in reflection. I bethought myself, and the beast, that Friday was a loyal servant, and that he had cast off the rituals his people had rais'd him within. He would no longer eat the flesh of men, and would not raise his hand against me. I long observ'd these things, and made them clear to the beast as well. When the moon rose for the second night, the beast was tamer in its mood, yet still did howl and race cross the hills, tho' I knew this was now in the manner of wolves, that it but establish'd its place as above Friday in our small family and second only to me.

The next day I return'd to the castle, where Friday was much reliev'd to see me, and bowed and made his many signs of thanks. He had scarce moved since I left, and had eaten nothing lest he upset me somehow by doing so. I gave him some milk and bread, and we went to the shore and found a turtle, the flesh of which pleas'd him. I show'd him how to cook the eggs in the shell, as it is call'd, and then told him I would need to spend one more night away so they would be his supper, to cook when he became hungry, and eat with another cake of bread. I was surpris'd that this announcement met with no cries this time, and Friday gave a solemn nod and smiled at me. I ask'd if he had been so worry'd afore about food. He shook his head and made it known that he had fear'd I was leaving him and would not return.

When I ask'd why this did not worry him now, he smiled at me again with his thin white teeth and pointed up into the sky, where the last full moon had already risen in the after noon sky. He tilted his head back and did give a low howl. Then he gave me a most meaningful look with his large, dark eyes, spread his long fingers to show the tiny webs of flesh betwixt them, and set it against my chest. Afore I could speak, he placed the hand against his own chest, then back to mine, and spoke a few words in the little English he had learnt so far. Altho' his words were few, his meaning was most clear to me.

He had no fear, for he knew we were both monsters.

Old beliefs, the moving island, the fallen

F riday began to talk pretty well and understand the names of almost every thing I had occasion to call for, and of every place I had to send him to. He talked a great deal to me. In short, I began now to have some use for my tongue again. Besides the pleasure of talking to him, I had a singular satisfaction in the fellow himself. His simple unfeigned honesty appeared to me more and more every day, and I began to love the creature. On his side, I believe he loved me more than it was possible for him ever to love any thing before.

I had a mind once to try if he had any hankering inclination to his own country again. Having taught him English so well he could answer me almost any question, I asked him whether the nation that he belonged to never conquered in battle? At which he smiled, and said, "Yes, yes, we always fight the better." That is, he meant, always get the better in fight. So we began the following discourse:

"You always fight the better," said I. "How came you to be taken prisoner then, Friday?"

"My nation beat much for all that," he replied.

"How beat? If your nation beat them, how came you to be taken?"

He struggled for words. "They more many than my nation in the place where me was. They take one, two, three, and me. My nation over-beat them in the yonder place, where me no was. There my nation take one, two, great thousand."

"But why did not your side recover you from the hands of your enemies then?"

"They run one, two, three, and me, and make go in the canoe. My nation have no canoe that time."

It came to my thoughts what the results of this great fight had been. "Well, Friday," said I, "and what does your nation do with the men they take? Do they carry them away and eat them, as these did?"

"Yes, my nation eat mans too." He nodded. "Eat all up."

"Where do they carry them?"

"Go to other place, where they think."

"Do they come hither?"

"Yes, yes, they come hither. Come other else place."

"Have you been here with them?"

"Yes, I have been here." And with this did he point to the south-west of the island, which was their side.

By this I understood my man Friday had been among the savages who used to come on shore on the farther part of the island, to the dark church and its totem, on the same man-eating occasions he was now brought for.

I have told this passage because it introduces what follows. After I had this discourse with him, I asked him how far it was from our island to the shore, and whether the canoes were not often lost. He told me there was no danger, no canoes ever lost. After a little way out to sea, there was a current and wind, always one way in the morning, the other in the afternoon.

This I understood to be no more than the sets of the tyde, as going out or coming in. I afterwards understood it was occasioned by the great draft and reflux of the mighty river Oroonoko, in the gulf of which river, as I found afterwards, our island lay. This land which I perceived to the west and north west was the great island Trinidad, on the north point of the mouth of the river. I asked Friday a thousand questions about the country, the inhabitants, the coast, and what nations were near. He told me all he knew, with the greatest openness imaginable. I asked him the names of the several nations of his sort of people, but could get no other name than Caribs, from whence I understood these were the Caribbees, which our maps place on the part of America which reaches from the mouth of the river Oroonoko to Guiana.

He told me up a great way beyond the moon, that was, beyond the setting of the moon, which must be west from their country, there dwelt white bearded men, like me, and pointed to my great whiskers, which I mentioned before. They had killed much mans. By all which I understood, he meant the Spaniards, whose cruelties in America had been spread over the whole country, and were remembered by all the nations, from father to son. I enquir'd if he could tell me how I might go from this island and get among those white men.

"Yes, yes," he told me, "you may go in two canoe." I could not understand what he meant, or make him describe to me what he meant by two canoe, till, at last, with great difficulty, I found he meant it must be in a large boat, as big as two canoes. This part of Friday's discourse began to relish with me very well. From this time I entertain'd some hopes that, one time or other, I might find an opportunity to make my way away from this cursed place, and this poor savage might be a means to help me.

During the long time Friday had now been with me, and he began to speak to me and understand me, I was wanting to lay a foundation of Christian knowledge in his mind. Particularly I asked him one time, Who made him? The poor creature did not understand me at all, but thought I had asked him who was his father. Once he understood my question, he told me it was one Great Kathooloo, that lived beyond all. He could describe nothing of this great person, but that he was very old, much older than the sea or the land, than the moon or the stars, and slept and dreamt for many years. At his mention of dreams, many of my old apprehensions did arise, and I did continue in a cautious manner.

I asked him then, if this old person had made all things, why did not all things worship him? He looked very grave, and said, "All things say O to him."

I asked him if the people who die in his country went away any where? "Yes, they all went to Kathooloo."

From these things I began to instruct him in the knowledge of the true God. I told him the great Maker of all things lived up there, pointing up towards heaven. He was omnipotent, and could do every thing for us, give every thing to us, and take every thing from us. Thus, by degrees, I opened his eyes. He listened with great attention, and received with pleasure the notion of Jesus Christ being sent to redeem us, and of the manner of making our prayers to God, and his being able to hear us, even in heaven. He told me one day if our God could hear us up beyond the sun, he must needs be a greater God than their Kathooloo, who slept but a little way off on another island, and yet could not hear till they went up to the great mountains to speak to him. I asked him if ever he went thither to speak to him?

He said, No. They never went that were young men. None went thither but the old men, whom he called their Walla-kay. That is, as I made him explain it to me, their religious, or clergy. They went to say O, so he call'd saying prayers, and then came back and told them what Kathooloo said.

I asked him if any went to where their Kathooloo slept to wake him, at which he seemed both terrified and amaz'd that I could ask such a thing. Great Kathooloo, he explain'd, could not awake or be awoken until "the stars is right." He said also there were none who knew where the island was now, which I took to mean no one remember'd. When I said this he shook his head and said "No" and did try to explain again. After many minutes, during which he moved shells and stones across the floor of my cave, I came to understand his words. The savages believ'd their Kathooloo's island had sunk beneath the waves in the distant past, as would a foundering ship, and now moved beneath the seas like some great whale or turtle, waiting to rise to the surface "when the stars is right." It could be anywhere beneath the sea, observ'd Friday, very distant or very near. Thus only their Walla-kay could know where the island was at a certain time and speak to their god.

By this I observ'd there was priestcraft even among the most blinded, ignorant pagans in the world. The policy of making a secret of religion, in order to preserve the veneration of the people to the clergy, was not only to be found in the Roman, but perhaps among all religions in the world, even among the most brutish and barbarous savages.

I endeavour'd to clear up this fraud to my man Friday. I told him islands could not move beneath the sea. The pretence of their old men going up to the mountains to their god Kathooloo was a cheat, and their bringing word from thence what he said was much more so. If they met with any answer, or spake with any one there, it must be with an evil spirit. Then I entered into a long discourse with him about the Devil, his rebellion against God, his enmity to man, the reason of it, his setting himself up in the dark parts of the world to be worshipped instead of God, and the many stratagems he made use of to delude mankind to their ruin.

I found it was not so easy to imprint right notions in his mind about the Devil as it was about the being of a God. The poor creature became insistent we again discuss'd his sleeping Kathooloo, and it was clear to me the two had become one in his mind, and it seem'd easiest to continue his lessons with such a belief.

He then so puzzled me by a question meerly natural and innocent, I scarce knew what to say to him. I had been talking a great deal to him of the power of God, his omnipotence, his aversion to sin, his being a consuming fire to the workers of iniquity, and Friday listened with great seriousness to me all the while.

After this, I had been telling him how Kathooloo was God's enemy in the hearts of men, and used all his malice and skill to defeat the good designs of Providence, and to ruin the kingdom of Christ in the world, and the like.

"Well," said Friday, "but you say God is so strong, so great. Is he not much strong, much might as Great Kathooloo?"

"Yes, yes," said I, "Friday, God is stronger than Kathooloo. God is above Kathooloo, and therefore we pray to God to tread him down under our feet and enable us to resist his temptations."

"But," said he again, "if God much stronger, much might as Kathooloo, why God no kill Great Kathooloo in his sleep, so make him no more do wicked?"

I was surprised at this question. After all, tho' I was now an old man, I was but a young doctor and ill qualified for a casuist, or a solver of difficulties. At first, I could not tell what to say, so I pretended not to hear him and asked him what he said. But he was too earnest for an answer to forget his question, so he repeated it in the very same broken words as above.

By this time I had recovered myself a little, and I said, "God will at last punish him severely. He is reserved for the judgment, and is to be cast into the bottomless pit to dwell with everlasting fire."

This did not satisfy Friday; but he returns upon me, repeating my words, *"Reserve at last!* Me no understand. Why not kill Great Kathooloo now? Why not kill great ago?"

"You may as well ask me," said I, "why God does not kill you and me when we do wicked things here that offend him. We are preserved to repent and be pardoned."

He mused some time on this. "Well, well," said he, "that well. So you, I, Kathooloo, all wicked, all preserve, repent, God pardon all."

Here I was run down again by him to the last degree. I therefore diverted the present discourse between me and my man, rising up as upon some sudden occasion of going out. Sending him for something a good way off, I prayed to God he would enable me to instruct this poor savage. When he came again to me, I entered into a long discourse with him upon the subject of the redemption of man by the Saviour of the world, and of the doctrine of the gospel preached from heaven. How the fallen angels had no share in the redemption, he came only to the lost sheep of the house of Israel, and the like.

I had, God knows, more sincerity than knowledge in all the methods I took for this poor creature's instruction. In laying things open to him, I really informed and instructed myself in many things that either I did not know or had not considered before. I had more affection in my inquiry after things upon this occasion than ever I felt before. Whether this poor wild wretch was the better for me or no, I had great reason to be thankful that ever he came to me.

In this thankful frame I continu'd all the remainder of my time. The conversation which employed the hours between Friday and me was such as made the three years which we lived there together perfectly and completely happy, if any such thing as complete happiness can be formed in a sublunary state. This savage was now a good Christian, a much better than I.

Talk of boats, bearded men,
my design

I acquainted Friday with my own history, or at least so much of it as related to my coming to this place. I let him into the mystery, for such it was to him, of gunpowder and bullet, and taught him how to shoot. I gave him a knife, which he was delighted with. I made him a belt with a frog hanging to it, such as in England we wear hangers in, and in the frog, instead of a hanger, I gave him a hatchet, which was not only as good a weapon, in some cases, but much more useful upon other occasions. He also took to wearing the great wooden broad-sword he had claimed from the other savage. It was carv'd of iron-wood and very heavy, yet he did swing it with grace like the most skill'd swords-man.

I gave him an account of the wreck which I had been on board of, told him of the beast killing the mate, the panic in the water, and showed him, as near as I could, the place where the ship lay. However, she was all beaten in pieces before, and gone. I showed him the ruins of our long-boat, which we lost when we escaped, and which

I could not stir with my whole strength then, but was now fallen almost all to pieces.

Upon seeing this boat, Friday stood musing a great while, and said nothing. I asked him what it was he studied upon?

At last, said he, "Me see such boat like come to place at my nation."

I did not understand him a good while, but at last, when I had examined farther into it, I understood by him a boat, such as that had been, came on shore upon the country where he lived. As he explain'd it, it was driven thither by stress of weather. I imagined some European ship must have been cast away upon their coast and the boat might get loose and drive ashore. But I was so dull I never once thought of men making their escape from a wreck thither, much less whence they might come, so I only inquired after a description of the boat.

Friday described the boat to me well enough, but brought me better to understand him when he added with some warmth, "We save the white mans from drown."

Then I presently asked him, if there were any white mans, as he called them, in the boat?

"Yes," he said, "the boat full of white mans." I asked him how many? He told upon his fingers seventeen, and I asked him then what became of them? He told me, "They live, they dwell at my nation."

This put new thoughts into my head. I imagined these might be the men belonging to the Spanish ship that was cast away in the sight of my island. Who, after the ship was struck on the black rocks, and they saw her lost, had saved themselves in their boat, and were landed upon that wild shore among the savages.

Upon this, I inquired of him more critically what was become of them. He assured me they lived still there. The savages let them alone and gave them victuals to live on. I asked him how it came to pass they did not kill them and eat them? He said, "No, they make brother with them." then he added, "They no eat mans but when make the war fight."

It was after this some considerable time, being upon the top of the hill, at the east side of the island, Friday looked towards the main land, and, in a kind of surprise, fell a jumping and dancing, and called out to me, for I was at some distance from him. I asked him what was the matter? "O joy!" said he. "O glad! there see my country, there my nation!"

I observ'd an extraordinary sense of pleasure appear'd in his face. His eyes sparkled, and his countenance discover'd a strange eagerness, as if he had a mind to be in his own country again. This observation of mine put a great many thoughts into me, which made me at first not so easy about my new man Friday as I was before. I made no doubt but that if Friday could get back to his own nation again, he would not only forget all his religion, but all his obligation to me, and would be forward enough to give his countrymen an account of me, and come back perhaps with a hundred or two of them and make a feast upon me.

But I wronged the poor honest creature very much, for which I was very sorry afterwards. One day, walking up the same hill, but the weather being hazy at sea so we could not see the continent, I called to him, and said, "Friday, do not you wish yourself in your own country, your own nation?"

"Yes," he said. "I be much glad to be at my own nation."

"What would you do there?" said I. "Would you turn wild again, eat men's flesh again, and be a savage as you were before?"

He looked full of concern, and shaking his head, said, "No, no, Friday tell them to live good. Tell them to pray God. Tell them to eat corn-bread, cattle-flesh, milk. No eat man again."

"Why then," said I to him, "they will kill you."

He looked grave at that, and then said, "No, no. They no kill me, they willing love learn." He meant by this, they would be willing to learn. He added, they learned much of the bearded mans that came in the boat. Then I asked him if he would go back to them. He smiled at that, and told me he could not swim so far. I told him, I would make a canoe for him. He told me he would go, if I would go with him.

"I go?" said I. "Why, they will eat me if I come there."

"No, no," said he. "Me make they no eat you. Me make they much love you." Then he told me how kind they were to seventeen white men, or bearded men, as he called them, who came on shore there in distress.

I confess I still had a mind to escape away from the island, and see if I could join with those bearded men, who, I made no doubt, were Spaniards and Portuguese. Upon the whole, I was by this time so fixed upon my design of going over with him to the continent and escaping the island, I told him we would go and make a boat and he should go home in it. He answered not one word, but looked very grave and sad. I asked him what was the matter with him? He asked me, "Why you angry mad with Friday? What me done?"

I asked him what he meant. I told him I was not angry with him at all.

"No angry!" said he, repeating the words several times. "Why send Friday home away to my nation?"

"Why," said I, "Friday, did not you say you wished you were there?"

"Yes, yes," said he. "Wish be both there. No wish Friday there, no master there." With a swift motion, he pulled out his great wooden sword and gave it to me.

"What must I do with this?" said I to him.

"You take kill Friday," said he.

"What must I kill you for?" said I again.

He return'd very quick, "What you send Friday away for? Take, kill Friday, no send Friday away." This he spoke so earnestly I saw tears stand in his eyes.

I told him then, and often after, that I would never send him away from me if he was willing to stay with me, for I knew now the depth of his loyalty to me and love for me.

Therefore, without any more delay, I went to work with Friday to find out a great tree proper to fell and make a large canoe to undertake the voyage. The main thing I looked at was to get one so near the water we might launch it when it was made.

At last, Friday pitched upon a tree. I found he knew much better than I what kind of wood was fittest for it. Friday was for burning the hollow of this tree out to make it for a boat, but I showed him how to cut it with tools. After I had showed him how to use these, he did very handily. In about a month's hard labour we finished it, and made it very handsome when, with our axes, we cut and hewed the outside into the true shape of a boat. After this, however, it cost us near a fortnight's time to get her along, as it were inch by inch, upon great rollers into the water. But when she was in, she would have carried twenty men with great ease.

When she was in the water, tho' she was so big, it amazed me to see with what dexterity and how swift my man Friday would manage her, turn her, and paddle her along. So I asked him if he would, and if we might venture over in her.

"Yes," he said, "we venture over in her very well, tho' great blow wind."

However, I had a farther design he knew nothing of, and that was to make a mast and a sail, and to fit her with an anchor and cable. As to a mast, that was easy enough to get. I pitched upon a straight young cedar tree which I found near the place. I set Friday to work to cut it down and gave him directions how to shape and order it. But as to the sail, that was my particular care. I knew I had old sails, or rather pieces of old sails enough. But as I had had them now six and twenty years by me, I did not doubt but they were all rotten, and, indeed, most of them were so. However, I found two pieces which appeared pretty good, and with these I went to work. With a great deal of pains and awkward stitching I, at length, made a three-cornered ugly thing, like what we call in England a shoulder of mutton sail, to go with a boom at bottom.

I was near two months performing this last work, viz. rigging and fitting my mast and sails. I finished them very complete, making a small stay, and a fore-sail to it, to assist, if we should turn to windward. More than all, I fixed a rudder to the stern of her to steer with. I was but a bungling shipwright, yet as I knew the usefulness and necessity of such a thing, I applied myself with so much pains to do it that at last I brought it to pass. Tho', considering the many dull contrivances I had for it that failed, I think it cost me almost as much labour as making the boat.

After all this was done, I had my man Friday to teach as to what belonged to the navigation of my boat. Tho' he knew very well how to paddle a canoe, he knew nothing what belonged to a sail and a rudder, and was the most amazed when he saw me work the boat to and again in the sea by the rudder. I say, when he saw this, he stood like one astonished and amazed. However, with a little use, I made all these things familiar to him, and he became an expert sailor.

The dark church again, my battle-orders, Friday's reunion

I was now entered on the six and twentieth year of my captivity in this place. Tho' the two last years I had this man with me ought rather to be left out of the account, my habitation being quite of another kind than in all the rest of the time. I kept the anniversary of my landing here with the same thankfulness to God for his mercies as at first. I had an invincible impression upon my thoughts that my deliverance was at hand, and I should not be another year in this place. I went on, however, with my digging, planting, and fencing as usual, and did every necessary thing as before.

The rainy season was, in the mean time, upon me, when I kept more within doors than at other times. We had stowed our new vessel as secure as we could, bringing her up into the creek, where, as I said in the beginning, I landed my rafts from the ship. Hauling her up to the shore at high-water mark, I made my man Friday dig a little dock, just big enough to hold her and just deep enough to give her water enough to float in. Then, when the tyde was out, we made a strong dam across the end of it, to keep the water out. She lay dry as to the tyde from the sea. To keep the rain off we laid a great many boughs of trees, so thick she was as well thatched as a house. Thus we waited for the months of November and December, in which I designed to make my escape.

When the settled season began to come in, as the thought of my design returned with the fair weather, I was preparing daily for the voyage. The first thing I did was to lay by a certain quantity of provisions, being the stores for our voyage. I intended in a week or a fortnight's time to open the dock and launch out our boat. I was busy one after noon upon something of this kind, when I called to Friday and bid him go to the sea-shore and see if he could find a tortoise, a thing which we generally got once a week, for the sake of the eggs as well as the flesh. Friday had not been long gone when he came running back and flew over my outer-wall like one that felt not the ground or the steps he set his feet on. Before I had time to speak to him, he cries out to me, "O master! O master! O sorrow! O bad!"

"What's the matter, Friday?" said I.

"O yonder, there," said he. "One, two, three canoe. One, two, three!"

"Well, Friday," said I, "do not be frightened." However, I saw the poor fellow was most scared, for nothing ran in his head but that they were come to look for him, and would cut him in pieces and eat him. The poor fellow trembled so I scarce knew what to do with him. I comforted him as well as I could, and told him I was in as much danger as he, and they would eat me as well as him. "But," said I, "Friday, we must resolve to fight them. Can you fight, Friday?!"

"Me shoot," said he. "But there come many great number."

"No matter," said I, again. "Our guns will fright them that we do not kill." So I asked him whether he would stand by me and do just as I bid him.

He said, "Me die when you bid die, master."

I went and fetched a good dram of rum. When he drank it, I made him take the two fowling-pieces, which we always carried. Then I took four muskets. My two pistols I loaded with a brace of bullets each. I hung my great sword naked by my side and gave Friday his hatchet and his wooden sword. When I had thus prepared myself, I took my perspective-glass and went up to the side of the hill to see what I could discover.

I found, by my glass, there were three canoes just reaching the south-west corner of the island, that place which I had named the dark church. There were no less than two dozen savages on board, tho' it was possible some of the figures were prisoners. They past from my sight as they reach'd the shore, yet I knew if they had made land at the dark church there could be only two purposes to this visit, viz. an awful feast of flesh, else more of their accursed rituals, and very possibly both.

This abhorrence of the inhuman errand these wretches came about fill'd me with such indignation, I came down again to Friday and told him I was resolv'd to go over to them and kill them all. I asked him again if he would stand by me. He told me, as before, he would die when I bid die.

In this fit of fury, I took and divided the arms which I had charged between us. I gave Friday one pistol to stick in his girdle and three guns upon his shoulder. I took one pistol and the other three guns myself. I took a small bottle of rum in my pocket and gave Friday a large bag with more powder and bullets. I charged him to keep close behind me, and not to stir or shoot or do any thing till I bid him. In the mean time, not to speak a word, and in this posture we set out at a run into the woods. My years on the island now served me well, for I knew each rock and tree and stump of the forest, and could run at a full pace with little noise. In a word, the beast itself would be impress'd if such a feeling were possible for it, tho' I did feel it within my skin, glorying in my own wild run the way it oft enjoy'd its own.

Friday, with his large feet and odd hunch, could not move with as little noise, but he did attempt it to his best and made a mighty effort to keep up.

While we were making this march, my former thoughts were returning, and I began to abate my resolution. I do not mean I entertained any fear of their number. As they were naked, unarmed wretches, it is certain I was superior to them. But it occurred to my thoughts, what occasion, much less what necessity, I was in to go and dip my hands in blood? It was true Friday might justify it, because he was a declared enemy, and in a state of war with those very particular people, and it was lawful for him to attack them, but I could not say the same with respect to myself. These things were so pressed upon my thoughts all the way as I went, I resolv'd I would only go and place myself near them that I might observe their barbarous feast and I would act then as God should direct.

It was at the moment of this resolution that Friday hissed and point'd up, and twixt the trees we saw a curl of black smoke rising up, for the savages had lit their fires by the great totem. We ran for yet another hour, till we came to the skirt of the wood on the side which was next to them, so only one corner of the wood lay between us and the area which I call'd the dark church.

There were one and twenty grey skinned savages, three prisoners, and three canoes. Their whole business seemed to be the triumphant banquet upon these three human bodies. A barbarous feast indeed, but nothing more than was usual with them. For now they twisted and bellowed around the fire and the totem, as was their way, and I could see that some among them were very monstrous and far more creatures than men, e'en for savages.

Here I call'd softly to Friday, and showing him a great tree which was just at the corner of the wood, I bade him go to the tree and bring me word if he could see there what they were doing. He did so and came back to me and told me they might be viewed there. They were all about their fire eating the flesh of one of their prisoners, and another lay bound upon the sand by the great totem, which, he said, they would kill next. He told me it was not one of their nation, but one of the bearded men he had told me of. I was fill'd with horror and, going to the tree, I saw by my perspective-glass a white man who lay upon the sand beneath the carv'd figure of the totem, with his hands and his feet tied with rushes. He was an European, and had cloathes on.

At this, whatever influence had clouded my mind with doubt was push'd away, and I resolv'd to kill them all. There was another tree, and a little thicket beyond it, about fifty yards nearer to them than the place where I was, which I saw I might come at undiscovered, and then I should be within half a shot of them. So I withheld my passion, tho' I was indeed enraged to the highest degree, and going back about twenty paces, I got behind some bushes, and then came to a little rising ground which gave me a full view of them at the distance of about eighty yards.

I had now not a moment to lose, for nineteen of the dreadful wretches now sat upon the ground all close huddled together, and had just sent the other two to butcher the poor Christian, and bring him, perhaps, limb by limb, to their fire. They were stooping down to untie the bands at his feet while the most of them pounded on the ground as a huge drum, in a most off-putting way, while still braying their dark chants.

I turned to Friday. "Now, Friday," said I, "do as I bid thee."

He nodded.

"Do exactly as you see me do. Fail in nothing." I set down one of the muskets and the fowling-piece upon the ground, and Friday did the like by his. With the other musket I took my aim at the savages, bidding him to do the like.

I asked, "Are you ready?"

"Yes."

"Then fire at them," said I, and the same moment I fired also.

Friday took his aim so much better than I. He kill'd two of them and wounded three more. On my side, I kill'd one, tho' it was the most monstrous creature of them all, and wounded two.

They were, you may be sure, in a dreadful consternation. All of them who were not hurt jumped upon their feet, but did not know which way to run or which way to look.

Friday kept his eyes close upon me, that he might observe what I did. As soon as the first shot was made I threw down the piece and took up the fowling-piece, and Friday did the like. "Are you ready, Friday?"

"Yes."

"Let fly, then, in the name of God!" We fired again among the amazed wretches. As our pieces were now loaden with what I called swan-shot, or small pistol-bullets, we found only two drop, but so many were wounded they ran about roaring and screaming like mad creatures, all bloody, whereof three more fell after, tho' not quite dead.

"Now, Friday," said I, laying down the discharged pieces and taking up the musket which was yet loaden, "follow me."

I rushed out of the wood and showed myself and Friday close at my foot. As soon as I perceived they saw me, I shouted as loud as I could and bade Friday do so too. Running as fast as I could, I made towards the poor victim. The two butchers had left him at the surprise of our first fire, fled in a terrible fright to the sea-side, and had jumped into a canoe. Three more of the rest made the same way. I turned to Friday and bade him fire at them. He understood, and running about forty yards, to be nearer them, he shot at them. I thought he had killed them all, for I saw them all fall of a heap into the boat, tho' I saw two of them up again quickly.

While my man Friday fired at them, I pulled out my knife and cut the rushes that bound the poor victim. Loosing his hands and feet, I lifted him up and asked him in the Portuguese tongue what he was. He answered in Latin, but was so weak and faint he could scarce stand or speak. I took my bottle out of my pocket, and gave it him, making signs he should drink, which he did. I gave him a piece of bread, which he ate. Then I asked him what countryman he was and he said Espagniole. Being a little recovered, he let me know, by all the signs he could make, how much he was in my debt for his deliverance.

"Seignior," said I, with as much Spanish as I could make up, "we will talk afterwards, but we must fight now. If you have any strength left, take this pistol and sword, and lay about you."

He took them very thankfully. No sooner had he the arms in his hands but, as if they had put new vigour into him, he flew upon his murderers like a fury and had cut two of them in pieces in an instant.

I kept my piece in my hand still without firing, being willing to keep my charge ready, because I had given the Spaniard my pistol and sword. I called to Friday and bade him run up to the tree from whence we first fired and fetch the arms which lay there that had been discharged, which he did with great swiftness. Then giving him my musket, I sat down myself to load all the rest again, and bade them come to me when they wanted. While I was loading these pieces, there happened a fierce engagement between the Spaniard and one of the grey skinned savages who made at him with one of their wooden swords, the same-like weapon that was to have killed him before if I had not prevented it. The Spaniard, who was as bold and brave as could be imagined, had fought this creature a good while and had cut him two great wounds on his head. But the savage being a stout, lusty fellow had thrown him down, being faint, and was wringing my sword out of his hand. The Spaniard, wisely quitting the sword, drew the pistol from his girdle, shot the savage through the body and killed him upon the spot.

Friday being now left to his liberty, pursued the flying wretches with his own great wooden sword in hand. With that he dispatched those three who were wounded at first and fallen, and all the rest he could come up with. The Spaniard pursued two of the savages and wounded them both, but as he was not able to run they both got from him into the wood. Friday pursued them and killed one of them with a swift cut which took off his head. But the other savage was too nimble for him. Tho' he was wounded, yet had plunged himself into the sea and swam with all his might off to those two who were left in the canoe. I could not help but observe what powerful swimmers some of the savages were, as I had observ'd with my man Friday and his pursuers on the day of his escape from a like fate, as I have said before.

Those that were in the canoe worked hard to get out of gun-shot, and tho' Friday made two or three shots at them, I did not find that he hit any of them. Friday would fain have had me take one of their canoes and pursue them. Indeed, I was very anxious about their escape, lest carrying the news home to their people they should come back perhaps with two or three hundred of the canoes and devour us by mere multitude. So I consented to pursue them by sea. Running to one of their canoes, I jumped in and bade Friday follow me.

But when I was in the canoe, I was surprised to find another poor creature lie there, bound hand and foot for the slaughter and almost dead with fear, not knowing what was the matter, for he had not been able to look up over the side of the boat. He was tied so hard, and had been tied so long, he had but little life in him.

I cut the twisted rushes which they had bound him with and would have helped him up. He could not stand or speak but groaned most piteously, believing, it seems, he was only unbound in order to be kill'd.

When Friday came to him, I bade him speak to him, and tell him of his deliverance. But when Friday came to hear him speak and look in his face, it would have moved any one to tears to have seen how Friday kissed him, embraced him, hugged him, cried, laughed, hallooed. It was a good while before I could make him speak to me, or tell me what was the matter. When he came a little to himself, he told me it was his father, whom he called Walla-kay.

Friday was so busy about his father, I could not find in my heart to take him off for some time. But after I thought he could leave him a little, I called him to me, and he came jumping and laughing, and pleased to the highest extreme. I asked him if he had given his father any bread. He shook his head, and said, "None, ugly frog eat all up self."

I then gave him a cake of bread, out of a little pouch I carried on purpose. I also gave him a dram for himself, but he would not taste it, but carried it to his father. I had in my pocket two or three bunches of raisins, so I gave him a handful of them for his father.

He had no sooner given his father these raisins but I saw him come out of the boat and run away as if he had been bewitched, he ran at such a rate. He was the swiftest fellow on his feet ever I saw, even with his odd gait. He was out of sight in an instant, and tho' I called and hallooed out after him, away he went.

This action put an end to our pursuit of the canoe with the other savages, who were now got almost out of sight. It was happy for us we did not, for it blew so hard within two hours after, and before they could be got a quarter of their way, and continued blowing so hard all night, I could not suppose their boat could live, or that they ever reached their own coast.

Yet at the time I did not know this. As I bethought myself my concerns, Friday's father raised a weak hand and pointed at the great totem of the dark church, the cuttel fish figure of my dreams. He cry'd out many words, which had an awful memory to me, and I did recall across the years those words my parrot Poll had cried out before his death. Altho' now one of these words was not foreign to me, for I had discust it with my man Friday many times, and that word was *Kathooloo*. This did cause me great discomfort, and the beast howl'd within my skin, and I was pleased when the old man let his hand drop and became silent again.

In a quarter of an hour I saw Friday come back again, tho' not so fast as he went. As he came nearer, I found his pace slacker, because he had something in his hand. When he came up to me, I found he had been to the summer house, which was nearer the dark church than my castle, for an earthen jug to bring his father some fresh water, and he had two more cakes or loaves of bread. The bread he gave me, but the water he carried to his father. The water revived his father more than all the rum or spirits I had given him, for he was just fainting with thirst.

When his father had drank, I called to him to know if there was any water left. He said "Yes," and I bade him give it to the poor Spaniard, who was in as much want of it as his father. I sent one of the cakes to the Spaniard too, who was indeed very weak and was reposing himself upon a not as red place under the shade of a tree, which had one of the old symbols carv'd in its bark. When I saw he sat up and drank and took the bread and began to eat, I went to him and gave him a handful of raisins. He look'd up in my face with all the gratitude and thankfulness that could appear in any countenance, but was so weak, notwithstanding he had so exerted himself in the fight, he could not stand up upon his feet. By way of signs he made it known to me that his name was Olegario, and I gave him my name as well, which brought a relieved smile to his face.

Friday came back to me presently, and we two stepped away to the great totem. It was plain he did not like the thing, for he look'd most reluctant to approach it. "Friday," said I, "do you know this man?"

He shook his head, which I first took as a denial of knowledge, but then reflected that he objected to my calling the cuttel fish figure of the totem a man. "What is this?" I asked.

Friday look'd at me with his large, dark eyes and trembled. "That great Kathooloo," said he, "who sleep and dream beneath the sea."

Tho' I suspected as much, this did make me tremble myself, and I repeat'd the question in the hope I had misunderstood my man, or he had misspoke to me. He said again the name, and seem'd at sorts to be confronted by his former god. After some moments his eyes met mine and he said "All things say O to him."

I was aware of a noise, and saw that the father, Walla-kay, again had his hand point'd at the totem and was repeating his words, altho' now as a penitent man says his prayers.

I spoke to Olegario, the Spaniard, to let Friday help him up if he could. But Friday, a strong fellow, took the man quite up upon his back and carry'd him away to the boat, and set him down upon the gunnel of the canoe with his feet in the inside of it. Then lifting him quite in, Friday set Olegario close to Walla-kay and launched the boat off, and paddled it along the shore faster than I could paddle my empty one. We brought them both safe into our creek an hour later. Friday then went to help our new guests out of the boat, but they were neither of them able to walk, so my poor man knew not what to do.

To remedy this, I went to work in my thought. Calling to Friday to bid them sit down on the bank while he came to me, I soon made a kind of a hand-barrow to lay them on, and Friday and I carried them both up together upon it between us.

But when we got them to the outside of our wall we were at a worse loss than before, for it was impossible to get them over, and I was resolv'd not to break it down. So I set to work again. Friday and I, in about two hours' time, made a very handsome tent, covered with old sails, and above that with boughs of trees, being in the space without our outward fence, and between, that and the grove of young wood which I had planted. Here we made them two beds of such things as I had.

As soon as I had secured my two weak rescued prisoners and given them shelter, I began to think of making some provision for them. The first thing I did, I ordered Friday to take a yearling goat, betwixt a kid and a goat, out of my particular flock to be killed. Then I cut off the hinder-quarter and, chopping it into small pieces, I set Friday to work to boiling and stewing and made them a very good dish of flesh and broth, having put some barley and rice also into the broth. I carry'd it all into the new tent, and having set a table there for them, I sat down and eat my dinner also with them. Friday was my interpreter to his father, and to Olegario too, for he spoke the language of the savages pretty well.

The uninhabitable island, the harvest, our boat sails away

After we had supped, I order'd Friday to take one of the canoes and go and fetch our muskets and other fire-arms, which, for want of time, we had left upon the place of battle. The next day I order'd him to go and burn the dead bodies of the savages, which lay open to the sun and would presently be offensive. I also order'd him to burn the horrid remains of their barbarous feast, which I knew were pretty much, and which I could not think of doing myself. The thought of the dark church and its totem now gave me great apprehensions, for I now suspected there may be more to Friday's god than a meer trick of savage priests.

It was also made clear to me at this time that Walla-kay was both a name and a title, for I did notice this was the same word Friday had used for the old clergy of his people. As we would call a man "captain" or "mate" so did the savages make this one and the same, and some would change names many times in their lives. Thus was Friday's father a priest of sorts, altho' I was not as quick to discredit their beliefs as I once had been, as I have said.

I then began to enter into a little conversation with my two new subjects. First, I set Friday to inquire of his father what he thought of the escape of the savages in that canoe, and whether we might expect a return of them with a power too great for us to resist. Walla-kay's first opinion was the savages in the boat never could live out the storm which blew that night they went off, but must be drowned or driven south to those other shores where they were as sure to be devoured as they were to be drowned. As to what they would do if they came safe on shore, he said he knew not. But it was his opinion they were so frighten'd with the manner of their being attacked, the sudden noise, and the fire, that he believed they would tell the people they were all kill'd by thunder and lightning, and the two which appear'd, viz. Friday and I, were two heavenly furies come down to destroy them, and not men. This he knew, because he heard them all cry out the word tynd-lo, which is the word in their language for a spirit which appears and kills.

In a little time, however, no more canoes appearing, the fear of their coming wore off. I began to take my former thoughts of an escape to the main into consideration, being likewise assured by Walla-kay I might depend upon good usage from their nation, on his account, if I would go. He had questions for me, as well, for he would not believe I had lived on this island for as many years as Friday and I told him.

"He say white mans cannot long live here," said Friday, interpreting his father's words. "This island strong for Kathooloo, weak for white mans. Only we people safe here." At which his father slapt his own chest with his hand, which was much like the hand of his son, tho' be it with longer nails and, I observ'd, more flesh between the long fingers. Walla-kay had the same grey skin as my man Friday, his son, but also a wider mouth above his white beard and larger eyes. He look'd to my eyes much like a grandfather frog, altho' I would never say as such to Friday.

I assured him that my numbers were true, and offer'd to show him my calendar, or post, on which I still mark'd the day every morning. The old man shook his head and made it known again that I could not live here. Then he and Friday enter'd into a long debate which I could not understand, that is to say, in their own language, and many times Friday did gesture at me and at the sky. Walla-kay's eyes open'd wide, which was very wide indeed, and he reach'd out to brush my brow with a fingertip. He then snifft his fingers, as a dog does take a scent, and I did see that he could smell the beast upon me. The old man found this acceptable and did not doubt my word again.

But my thoughts were a little suspended when I had a serious discourse with Olegario, and when I understood there were sixteen more of his countrymen and Portuguese, who, having been cast away, lived there at peace with the savages but were very sore put to it for necessaries and indeed for life.

I asked him all the particulars of their voyage and found they were a Spanish ship, bound from the Rio de la Plata to the Havana, being directed to leave their loading there and to bring back what European goods they could meet with there. They had five Portuguese seamen on board, whom they took out of another wreck. Five of their own men were drown'd when first the ship was lost, and these escaped through infinite dangers and hazards and arrived on the cannibal coast, where they expected to have been devour'd every moment. He told me they had some arms with them, but they were useless for they had neither powder nor ball.

I asked him what he thought would become of them there and if they had formed any design of making their escape. Olegario said they had many consultations about it, but having neither vessel, nor tools to build one, nor provisions of any kind, their councils always ended in tears and despair. I asked him how he thought they would receive a proposal from me which might tend towards an escape, and whether it might not be done. I feared mostly their treachery and ill usage of me if I put my life in their hands. Many is the sailor who would see a man of the beast, as myself, as less than a man and worth no debt or promise, or that they could be even more than hostile to me. Gratitude was no inherent virtue, nor did men always square their dealings by the obligations they had received so much as they did by the advantages they expected. These were my thoughts, altho' I did not explain them all to Olegario at this time. I told him it would be very hard that I should be the instrument of their deliverance and they should afterwards make me their prisoner in New Spain. I had rather be deliver'd up to the savages and be devoured alive than fall into the merciless claws of the priests and be carry'd into the Inquisition.

I added, that otherwise I was persuaded, if they were all here, we might with so many hands build a bark large enough to carry us all away, either to the Brasils, to the islands, or Spanish coast. But if they should carry me by force among their own people, I might be ill used for my kindness to them and make my case worse than it was before.

He answer'd, with a great deal of candour and ingenuousness, their condition was so miserable, and they were so sensible of it, he believed they would abhor the thought of using any man unkindly that should contribute to their deliverance. If I pleased, he would go to them with the old man (for the other savages might be displeased if he return'd alone) and discourse with them about it and return again and bring me their answer. He would make conditions with them upon their solemn oath that they should be absolutely under my leading, as their commander and captain. They should swear upon the holy sacraments and gospel to be true to me, and to be directed wholly and absolutely by my orders till they were landed in such country as I intended. He would bring a contract from them for that purpose. Then he told me he would first swear to me himself that he would never stir from me as long as he lived till I gave him orders. He would take my side to the last drop of his blood if there should happen the least breach of faith among his countrymen. He told me they were all of them very civil, honest men, and they were under the greatest distress imaginable, having neither weapons or cloathes, nor any food, but at the mercy and discretion of the savages. He was sure if I would undertake their relief they would live and die by me.

Upon these assurances, I resolv'd to relieve them, if possible, and to send the old savage and Olegario over to them to treat. But when we had got all things in readiness to go, Olegario himself started an objection, which had so much prudence in it on one hand, and so much sincerity on the other hand, I could not but be very well satisfy'd in it.

By his advice, put off the deliverance of his comrades for at least half a year. The case was thus. He had been with us now about a month, during which time I had let him see in what manner I had provided for my support. He saw what stock of corn and rice I had laid up, which, tho' it was more than sufficient for myself, it was not sufficient, without good husbandry, for my family now it was increased to four. But much less would it be sufficient if his countrymen, who were, as he said, sixteen still alive, should come over. Least of all would it be sufficient to victual our vessel, if we should build one, for a voyage to any of the Christian colonies of America. So he told me he thought it would be more advisable to let him and the other two dig and cultivate some more land, as much as I could spare seed to sow, and we should wait another harvest, that we might have a supply of corn for his countrymen when they should come. For want might be a temptation to them to disagree.

"You know," said he, "the children of Israel, tho' they rejoiced at first for their being delivered out of Egypt, yet rebelled even against God himself when they came to want bread in the wilderness."

His caution was so seasonable, and his advice so good, I could not but be very well pleased with his proposal, as well as I was satisfied with his fidelity. So we fell to digging all four of us, as well as the wooden tools we were furnished with permitted. In about a month's time we had got as much land cured and trimmed up as we sowed two and twenty bushels of barley on and sixteen jars of rice. In short, all the seed we had to spare. Nor, indeed, did we leave ourselves barley sufficient for our own food for the six months we had to expect our crop.

It is worth mentioning that for these months the moon still rose and I still let the beast run free on those three nights it shone full in the sky. On the first night, which was a good week before Olegario had ask'd me to delay our voyage, the Spaniard was much concern'd that I was to wander into the woods for the night. He, too, had heard the same stories of this island as Friday had once told me, and could not picture an older gentlemen, as I now was, going unarmed into the woods where savage creatures hunted. Indeed, he asked such things several times as to how I had survived so long in such an awful place. It pleas'd me when Friday told him the same almost true story that I had once told to my man, that I was, in a word, the master of the beast, and went to set it free for the few nights necessary to keep it docile. Walla-kay, when ask'd, confirmed this as well, and said in his sage way that he believed the beast would never harm me. Thus did we three keep my nature as a secret from Olegario, altho' I believe in the end he did suspect the truth.

Having now number being sufficient to put us out of fear of the savages, we went all over the island, whenever we found occasion. Altho' none of us would go to the south west corner, where the dark church still stood, except for Walla-kay, who still kept his faith in his god and would sometimes go there to pray, and would berate my man Friday, his son, for not joining him. This did cause a rift tween them, tho' not, I believed, one of great consequence. I confess this faith did make me suspicious and Walla-kay never did earn my trust as well as had Friday.

As we had our escape, or deliverance, upon our thoughts, it was impossible to have the means of it out of mine. For this purpose I mark'd out several trees which I thought fit for our work, and I set Friday and his father to cutting them down, tho' I may note I did not choose any tree which had been mark'd by the savages at one time, even if those marks had been removed. Then I caused the Spaniard, to whom I imparted my thoughts on that affair, to oversee and direct their work. I showed them with what pains I had hewed a large tree into single planks, and I caused them to do the like, till they had made about a dozen large planks of good oak, near two feet broad, thirty-five feet long, and from two inches to four inches thick. What prodigious labour it took up any one may imagine.

At the same time, I contrived to increase my little flock of tame goats as much as I could. For this purpose, I made Friday and Olegario go out one day, and myself with Friday the next day (for we took our turns), and by this means we got about twenty young kids to breed up with the rest. Whenever we shot the dam, we saved the kids and added them to our flock. But, above all, the season for curing the grapes coming on, I caused such a prodigious quantity to be hung up in the sun I believe we could have fill'd sixty or eighty barrels. These, with our bread, was a great part of our food and was very good living too, I assure you, for it is exceeding nourishing.

It was now harvest, and our crop in good order. It was not the most plentiful increase I had seen in the island, but it was enough to answer our end. From twenty-two bushels of barley we brought in and thresh'd out above two hundred and twenty bushels, and the like in proportion of the rice.

When we had thus housed and secured our magazine of corn, we fell to work to make more wicker-ware in which we kept it. Olegario was very handy and dexterous at this part, and often blamed me that I did not make some things for defence of this kind of work. Indeed, in the final weeks of our harvest he had grown very sullen and angry, and did not sleep well.

Walla-kay advised me in private that in the same way the beast shared its nature with me, so did this island share its nature with those upon it, which is why he at first could not believe I had lived here my many years. He and his son, Friday, were protected as children of the sea, and I had the protection of the beast, but our Spanish friend had none to guard him from the island.

Now having a full supply of food for all the guests I expected, I gave Olegario leave to go over to the main to see what he could do with those he had left behind them there, and to free him from the nature of the island. I gave him a strict charge not to bring any man with him who would not first swear, in the presence of himself and the old savage, that he would no way injure, fight with, or attack the person he should find in the island, and this should be put in writing, and sign'd with their hands. Under these instructions, Olegario and Walla-Kay went away in the boat my man Friday and I had spent so many weeks making. I gave each of them a musket with a firelock on it and about eight charges of powder and ball, charging them to be very good husbands of both and not to use either of them but upon urgent occasions.

I gave them provisions sufficient for themselves for many days, and sufficient for all the Spaniards for about eight days' time. Wishing them a good voyage, I saw them go. They went away with a fair gale on the day the moon was at full, by my account in the month of October, but as for an exact reckoning of days, after I had once lost it I could never recover it again.

Another ship, captives,
my first victory

The day Olegario and Walla-Kay left was the second full moon of October, a rare enough thing to be worth noting, and the beast did seem pleas'd to have the new arrivals gone, for it had ne'er warmed to Friday's father as it had to my man himself. On reflection, I took this to be because Walla-Kay did not renounce his religion to the thing they call'd Kathooloo, and in this, the beast and I were in agreement.

It was no less than eight days all together I had waited for them when again a strange and unforeseen accident intervened, of which the like has not perhaps been heard of in history. I was fast asleep in my hutch one morning, when my man Friday came running in to me, and called aloud, "Master, master, they are come, they are come!"

I jumped up and I went out as soon as I could get my cloathes on. I was surprised when, turning my eyes to the sea, I saw a boat at about a league and a half distance, standing in for the shore, with a shoulder of mutton sail and the wind blowing pretty fair to bring them in. I observ'd they did not come from that side which the shore lay on, but from the southernmost end of the island. I called Friday and bade him lie close, for these were not the people we looked for, and we might not know yet whether they were friends or enemies. I went in to fetch my perspective-glass to see what I could make of them. I climbed up to the top of the hill, to take my view the plainer without being discovered. I had scarce set my foot upon the hill when my eye plainly discover'd a ship lying at an anchor, about two leagues and a half distance from me but not above a league and a half from the shore. By my observation, it appear'd to be an English ship, and the boat appear'd to be an English long-boat.

I cannot express the confusion I was in. The joy of seeing a ship, and one I had reason to believe was manned by my own countrymen, was such as I cannot describe. Yet I had some secret doubts hung about me, I cannot tell from whence they came, bidding me keep upon my guard. In the first place, it occur'd to me to consider what business an English ship could have in that part of the world, since it was not the way to or from any part of the world where the English had any traffic. I knew there had been no storms to drive them in there. If they were English, it was most probable they were here upon no good design. I had better continue as I was than fall into the hands of pirates and murderers.

I had not kept myself long in this posture but I saw the boat draw near the shore, as if they looked for a creek to thrust in at for the convenience of landing. However, as they did not come quite far enough, they did not see the little inlet where Friday and I docked our vessels, but run their boat on shore upon the beach, at about a mile from me, which was very happy for me. Otherwise they would have landed just at my door, and would soon have beaten me out of my castle and perhaps have plundered me of all I had.

When they were on shore, I was satisfy'd they were Englishmen, at least most of them. There were in all eleven men, where of three of them I found were unarmed and bound. When the first four or five of them were jumped on shore, they took those three out of the boat as prisoners. One of the three I could perceive using the most passionate gestures of entreaty, affliction, and despair, even to a kind of extravagance. The other two, I could perceive, lifted up their hands sometimes, and appeared concerned, indeed, but not to such a degree as the first.

I was confounded at the sight, and knew not what the meaning of it should be. Friday called out to me, "O master! you see English mans eat prisoner as well as savage mans."

"Why, Friday," said I, "do you think they are going to eat them then?"

"Yes," said Friday. "They will eat them."

"No, no," said I. "Friday, I am afraid they will murder them, indeed, but you may be sure they will not eat them."

All this while I had no thought of what the matter was, but stood expecting every moment when the three prisoners should be killed. Once I saw one of the villains lift up his arm with a great cutlass to strike one of the poor men. I expect'd to see him fall every moment. I wished now I had any way to have come undiscovered within shot of them, that I might have rescued the three men, for I saw no fire-arms they had among them. After I had observ'd the outrageous usage of the three men by the insolent seamen, I observ'd the fellows run scattering about the island as if they wanted to see the country. I observ'd the three other men had liberty to go also where they pleased, but they sat down all three upon the ground, very pensive, and looked like men in despair. This put me in mind of the first time when I came on shore and began to look about me. How I gave myself over for lost, how wildly I looked round me, what dreadful apprehensions I had.

It was just at the top of high water when these people came on shore. While they rambled about to see what kind of a place they were in, they had carelessly staid till the tyde was spent and the water was ebb'd away, leaving their boat aground. They had left two men in the boat, who, having drank a little too much brandy, fell asleep. However, one of them waking a little sooner than the other, and finding the boat too fast aground for him to stir it, hallooed out for the rest. They all soon came to the boat, but it was past all their strength to launch her, the boat being very heavy, and the shore on that side being a soft oozy sand, almost like a quicksand. In this condition, like true seamen, who are perhaps the least of all mankind given to forethought, they gave it over, and away they strolled about the country again. I heard one of them say aloud to another, calling them off from the boat, "Why, let her alone, Jack, can't you? She'll float next tyde."

All this while I kept myself very close, not once daring to stir out of my castle any farther than to my place of observation near the top of the hill. Very glad I was to think how well it was fortify'd. I knew it was no less than ten hours before the boat could float again, and by that time it would be dark and I might be at more liberty to see their motions and to hear their discourse, if they had any. In the mean time, I fitted myself up for a battle as before, tho' with more caution, knowing I had to do with another kind of enemy than I had at first. I ordered Friday also to load himself with arms. My figure, indeed, was very fierce. I had my formidable goat-skin coat on, with the great cap I have mention'd, a naked sword by my side, two pistols in my belt, and a gun upon each shoulder.

It was my design, as I said above, not to have made any attempt till it was dark. But about two o'clock, being the heat of the day, I found they were all gone straggling into the woods, and, as I thought, laid down to sleep. The three poor distress'd men, too anxious for their condition to get any sleep, however, sat down under the shelter of a great tree at about a half of a mile from me, and, as I thought, out of sight of any of the rest. Upon this I resolv'd to discover myself to them and learn something of their condition. I marched in the figure as above, my man Friday at a good distance behind me, as formidable for his arms as I, but making quite more an apprehending figure as I did with his gray skin and sharp teeth.

I came as near them undiscovered as I could, and then, before any of them saw me, I let out a sharp howl in the nature of the beast. They started up at the noise, but were ten times more confounded when they saw me and the uncouth figure I made. They made no answer at all, but I thought I perceived them just going to fly from me, when I spoke to them in English.

"Gentlemen," said I, "do not be surprised at me. Perhaps you may have a friend near when you did not expect it."

"He must be sent directly from Heaven then," said one of them very gravely to me, and pulling off his hat at the same time, "for our condition is past the help of man."

"All help is from Heaven, sir," said I. "But can you put a stranger in the way how to help you? You seem to be in some great distress. I saw you when you landed, and when you seemed to make application to the brutes that came with you, I saw one of them lift up his sword to kill you."

The poor man, with tears running down his face, and trembling, looking like one astonished, returned, "Am I talking to God or man? Is it a real man or an angel?"

"Be in no fear about that, Sir," said I. "If God had sent an angel to relieve you, he would have come better cloathed and armed. Pray lay aside your fears. I am an Englishman and disposed to assist you. You see I have one servant only. We have arms and ammunition. Tell us freely, can we serve you? What is your case?"

"Our case, sir," said he, "is too long to tell you while our murderers are so near us. But, in short, I, Hammond Burke, was commander of that ship and my men have mutinied against me. They have been hardly prevailed on not to murder me. At last, they have set me on shore in this desolate place, with these two men with me, one my mate, Turner, the other a passenger, Sir Wade Jermyn. We expected to perish, believing the place to be uninhabited, and know not yet what to think of it."

"Where are these brutes, your enemies?" said I. "Do you know where they are gone?"

"There they lie, sir," said he, pointing to a thicket of trees. "My heart trembles for fear they have seen us and heard you speak. If they have, they will murder us all."

"Have they any fire-arms?" said I.

"They had only two pieces, one of which they left in the boat."

"Well then," said I, "leave the rest to me. I see they are all asleep, it is an easy thing to kill them all, but shall we rather take them prisoners?"

Burke told me there were two desperate villains among them it was scarce safe to show any mercy to. But if they were secured, he believed all the rest would return to their duty. I asked him which they were? He told me he could not at that distance distinguish them, but he would obey my orders in any thing I would direct.

"Well," said I, "let us retreat out of their view or hearing, lest they awake, and we will resolve further." So they went back with me till the woods covered us from them.

"Look you, sir," said I, "if I venture upon your deliverance, my conditions are but two. First, while you stay in this island with me, you will not pretend to any authority here. If I put arms in your hands, you will, upon all occasions, give them up to me, and do no prejudice to me or mine upon this island, and be governed by my orders. Secondly, if the ship is or may be recovered, you will carry me and my man to England, passage free."

Burke gave me all the assurances the invention or faith of man could devise that he would comply with these most reasonable demands. Besides, he would owe his life to me and acknowledge it upon all occasions as long as he lived. "Well then," said I, "here are three muskets for you, with powder and ball. Tell me next what you think is proper to be done."

He offered to be wholly guided by me. I told him I thought it was hard venturing any thing, but the best method I could think of was to fire upon them at once as they lay, and if any were not killed at the first volley, and offer'd to submit, we might save them. He said he was loth to kill them if he could help it, but those two had been the authors of all the mutiny, and if they escaped we should be undone still. They would go on board and bring the whole ship's company and destroy us all. "Well then," said I, "necessity legitimates my advice, for it is the only way to save our lives." However, seeing him still cautious of shedding blood, I told him they should go themselves, and manage as they found convenient.

In the middle of this discourse we heard some of them awake and soon after we saw two of them on their feet. Asked I, "Are either of them the heads of the mutiny?"

"No," said Burke.

"Well then," said I, "you may let them escape. Providence seems to have awakened them on purpose to save themselves. Now if the rest escape you, it is your fault." Animated with this, the captain took the musket I had given him in his hand and a pistol in his belt, and his two comrades with him, with each a piece in his hand. The two men who were with him going first, made some noise, at which one of the seamen who was awake turned about, and seeing them coming, cried out to the rest. But it was too late then, for the moment he cried out they fired. They had so well aimed their shot at the men, one of them was killed on the spot and the other very much wounded. Not being dead, he started up on his feet, and called for help to the other. Captain Burke, stepping to him, told him, "It is too late to call for help. You should call upon God to forgive your villainy." With that word he knocked the man down with the stock of his musket, so he never spoke more.

There were three more in the company, and one of them was also wounded. By this time I was come. When they saw their danger, and that it was in vain to resist, they begged for mercy. Burke told them he would spare their lives if they would give him any assurance of their abhorrence of the treachery they had been guilty of, and would swear to be faithful to him in recovering the ship. They gave him all the protestations of their sincerity that could be desired, and he was willing to spare their lives, which I was not against, only I obliged him to keep them bound hand and foot while they were on the island.

While this was doing, I sent Friday with Turner, the captain's mate, to the boat with orders to secure her and bring away the oars and sails, which they did. By and by three straggling men that were (happily for them) parted from the rest, came back upon hearing the guns fired. Seeing the captain who before was their prisoner now their conqueror, they submitted to be bound also. And so our victory was complete.

My new allies, villains,
fear the island

It now remained that Captain Burke and I should inquire into one another's circumstances. I began first, and told him my whole history, leaving out certain particulars of my nature and the nature of the island, to be certain. Indeed, as my story is a whole collection of wonders e'en without these particulars, it affected him deeply. But when he reflected from thence upon himself, and how I seem'd to have been preserved there on purpose to save his life, the tears ran down his face and he could not speak a word more. After this communication was at an end, I carried him and his two men into my apartment, where I refresh'd them with such provisions as I had, and showed them all the contrivances I had made during my long, long inhabiting that cursed place.

Above all, Burke admired my fortification, and how I had conceal'd my retreat with the growth about my fence, which, having been now planted near twenty years, was become a little wood. I told him this was my castle and my residence, but I had a seat in the country, as most princes have, and I would show him that too another time.

At present our business was to consider how to recover the ship. He agreed with me, but told me he was at a loss what measures to take, for there were still six and twenty hands on board who would be hardened in it now by desperation, knowing if they were subdued they would be brought to the gallows as soon as they came to England or to any of the English colonies. Therefore, there would be no attacking them with so small a number as we were.

I mused for some time upon what he had said, and found it was a very rational conclusion. Therefore, something was to be resolv'd on speedily, as well to draw the men on board into some snare for their surprise as to prevent their landing upon us and destroying us. It occurred to me in a little while the ship's crew, wondering what was become of their comrades and of the boat, would come on shore in their other boat to look for them. Perhaps they might come armed and be too strong for us. Upon this, I told him the first thing we had to do was to stave the boat which lay upon the beach, so they might not carry her off, and leave her so far useless as not to be fit to swim. Accordingly we went on board, took the arms which were left on board out of her, and whatever else we found there.

When we had carried all these things on shore, we knock'd a great hole in her bottom, that if they had come strong enough to master us, yet they could not carry off the boat. Indeed, it was not much in my thoughts we could be able to recover the ship. My view was if they went away without the boat, I did not much question to make her fit again to carry us to the Leeward Islands, and call upon our friends the Spaniards in my way, for I had them still in my thoughts.

While we were thus preparing our designs, and had by main strength heaved the boat upon the beach so high the tyde would not float her off at high water mark, and besides, had broke a hole in her bottom too big to be stopped, we heard the ship fire a gun and saw her make a waft with her ensign as a signal for the boat to come on board. But no boat stirred. They fired several times, making other signals for the boat. At last, when all their signals and firing proved fruitless, we saw them, by the help of my glasses, hoist another boat out and row towards the shore. We found, as they approached, there were no less than ten men in her, and they had fire-arms with them.

As the ship lay almost two leagues from the shore, we had a full view of them as they came, and a plain sight even of their faces. Because the tyde having set them a little to the east of the other boat, they rowed up under shore to come to the same place where the other had landed and where the boat lay. Captain Burke knew the persons and characters of all the men in the boat, of whom, he said, there were three very honest fellows who he was sure were led into this conspiracy by the rest, being overpowered and frightened. As for the boatswain, Slaader, a Moorish pirate who it seemed was the chief officer among them, and all the rest, they were as outrageous as any of the ship's crew, and were no doubt made desperate in their new enterprise. Terribly apprehensive he was they would be too powerful for us.

I smiled at him. "Men in our circumstances are past the operation of fear," I told him. "And where, Sir, is your belief of my being preserved here on purpose to save your life, which elevated you a little while ago? For my part, there seems to me but one thing amiss in all the prospect of it."

"What is that?" said he.

"Why," said I, "it is, that as you say there are three or four honest fellows among them which should be spared. Had they been all of the wicked part of the crew, I should have thought God's providence had singled them out to deliver them into your hands. Depend upon it," I told him, "every man that comes ashore are our own, and shall die or live as they behave to us."

As I spoke this with a raised voice and cheerful countenance, I found it encouraged him. So we set vigorously to our business.

We had, upon the first appearance of the boat's coming from the ship, consider'd of separating our prisoners. We had, indeed, secured them effectually. Two of them, of whom Burke was less assured than ordinary, I sent with Friday, and one of the three deliver'd men to my cave, where they were remote enough and out of danger of being heard or discovered, or of finding their way out of the woods if they could have deliver'd themselves. Here they left them bound, but gave them provisions and promised them if they continued there quietly to give them their liberty in a day or two. If they attempted their escape, they should be kill'd by the beast of the island without mercy. As Friday's countenance can be most fierce if he wills it, they dreaded at the thought of something more bestial than he. They promised faithfully to bear their confinement with patience, and were very thankful they had such good usage as to have provisions and light left them.

The other prisoners had better usage. Two of them were kept pinioned, because the captain was not free to trust them. The other two were taken into my service, upon Burke's recommendation and upon their solemnly engaging to live and die with us. With them and the three honest men we were seven men well armed, and I made no doubt we should be able to deal well enough with the ten that were coming, considering the captain had said there were three or four honest men among them also.

As soon as the mutineers got to the place where their other boat lay, they ran their boat into the beach and came all on shore, hauling the boat up after them, which I was glad to see. I was afraid they would rather have left the boat at an anchor, some distance from the shore, with some hands in her to guard her, and so we should not be able to seize the boat. Being on shore, the first thing they did, they ran all to their other boat. It was easy to see they were under a great surprise to find her stript of all that was in her and a great hole in her bottom.

After they had mused a while upon this, they set up two or three great shouts, hallooing with all their might to try if they could make their companions hear, but all was to no purpose. Then they came all close in a ring and fired a volley of their small arms, and the echoes made the woods ring. But those in the cave we were sure could not hear and those in our keeping, tho' they heard it well enough, yet durst give no answer to them. The men were so astonished at the surprise of this, they resolv'd to go all on board again and let them know the men were all murdered and the long-boat staved. Accordingly, they immediately launched their boat again and got all of them on board.

Captain Burke was amazed, and even confounded at this, believing they would go on board the ship again and set sail, giving their comrades over for lost, and so he should still lose the ship, which he was in hopes we should have recovered. But he was quickly as much frightened the other way.

They had not been long put off with the boat but we perceived them all coming on shore again. With this was a new measure in their conduct, which it seemed they consulted together upon, viz. to leave three men in the boat, and the rest to go up into the country to look for their fellows. This was a great disappointment to us, for now we were at a loss what to do. Our seizing those seven men on shore would be no advantage to us if we let the boat escape, because they would then row away to the ship and then the rest of them would be sure to weigh and set sail, so our recovering the ship would be lost. However, we had no remedy but to wait and see what the issue of things might present. The seven men came on shore and the three who remained in the boat put her off to a good distance from the shore, and came to an anchor to wait for them. Friday was quite sure he could reach the boat swimming, and of this I had no doubts, but were he to do so it was my belief those on the ship would observe his attack and, again, weigh and set sail. So it was impossible for us to come at them in the boat.

Those that came on shore kept close together, marching towards the top of the little hill under which my habitation lay. We could see them plainly, tho' they could not perceive us. Slaader, who was the principal ringleader of the mutiny, was a large and fit man with hair like tar, much like all the Moors, and his tann'd skin had been ink'd with many pictures, as was common among the more superstitious sailors, which was many of them. Altho' I did not think of it at the time, I did realize upon reflection I had seen many of the symbols ink'd on Slaader's skin upon the trees and stones of this island in the past years.

When they were come to the brow of the hill, where they could see a great way into the valleys and woods, which lay towards the north-east part and where the island lay lowest, they shouted and hallooed till they were weary. Not caring to venture far from the shore, nor far from one another, they sat down together under a tree to consider of it. Had they thought fit to have gone to sleep there, as the other part of them had done, they had done the job for us. But they were too full of apprehensions of danger to venture to go to sleep, tho' they could not tell what the danger was they had to fear neither.

At length I told Friday, Burke, Sir Wade, and the others that there would be nothing done, in my opinion, till night. If they did not return to the boat, perhaps we might find a way to get between them and the shore, and so might use some stratagem with them in the boat to get them on shore. We waited a great while, tho' very impatient for their removing, and were very uneasy when, after long consultations, we saw them all start up and march down to-wards the sea. It seemed they had such dreadful apprehensions upon them of the danger of the place, they resolv'd to go on board the ship again, give their companions over for lost, and so go on with their intended voyage with the ship.

Captain Burke, as soon as I told him my thoughts, was ready to sink at the apprehensions of it, but I presently thought of a stratagem to fetch them back again. I ordered Friday and Turner to go over the little creek westward, towards the place where the savages came on shore when Friday was rescued, and as soon as they came to a little rising ground, at about half a mile distance, I bade them halloo out as loud as they could, and wait till they found the seamen heard them. As soon as ever they heard the seamen answer them they should return it again. Then keeping out of sight, always answering when the others hallooed, draw them as far into the island among the woods as possible, then wheel about again to me.

The pirates were just going into the boat when Friday and the mate hallooed. They heard them, and answering, ran along the shore westward towards the voice they heard, when they were presently stopped by the creek, where the water being up they could not get over. Slaader called for the boat to come up, as I expected. When they had set themselves over, I observ'd the boat being gone a good way into the creek and in a harbour within the land. The Moorish pirate took one of the three men out of her to go along with them and left only two in the boat, having fasten'd her to the stump of a little tree on the shore. This was what I wished for.

Leaving Friday and the captain's mate to their business, I took the rest with me and, crossing the creek out of their sight, we surprised the two men before they were aware. One of them lying on the shore and the other being in the boat. The fellow on shore was between sleeping and waking and going to start up. The captain, who was foremost, ran in upon him and knocked him down, then called out to him in the boat to yield or he was a dead man. There needed very few arguments to persuade a single man to yield when he saw five men upon him and his comrade knocked down. Besides, this was one of the three who were not so hearty in the mutiny as the rest of the crew, and therefore was persuaded not only to yield but afterwards to join with us.

In the mean time, Friday and Turner so well managed their business with the rest they drew them from one hill to another and from one wood to another, till they not only tired them, but left them stranded on the edge of the shadow'd valley. Of the eight which Friday led away to that awful place, only half ever returned, and the fate of the others was never learnt by any of us there.

More battles, the unseen ruler, the body

We had nothing now to do but to watch for them in the dark, and to fall upon them so as to make sure work with them. It was past midnight before the lucky four came back to their boat, having escap'd the shadow'd valley. We could hear Slaader, the foremost of them, long before they came quite up, calling to those behind to come along. We could also hear them answer and complain how tired they were and not able to come any faster, and in their voices was a tremble of fear. At length they came up to the boat, but it is impossible to express their confusion when they found the boat fast aground in the creek, the tyde ebbed out, and their two men gone. We could hear them call to one another in a most lamentable manner, telling one another they were got into an enchanted island. Either there were inhabitants in it, and they should all be murdered, or else there were devils and spirits in it, and they should be all carried away and devoured. My man Friday and I did take pleasure at such words, and shared a smile. The mutineers hallooed again, and called their two comrades by their names a great many times, but no answer.

After some time, we could see them, by the little light there was, run about, wringing their hands like men in despair. Sometimes they would go and sit down in the boat to rest themselves, then come ashore again and walk about again and so the same thing over again. My men would fain have had me give them leave to fall upon them at once in the dark. I was willing to take them at some advantage, so to spare them, and kill as few of them as I could. I was unwilling to hazard the killing any of our men, knowing the others were very well armed. I resolv'd to wait to see if they did not separate. To make sure of them, I drew my ambuscade nearer and ordered Friday and Burke to creep upon their hands and feet, as close to the ground as they could that they might not be discovered, and get as near them as they could before they offered to fire.

They had not been long in that posture when the piratical boatswain, Slaader, came walking towards them with two more of the crew. Burke was so eager at having this rogue so much in his power he could hardly have patience to let him come so near as to be sure of him. When they came nearer, the captain and Friday let fly at them. Slaader was killed upon the spot. The next man was shot in the body and fell just by him, tho' he did not die till an hour or two after. The third run for it.

At the noise of the fire, I advanced with my whole army, which was now eight men. We came upon them in the dark so they could not see our number. I made the man they had left in the boat, who was now one of us, to call them by name, to try if I could bring them to a parley. So he called out as loud as he could, to one of them, "Tom Smith! Tom Smith!"

Tom Smith answered, "Is that Roberts?" For it seemed he knew the voice.

The other answered, "Aye aye. For God's sake, Tom Smith, throw down your arms and yield, or you are dead men this moment."

"Who must we yield to? Where are they?" said Smith again.

"Here they are," said he. "Captain Burke, and fifty men with him, have been hunting you these two hours. Slaader is killed, Will Fry is wounded, and I am a prisoner. If you do not yield, you are all lost."

"Will they give us quarter then?" said Smith.

"I'll go and ask, if you promise to yield," said Roberts.

Burke himself then called out, "You, Smith, you know my voice. If you lay down your arms immediately, and submit, you shall have your lives, but not Will Atkins."

Upon this Atkins cried out, "For God's sake, captain, give me quarter! What have I done? They have all been as bad as I!" Which was not true neither, for this Atkins was all but a pirate himself, and the first man that laid hold of the captain when they mutinied and used him barbarously. However, the captain told him he must lay down his arms at discretion and trust to the governor's mercy. For they all called me governor.

In a word, they both laid down their arms and begged their lives. I sent the man that had parleyed with them, and two more, who bound them. Then my great army came up and seized upon them and upon their boat.

Our next work was to repair the first boat and think of seizing the ship. As for Burke, now he had leisure to parley with them, he expostulated with them upon the villainy of their practices with him, and how it must bring them to the gallows.

They all appear'd very penitent and begged hard for their lives. As for that, he told them they were none of his prisoners, but the commander's of the island. They thought they had set him on shore in a barren, uninhabited island. But it had pleased God so to direct them, that it was inhabited, and the governor was an Englishman. He might hang them all there, if he pleased. But as he had given them all quarter, he supposed he would send them to England, to be dealt with there as justice required, except Atkins, whom he was commanded by the governor to advise to prepare for death, for he would be hanged in the morning.

Tho' this was all but a fiction of his own, yet it had its desired effect. Atkins fell upon his knees to beg the captain to intercede with the governor for his life. All the rest begged of him, for God's sake, that they might not be sent to England.

It now occurred to me the time of our deliverance was come, and it would be a most easy thing to bring these fellows in to be hearty in getting possession of the ship. I retired in the dark, that they might not see what kind of a governor they had, and called the captain to me. When I called, as at a good distance, one of the men was ordered to speak again, and said to Burke, "Captain, the commander calls for you."

Presently he replied, "Tell his Excellency I am just a coming." This amused them, and they all believed the commander was just by with his fifty men.

Upon Burke's coming to me, I was struck with an uneasy sense. It was part my own awareness, part that of the beast, which had lurk'd just beneath my skin while we ran and hunted these villains cross the island. It had observ'd some thing thru my eyes which bother'd it, which meant, in a word, it was a thing I had observ'd as well, tho' I knew not what it was.

Putting such reflections aside for the moment, I told Burke my project for seizing the ship, which he liked wonderfully well, and resolv'd to put it in execution the next morning.

But, in order to execute it and to be secure of success, I told him we must divide the prisoners, and he should go and take Atkins and two more of the worst of them and send them pinioned to the cave where the others lay. This was committed to Friday, Turner, and Sir Wade. They conveyed them to the cave, as to a prison. It was, indeed, a dismal place to men in their condition. The others I ordered to my bower. As it was fenced in and they pinioned, the place was secure enough, considering they were upon their behaviour.

It was at this point, as the men scatter'd upon their tasks, that I observ'd what the beast had seen which foul'd its mood. Or, in a word, what it had not seen.

The body of Slaader had vanish'd.

I spoke with the men, but none had remov'd it from the shore, and this did feed the fear many of them had felt for this island as its nature did work upon them. There were much talk of Carrib rituals and vampyre and one man spoke of the *ghul*, a word I had heard long, long ago from the wise men of Sallee.

When I spoke of the missing body to Friday, he was very put out, and look'd to the south west, to the dark church. "What is it, Friday?" I asked of him.

He shook his head in shame, but would not say. When I ask'd again, he raised his dark eyes to mine. "All things say O to him," said my man. And he would say no more that night.

Prisoners and hostages, taking the ship,
the beast fights death

I n the morning I sent Burke to our prisoners, who was to
enter into a parley with them. In a word, to try them and
tell me whether he thought they might be trusted or no to
go on board and surprise the ship. He talked to them of the injury
done him, of the condition they were brought to, and tho' the
governor had given them quarter for their lives as to the present
action, yet if they were sent to England they would all be hanged
in chayns, to be sure. But if they would join in so just an attempt
as to recover the ship, he would have the governor's engagement
for their pardon.

Any one may guess how such a proposal would be accepted by
men in their condition. They fell down on their knees to Burke and
promised they would be faithful to him to the last drop, and they
should owe their lives to him and would go with him all over the
world. They would own him as a father as long as they lived.

"Well," said he, "I must go and tell the governor what you say, and
see what I can do to bring him to consent to it." So he brought me

an account of the temper he found them in, and he believed they would be faithful.

However, that we might be very secure, I told Burke he should go back again and choose out five that they might see he was not wanting for men, and tell them he would take out those five to be his assistants. The governor would keep the other two, and the three that were sent prisoners to the castle (my cave) as hostages for the fidelity of those five. If they proved unfaithful in the execution, the five hostages should be hanged in chayns alive on the shore.

This look'd severe and convinced them the governor was in earnest. However, they had no way left them but to accept it. It was now the business of the prisoners, as much as of Burke, to persuade the other five to do their duty.

I asked him if he was willing to venture with these hands on board the ship. As for me and my man Friday, I did not think it was proper for us to stir, having seven men left behind. It was employment enough for us to keep them asunder and supply them with victuals.

As to the five in the cave, I resolv'd to keep them fast, but Friday went in twice a day to them, to supply them with necessaries. I made the other two carry provisions to a certain distance, where Friday was to take it.

When I show'd myself to the two hostages, it was with Burke, who told them I was the person the governor had ordered to look after them. It was the governor's pleasure they should not stir any where but by my direction. If they did, they would be fetch'd into the castle and be laid in irons, or, far worse, set free in the wood to be hunted by the beast of the island. I now appeared as another person and spoke of the governor, the garrison, the castle, and the like, upon all occasions.

Burke now had no difficulty before him but to furnish his two boats, stop the breach of one, and man them. He made young Sir Wade captain of one, with four of the men. Himself, Turner, and five more, went in the other. They contrived their business very well, for they came up to the ship about midnight. As soon as they came within call of the ship, he made Roberts hail the mutineers and tell them they had brought off the men and the boat, holding them in a chat till they came to the ship's side. Burke and Turner, entering first, knock'd down the second mate and carpenter with the butt end of their muskets, being seconded by their men.

They secured all the rest that were upon the mainland quarter-decks, and began to fasten the hatches to keep them down that were below. The other boat and their men, entering at the fore-chains, secured the forecastle of the ship, and the scuttle which went down into the cook-room, making three men they found there prisoners. When this was done, and all safe upon deck, Burke ordered the mate, with three men, to break into the round-house, where the mutineer captain, Doyle, lay.

Having taken the alarm, Doyle had got up and, with two men and a boy, had got fire-arms in their hands. When Turner split open the door with a crow, the false captain and his men fired boldly among them. They wounded the mate with a musket ball, which broke his arm, and wounded two more of the men, but killed nobody.

Turner, calling for help, rush'd into the round-house, wounded as he was, and with his pistol shot Doyle thru the head, so he never spoke a word more. Upon which the rest yielded, and the ship was taken without any more lives lost.

As soon as the ship was thus secured, Captain Burke ordered seven guns to be fired, which was the signal agreed upon with me to give me notice of his success, which you may be sure I was very glad to hear. Having thus heard the signal, I did head away from the shore to my castle for sleep, it having been a day of great fatigue to me. Yet I had not cover'd half the distance when one stepped from the trees to confront me with a drawn broad sword, or cutlass, and made me set my hand upon my own.

At first, I bethought myself this was one of the four pirates lost in the shadow'd valley. And then the quarter moon did come from behind a cloud and cast some light upon the shore, and I saw the Moor Slaader before me. An awful wound marr'd his features, and show'd the skull and teeth below his flesh, for Burke's weapon had ruin'd much of his face. Indeed, it had kill'd him, of this I would be sure even if the beast did not assure me of it from beneath my skin with furious snarls. Yet before me he stood, and many of the dark symbols ink'd in his skin did burn and gleam like lamp light.

"Robin Crusoe," said Slaader, and his voice was that of the grave, "there you are." His brow did wrinkle in anger, tho' he was beyond all such feeling, and he point'd a stern finger at me. "You shall not leave, Robin Crusoe! Your soul *will* feed the Great Dreamer! *You shall not leave!!*"

At this he lunged at me with his cutlass. I drew my own sword and leapt aside. The boatswain follow'd, swinging his great weapon. The blades met, but I was no swords man, and Slaader had a furious strength upon him. Our swords met twice, high and low, and twice again, side to side, and then the pirate knock'd my blade from my hand and it flew far from my grasp. Now from his mouth came the words, the awful words of Poll and the savages and Walla-Kay, Friday's father. The dark prayers of Kathooloo. The ink of his skin did flicker and flare with his words, like a lantern being brush'd with a breeze.

Within my skin the beast did howl for freedom, for the words of Slaader anger'd it, as the like words of Poll had years and years ago, as I have said.

I dodged a swipe of his cutlass and felt a great freedom come across me, as a man must when he sees the door of his prison open'd after many, many years, yet the feeling was not mine but that of the beast. The moon was of no consequence, for the years alone had made us too close for such things to matter, and like in the stories I had heard of my father's father, I call'd to the beast and set it free.

The mantle of the beast fell upon me, and through the smok'd lens did I see the look of surprise come across the face of Slaader. I felt the beast's displeasure at my cloathes, and its hunger for flesh, and its rage at the dead boatswain.

In the moments it took for the beast to take my form, Slaader brought his sword down in a mighty swing, as a man takes an axe to a tree. The blow did catch us in the shoulder, splitting bone and flesh, but the beast had enough of me at that point that the wound did heal over, in a word like a baking pie which closes itself up with only a faint scar, and even that was hidden by the beast's fur.

The beast's claws lash'd out as a whip, tearing open the boatswain's stomach to spill his innards cross the shore. Yet Slaader noticed the wound no more than the beast had its, and swung his cutlass again. The beast swept away the blade as a man sweeps away flies, and its claws cut at the boatswain's flesh once more, yet again he ignored it.

Slaader brought his own hand around in a fist to strike the beast and O the pain! The man wore a ring of purest silver, tho' he knew not the power it gave him, for he raised his cutlass again as the beast reel'd back. Recovering, it leapt forward and closed its mighty jaws on the man's arm, tearing at flesh and crushing bone, and Slaader's arm fell to the sand, the cutlass still clutch'd in its hand.

At this the man sent forth a mighty blow with his undamaged hand, his ringed hand, and this strike sprawl'd the beast back cross the shore, and it yelpt like a dog which had been beaten, tho' only for a moment. It turned and snarl'd. The boatswain grabb'd his sword with his other hand.

Slaader stepped forward again and then, most suddenly, did his head burst like an over ripe melon dropp'd from the vine. His body stagger'd on the sand and rais'd the cutlass once more, and then the lamp light from his ink grew dim and he fell.

A few yards away, Friday stood with his musket at the shoulder, his aim once again shown to be true and good. He look'd at the beast for a moment, and thru the smok'd lens I was pleased to see Friday did not appear as meat, but as a member of the pack to be protected. And this thought, nay, this vague impression, was scarce cross my mind when I observ'd I was gazing upon my man with my own eyes and not those of the beast. My legs were weak and I fell to the sand, not far from the headless body of Slaader.

"Master," said Friday with a glare at the piratical boatswain's body. "Is you safe?"

I felt the beast settle beneath my skin and met my faithful servant's gaze. "We are safe, Friday," said I to him. "We are safer than ever we have been before." At which we burnt the body of Slaader there on the shore where it lay, and then Friday helped me to our castle and got me into my hammock, which had once belong'd to a long dead mate whose name I had never learnt.

Final preparations, those left behind, my deliverance

I slept very sound, till I was something surprised with the noise of a gun. Presently starting up, I heard a man call me by the name of "Governor, Governor," and I knew Burke's voice. When climbing up to the top of the hill, there he stood, and, pointing to the ship, he embraced me in his arms. "My dear friend and deliverer," said he, "there's your ship, for she is all yours, and so are we, and all that belong to her."

I cast my eyes to the ship, and there she rode within little more than half a mile of the shore. They had weighed her anchor as soon as they were masters of her, and the weather being fair, had brought her to just against the mouth of the little creek. The tyde being up, the captain had brought the pinnacle in near the place where I at first landed my rafts, and so landed just at my door.

I saw my deliverance, indeed, visibly put into my hands. A large ship just ready to carry Friday and me away whither I pleased to go. At first, for some time, I was not able to answer Burke one word. He perceived the surprise, and pulled a bottle out of his pocket, and gave me a dram of cordial which he had brought on purpose for me. After I had drank it, I sat down upon the ground.

All this time the poor man was in as great an ecstasy as I, only not under any surprise as I was. He said a thousand kind and tender things to me, to compose and bring me to myself. But such was the flood of joy in my breast, it put all my spirits into confusion. At last it broke out into tears, and in a little while after I recovered my speech. I then took my turn and embraced him as my deliverer, and we rejoiced together.

When we had talked a while, the captain told me he had brought me some little refreshment, such as the ship afforded, and such as the wretches that had been so long his masters had not plundered him of. Upon this he called aloud to the boat and bade his men bring the things ashore that were for the governor. Indeed, it was a present as if I had been one that was not to be carried away with them, but as if I had been to dwell upon the island still.

First, he had brought me a case of bottles full of excellent cordial waters, six large bottles of Madeira wine, two pounds of excellent tobacco, twelve good pieces of the ship's beef, and six pieces of pork, with a bag of peas, and about a hundred weight of bisket.

But, besides these, and what was a thousand times more useful to me, he brought me clean shirts, very good neckcloths, gloves, shoes, a hat, and one pair of stockings, with a very good suit of cloathes of his own which had been worn but very little. In a word, he cloathed me from head to foot. It was a very kind and agreeable present to one in my circumstances, but never was any thing in the world of that kind so unpleasant, awkward, and uneasy, as it was to me to wear such cloathes at their first putting on after so many years.

After these ceremonies were past, and after all his good things were brought into my little apartment, we began to consult what was to be done with the prisoners we had. It was worth considering whether we might venture to take them away with us or no, especially two of them, whom he knew to be incorrigible and refractory to the last degree. Burke said he knew they were such rogues there was no obliging them. If he did carry them away, it must be in irons, to be delivered over to justice at the first English colony he could come at. I found the captain himself was very anxious about it.

Upon this I told him if he desired it, I would undertake to bring the two men he spoke of to make it their own request he should leave them upon the island, tho' I did warn him this was but a sentence of a different kind. "I should be very glad of that," said the captain, "with all my heart."

"Well," said I, "I will send for them up, and talk with them for you." So I caus'd Friday and the two hostages to go to the cave and bring up the five men to the bower, and keep them there till I came.

After some time, I came thither dressed in my new habit, and now I was called governor again. Being all met, and Burke with me, I caused the men to be brought before me. I told them I had got a full account of their villainous behaviour to the captain, and how they had run away with the ship and were preparing to commit farther piracy. But Providence had ensnared them in their own ways, and they were fallen into the pit which they had dug for others.

I let them know by my direction the ship had been seized. She lay now in the road, and they might see their new captain, Doyle, had received the reward of his villainy. They would see him hanging at the yard-arm.

I wanted to know what they had to say, why I should not execute them as pirates, as by my commission they could not doubt but I had authority so to do.

One of them answered in the name of the rest that they had nothing to say but this— when they were taken, Burke promised them their lives, and they implored my mercy. But I told them I knew not what mercy to show them. As for myself, I had resolv'd to quit the island with all my men, and had taken passage to go for

England. As for Burke, he could not carry them to England other than as prisoners to be tried for mutiny, the consequence of which would be the gallows. I could not tell what was best for them, unless they had a mind to take their fate on the island. If they desired, I had some inclination to give them their lives, if they thought they could shift on shore, tho' I did warn them it was a dark place and no true mercy.

They seemed very thankful for it, and said they would much rather venture to stay there than be carried to England to be hanged. I left it on that issue.

However, Burke pretended to make some difficulty of it, as if he durst not leave them there. Upon this I seemed a little angry with the captain, and told him they were my prisoners, not his. Seeing I had offer'd them so much favour, I would be as good as my word. If he did not think fit to consent to it, I would set them at liberty, as I found them. He might take them again if he could catch them.

Upon this they appeared very thankful, and I set them at liberty and bade them retire into the woods to the place whence they came. I would leave them some fire-arms, some ammunition, and some directions how they should live very well, if they thought fit.

Upon this I prepared to go on board the ship, but told Burke that Friday and I would stay that night to prepare my things. When the captain was gone, I sent for the men up to me to my apartment, and enter'd seriously into discourse with them on their circumstances. I told them I thought they had made a right choice, tho' a dangerous one. If the captain had carry'd them away, they would be hanged. I showed them the false captain hanging at the yard-arm of the ship and told them they had nothing less to expect.

When they had all declared their willingness to stay, I then told them I would let them into the story of my living there, and put them into the way of making it easy to them, or as easy as could be. Accordingly, I gave them the history of the place, and of my coming to it. I warn'd them of the dark church and the dream lord

Kathooloo, and to be cautious of all thoughts in that place, and of the very nature of the island. Also I showed them my fortifications, the way I made my bread, planted my corn, cured my grapes. In a word, all that was necessary to make them survive for as long a time as they would. I told them also the story of the seventeen Spaniards that were to be expected, for whom I left a letter, and made them promise to treat them in common with themselves. Here it may be noted, Burke had ink on board, and was greatly surprised I never hit upon a way of making ink of charcoal and water, as I had done things much more difficult.

I left them my fire-arms and three swords. I had above a barrel and a half of powder left. I gave them a description of the way I managed the goats and directions to milk and fatten them, and to make both butter and cheese. I gave them every part of my own story, and told them I should prevail with Burke to leave them two barrels of gunpowder more and some garden seeds, which I told them I would have been very glad of. I gave them the bag of peas which the captain had brought me to eat and bade them be sure to sow and increase them.

Having done all this, and warned yet again against the dark church, I left them the next day and went on board the ship. We prepared to sail, but did not weigh that night.

The next morning, two of the five men came swimming to the ship's side, and making a most lamentable complaint of the island, begged to be taken into the ship, for God's sake, for they should be taken by the dream lord Kathooloo, and begged Burke to take them on board e'en if he hanged them immediately.

Upon this, he pretended to have no power without me. After some difficulty, and after their solemn promises of amendment, they were taken on board, and were some time after whipped and pickled. After which they proved very honest and quiet fellows.

Some time after this, the long-boat was order'd on shore, the tyde being up, with the things promised to the men. Burke, at my intercession, caused their chests and cloathes to be added, which they took, and were very thankful for. I also encouraged them by telling them if it lay in my power to send any vessel to take them in, I would not forget them.

When I took leave of this island, I carried on board, for a relique, the great goat-skin cap I had made, and also I forgot not to take the money I formerly mention'd, which had lain by me so long useless it was grown rusty or tarnish'd. Also the money I found in the wreck of the Spanish ship. Friday brought naught but his great wooden sword, which he wore on his hip through his goat-skin belt.

And thus we left my sanctuary, my prison, the Island of Despair, the 19th of December, as I found by the ship's account, in the year 1686. I had been upon it seven and twenty years, two months, and nineteen days, deliver'd from this second captivity the same day of the month I first made my escape from among the Moors of Sallee.

My return, old friends,
my fortunes reverse

◉

In this vessel, after a long voyage, I arrived in England the 11th of June, in the year 1687, having been thirty-five years absent. No less than five moons were spent on board, yet Burke did not see to question my sometimes solitary nature, nor would any cross Friday as he stood guard without my cabin with his great wooden sword.

When I came to England, I was as perfect a stranger to all the world as if I had never been known there. I went down afterwards into Yorkshire, but my father was dead and my mother and all the family extinct. I found two sisters and two nephews by the name of Marsh. As I had been long ago given over for dead, there had been no provision made for me. In a word, I found nothing to relieve or assist me, and the little money I had would not do much for me as to settling in the world.

I met with one piece of gratitude, indeed, which I did not expect. Burke, whom I had so happily deliver'd, and by the same means saved the ship and cargo, did give a very handsome account to the owners of the manner how I had saved the lives of the men and the ship. They invited me to meet them and some other merchants concerned, and all together made me a very handsome compliment upon the subject and a present of almost £200 sterling.

But after making several reflections upon the circumstances of my life, and how little way this would go towards settling me in the world, I resolv'd to go to Lisbon and see if I might not come by some information of the state of my plantation in the Brasils, and of what was become of my partner, who, I had reason to suppose, had some years past given me over for dead.

When I arrived, April following, in Lisbon I found, to my particular satisfaction, my friend Captain Amaral who first took me up at sea off the shore of Africk. He was now grown old, and had left off going to sea, having put his son, Zachary, who was far from a young man, into his ship and who still used the Brasil trade.

After some passionate expressions of the old acquaintance between us, I inquired after my plantation and my partner. Amaral told me he had not been in the Brasils for about nine years, but he could assure me when he came away my partner was living. The trustees, whom I had joined with him to take cognizance of my part, were both dead. However, he believed I would have a very good account of the improvement of the plantation. Upon the general belief of my being cast away and drowned, my trustees had given in the account of the produce of my part of the plantation to the procurator-fiscal, who had appropriated it, in case I never came to claim it, one-third to the king, and two-thirds to the monastery of St. Augustine, to be expended for the benefit of the poor, and for the conversion of the Indians to the Catholic faith.

I asked him if he knew to what height of improvement he had brought the plantation, and whether he thought it might be worth looking after.

Amaral told me he knew my partner was grown exceeding rich upon the enjoying his part of it. As to my being restored to a quiet possession of it, there was no question to be made of that, my partner being alive to witness my title and my name being also enrolled in the register of the country. Also the old captain told me the survivors of my two trustees were very fair honest people and very wealthy. He believed I would not only have their assistance for putting me in possession, but would find a very considerable sum of money in their hands for my account.

I showed myself a little concerned at this account, and inquired of Amaral how it came to pass the trustees should thus dispose of my effects when he knew I had made my will and had made him my universal heir. He told me that was true, but as there was no proof of my being dead, he could not act as executor. Besides, he was not willing to intermeddle with a thing so remote.

"But," said the old man, "I have one piece of news to tell you, which perhaps may not be so acceptable to you as the rest. Believing you were lost, your partner and trustees did offer to account with me, in your name, for six or eight of the first years' profits, which I received. There being at that time great disbursements, it did not amount to near so much as afterwards it produced. However," said the old man, "I shall give you a true account of what I have received, and how I have disposed of it."

The good man then began to explain his misfortunes, having lost his ship coming home to Lisbon about eleven years after my leaving the place. He had been obliged to make use of my money to recover his losses and buy him a share in a new ship. "However, my old friend," said he, "you shall not want a supply in your necessity. As soon as my son returns, you shall be fully satisfied." Upon this, he pulled out an old pouch, and gave me one hundred and sixty Portugal moidores in gold and giving the writings of his title to the ship, which his son was gone to the Brasils in, of which he was a quarter-part owner, and his son another, he put them both into my hands for security of the rest.

I was too much moved with the honesty and kindness of the poor man to be able to bear this. Remembering what he had done for me, how he had taken me up at sea, and how generously he had used me on all occasions, and how sincere a friend he was now to me, I could hardly refrain weeping at what he had said to me. I asked him if his circumstances admitted him to spare so much money at that time, and if it would not straiten him?

"I could not say," he told me. "However, it is your money, and you might want it more than I."

"And your son? Shall he not be displeased to find his ship sold from beneath his heels?"

At which Amaral became most reflective, and confided in me that his son did have a great hatred of me already, which surprised me to no end, for I had never met the youth. "Fear often turns to hate over time," he told me, "and Zachary had much call to fear you as a child, as he often told me."

Still was I confused, and now worried Amaral had mistook me for some other acquaintance, and then he told me that before taking the Christian name of Zachary, after Zachariah, his adopted son had been called Xury, the boy he had bought from me and whom he had come to love as much as any father loves their son. As Xury had learnt more and better English, he had told his father of the *almustazeb*, and of the awful things he saw on our voyage along the coast of Africk, and sometimes the boy would wake screaming and in tears with fright.

This shamed me, for I had not given much thought to Xury over the years, tho' without him I would still be a prisoner of Sallee, or dead, and I had no words to express my sadness that he had been haunted by the beast for so many years.

At this, tho', my man Friday stepped forward, for he had been there at my side all along, and spoke sharply to my defense. "Master is good man," said he. "The best mans. The beast keep him alive on island and protect him and save many lifes." Even cloathed now in the good fashions of Europe, Friday was most intimidating, and still wore his great wooden sword.

His loud words did start Amaral for a moment, but the old captain shook them off and assured us he did not seek to lay blame or to expose secrets. He was a happy man who loved his son, and wish'd only to repay an old friend for bringing them together. While he knew of my hidden nature, he could not see evil in that which had brought a son to him, nor could he find any but love in his heart for me because of it.

Every thing the good man said was full of affection, and I could hardly refrain from tears while he spoke. I took one hundred of the moidores and return'd him the rest, and told him if ever I had possession of the plantation, I would return the other to him also. As to the bill of sale of his part in his son's ship, I would not take it by any means. If I wanted the money, I found he was honest enough to pay me. If I came to receive what he gave me reason to expect, I would never have a penny more from him. I also swore to write a letter to his son Zachary, who had been Xury, and beg the grown man's forgiveness for the fears of his childhood.

When this was pass'd, Amaral asked me if he should put me into a method to make my claim to my plantation? I told him I thought to go over to it myself. He said I might do so if I pleased. If I did not, there were ways enough to secure my right and to appropriate the profits to my use. As there were ships in the river of Lisbon just ready to go away to Brasil, he made me enter my name in a public register, with his affidavit affirming upon oath that I was alive, and I was the same person who took up the land for the planting of said plantation at first.

Never was any thing more honourable than the proceedings upon this procuration. In less than seven months I received a large packet from the survivors of my trustees, in which were the following particular letters and papers enclosed.

First, There was the account-current of the produce of my farm or plantation, from the year when their fathers had balanced with Captain Amaral, being for six years. The balance appeared to be 1,174 moidores in my favour.

Secondly, There was the account of four years more before the government claimed the administration, as being the effects of a person not to be found, which they called civil death. The balance of this amounted to 19,446 crusadoes, being about 3,241 moidores.

Thirdly, There was the prior of Augustine's account, who had received the profits for above fourteen years. Not being able to account for what was disposed of by the hospital, declared he had 872 moidores not distributed, which he acknowledged to my account.

There was a letter of my partner's, congratulating me upon my being alive, giving me an account how the estate was improved, and inviting me very passionately to come over and take possession of my own. It concluded with a hearty tender of his friendship and that of his family. Also he sent me, as a present, seven fine leopards' skins, five chests of sweetmeats, and a hundred pieces of gold uncoin'd, not quite so large as moidores. By the same fleet, my two merchant-trustees shipped me 1,200 chests of sugar, 800 rolls of tobacco, and the rest of the whole account in gold.

I was now master, all on a sudden, of above five thousand pounds sterling in money, and had an estate, as I might well call it, in the Brasils, of above a thousand pounds a year, as sure as an estate of lands in England. In a word, I was in a condition which I scarce knew how to understand, or how to compose myself for the enjoyment of it.

The first thing I did was to recompense my original benefactor, my good old Captain Amaral, who had been first charitable to me in my distress, kind to me in my beginning, and honest to me at the end. It now lay on me to reward him, which I would do a hundredfold. I first return'd to him the hundred moidores I had received of him. Then I sent for a notary and caused a procuration to be drawn, empowering him to be my receiver of the annual profits of my plantation, and appointing my partner to account with him, with a clause in the end, being a grant of 100 moidores a year to him during his life and 50 moidores a year to his son, Zachary, for his life. Thus I requited my old man and my former savior.

I was now to consider which way to steer my course next, and what to do with the estate Providence had thus put into my hands. Indeed, I had more care upon my head now than I had in my silent state of life in the island, where I wanted nothing but what I had, and had nothing but what I wanted. I had now a great charge upon me, and my business was how to secure it. I had never a cave now to hide my money in, or a place where it might lie without lock or key, till it grew mouldy and tarnish'd before any body would meddle with it. On the contrary, I knew not where to put it, or whom to trust with it. My old patron, Captain Amaral, indeed, was honest, and was the only refuge I had.

I had once a mind to have gone to the Brasils, and have settled myself there, for I was, as it were, naturalized to the place. But now I could not tell how to think of going thither till I had settled my affairs, and left my effects in some safe hands behind me. It was some months, however, before I resolv'd upon this. I resolv'd, at last, to go to England with it, where, if I arrived, I concluded I should make some acquaintance, or find some relations that would be faithful to me. Accordingly, I prepared to go to England with all my wealth.

My travels, loup garou,
my awful damnation

Having settled my affairs, sold my cargo, and turned all my effects into good bills of exchange, my next difficulty was which way to go to England. I had been accustomed enough to the sea, and yet I had a strange aversion to go to England by sea at that time. It was an aversion the beast shared with me, as it had oft been disturbed by the dark church, and even Friday seemed put out by the idea. He and I spoke of this, and agreed that while some things were very strong on the island, it did not mean they could not be strong in other places and at other times.

Captain Amaral pressed me not to go by sea if I were so averse, but either to go by land and cross over the Bay of Biscay to Rochelle, from whence it was but an easy and safe journey by land to Paris, and so to Calais and Dover. Or to go up to Madrid, and so all the way by land through France. In a word, I was so prepossessed against my going by sea at all, except from Calais to Dover, I resolv'd to travel all the way by land. As I was not in haste and did not value the charge, it was by much the pleasanter way. To make it more so, my old captain brought an English gentleman, the son of a merchant in Lisbon, who was willing to travel with me. We picked up two more English merchants also, and two young Portuguese gentlemen, the last going to Paris only. In all there were six of us, and five servants. The two merchants and the two Portuguese contented themselves with one servant between two, to save the charge. As for me, I got an English sailor to travel with me as a servant beside my man Friday, who was too much a stranger to be capable of supplying the place of a servant on the road, and was very oft looked at as a sport for his dusky appearance.

In this manner I set out from Lisbon. Our company being very well mounted and armed, we made a little troop, whereof they did me the honour to call me captain, as well because I was the oldest man as because I had two servants, and, indeed, was the original of the whole journey.

As I have troubled you with none of my sea journals, so I shall trouble you now with none of my land journal. But some grim and horrible adventures happened to us in this journey I must not omit.

When we came to Madrid, we being all of us strangers to Spain, were willing to stay some time. Alas, the moon was due at the end of the month, and already my loyal Friday attracted much unwanted attention. Rather than risk my taking on the mantle of the beast within a city of the Inquisition, we set out from Madrid about the middle of October. When we came to the edge of Navarre, we were alarm'd with an account that so much snow was fallen on the French side of the mountains several travelers were obliged to come back to Pampeluna after having attempted, at an extreme hazard, to pass on.

When we came to Pampeluna itself we found it so indeed. To me, that had been always used to a hot climate, and to countries where I could scarce bear any cloathes on, the cold was insufferable. Nor, indeed, was it more painful than surprising, to come but ten days before out of Old Castile and to feel a wind so cold as to be intolerable.

Poor Friday was frightened when he saw the mountains all cover'd with snow and felt cold weather, which he had never seen or felt before in his life. That he could be brave in so many things, yet scared at the sight of snow, I found very amusing, and eventually he did laugh with me, tho' I could tell the cold did have a severe affect on one of his nature.

To mend the matter, when we came to Pampeluna, it continued snowing with so much violence the people said winter was come before its time. The roads which were difficult before were now quite impassable. In a word, the snow lay in some places too thick for us to travel, and being not hard frozen, as is the case in the northern countries, there was no going without being in danger of being buried alive every step.

We stayed no less than twenty days at Pampeluna. Much to his displeasure, Friday spent the three nights of the moon within a barn with only a small fire to warm his cold limbs. These same nights I spent myself bound to the beams of the barn, for I had shewn my man the tricks of silver coins and knots my father had long ago taught me. Most pleased were we both when these nights ended and we could rejoin to the inn, altho' it was clear the beast found such weather to its liking.

When seeing the winter coming on, and no likelihood of its being better, I proposed our little company should all go away to Fontarabia and there take shipping for Bourdeaux, which was a little voyage.

But while I was considering this, there came in four French gentlemen, who having been stopped on the French side of the passes, had found out a guide who had brought them over the mountains by such ways they were not much incommoded with the snow. Where they met with snow in any quantity, they said it was frozen hard enough to bear them and their horses.

We sent for this guide, a man named Etienne, who told us he would undertake to carry us the same way with no hazard from the snow, provided we were armed sufficiently to protect ourselves from wild beasts.

"For," he said, "upon these great snows it is frequent for some wolves to show themselves at the foot of the mountains, being made ravenous for want of food." We told him we were well enough prepared for such creatures as they were. One of the young Portuguese gentlemen, by name of Dacosta, then ask'd if our guide would ensure us from a kind of two-legged wolves which he had been told we were in most danger from on the French side of the mountains by Languedoc, and at which I saw Friday narrow his eyes in concern. My man's hand wrapt on the hilt of his wooden sword, yet I assur'd him with a glance and a shake of my head that this was meer folklore and no threat to us.

Etienne satisfy'd us there was no danger of that kind in the way we were to go. So we agreed to follow him, as did also twelve other gentlemen, with their servants.

Accordingly, we set out from Pampeluna, with our guide, on the 15th of November. I was surprised, when, instead of going forward, he came back with us on the same road we came from Madrid, about twenty miles. When having passed two rivers and come into the plain country, we found ourselves in a warm climate again where the country was pleasant and no snow to be seen. Turning to his left, Etienne approached the mountains another way. Tho' it is true the hills and precipices looked dreadful, yet he made so many tours, such meanders, and led us by such winding ways, we past the height of the mountains without being much encumber'd with the snow. All on a sudden, he show'd us the pleasant fruitful provinces of Languedoc and Gascony, all green and flourishing, tho', indeed, at a great distance, and we had some rough way to pass still.

We were a little uneasy, however, when we found it snowed one whole day and a night so fast we could not travel. Etienne bid us be easy. We should soon be past it all. We found, indeed, we began to descend every day and to come more north than before.

It was about two hours before night when, Etienne being something before us and not just in sight, out rush'd three wolves of a
hollow way adjoining to a thick wood. Two of the wolves made at
the guide, and had he been far before us he would have been devoured before we could have helped him. One of them fastened
upon his horse and the other attacked the man with such violence
that he had not time to draw his pistol, but hallooed and cried out
to us. My man Friday being next me, I bade him ride up and see
what was the matter. As soon as Friday came in sight of the man, he
hallooed out as loud as the other, "O master! O master!" but, like a
bold fellow, rode up to the poor man.

It was happy for Etienne it was my man Friday, for he having
been used to the beast after so many years had no fear upon him,
but went close up to him and with his pistol shot the wolf that
attacked Etienne in the head. Any other of us would have fired
at a distance, and perhaps either missed the wolf or endangered
shooting the man.

But it was enough to have terrify'd a bolder man than I. Indeed,
it alarmed all our company, when, with the noise of Friday's
pistol, we heard on both sides the most dismal howling of wolves.
The noise, redoubled by the echo of the mountains, appeared to
us as if there had been a prodigious number of them. However,
as Friday had kill'd this wolf, the other that had fastened upon
the horse left him and fled without doing the horse any damage,
having fastened upon his head where the bosses of the bridle had
stuck in his teeth. But Etienne was most hurt, for the raging creature had bit him twice, once in the arm, and the other time a little
above his knee. Tho' he had made some defence, he was just as it
were tumbling down by the disorder of his horse, when Friday
came up and shot the wolf.

At the noise of Friday's pistol we all mended our pace and rode
up as fast as the way would give us leave to see what was the matter.
As soon as we came clear of the trees, which blinded us before, we

saw what had been the case, and how Friday had disengaged poor Etienne, tho' we did not presently discern what kind of creature it was he had kill'd.

Friday had delivered our guide, and when we came up to him he was helping him off from his horse, for Etienne was both hurt and frighten'd.

We were still in a wild place, and our guide very much hurt, and what to do we hardly knew. The howling of wolves ran much in my head and, indeed, except the noise I once heard on the shore of Africk, I never heard any thing that fill'd me with such strange vigour.

These things, and the approach of night, called us off. We had near three leagues to go, and Etienne hastened us down into Languedoc.

The ground was still covered with snow, tho' not so deep and dangerous as on the mountains. The ravenous creatures, as we heard afterwards, were come down into the forest and plain country to seek for food, and had done a great deal of mischief in the villages. They kill'd a great many sheep and horses, and some people too.

We had one dangerous place to pass, which Etienne told us, if there were more wolves in the country we should find them there. This was a small plain, surrounded with woods on every side, and a long narrow defile, or lane, which we were to pass to get through the wood. Then we should come to the village where we were to lodge.

It was a little after sunset when we came into the plain. We met with nothing in the first wood, except in a little plain within the wood, which was not above two furlongs over, we saw five great wolves cross the road, full speed, one after another, as if they had been in chase of some prey. They took no notice of us and were gone out of sight in a few moments. Upon this Etienne bid us keep in a ready posture, for he believed there were more wolves a coming.

We kept our arms ready, and our eyes about us, but we saw no more wolves till we came through that wood and entered the plain. As soon as we came into the plain, we had occasion enough to look about us. The first object we met with was a dead horse which the wolves had killed, and at least a dozen of them at work. We could not say eating of him, but picking of his bones rather. They had eaten up all the flesh before.

The night was coming on, and the light began to be dusky, which made it worse on our side. The noise increasing, we could perceive it was the howling and yelling of those hellish creatures. On a sudden we observ'd 2 or 3 wolves, one on our left, one behind us, and one in our front, so we seem'd to be surrounded with them. However, as they did not fall upon us, we kept our way forward, as fast as we could make our horses go, which was only a good hard trot. In this manner we came in view of the entrance of a wood at the farther side of the plain.

On a sudden, at another opening of the wood, we heard the noise of a gun, and looking that way, out rushed a horse with a saddle and a bridle on him, flying like the wind, and sixteen or seventeen wolves after him, full speed.

Here we had a most horrible sight. Riding up to the entrance where the horse came out, we found the carcasses of another horse and of two men, devoured by the ravenous creatures. One of the men was no doubt the same whom we heard fire the gun, for there lay a gun just by him. His head and the upper part of his body were eaten up.

This fill'd us with horror, and we knew not what course to take. But the creatures resolv'd us soon, for they gathered about us in hopes of prey. I believe there were three hundred of them. It happened very much to our advantage, that at the entrance into the wood, but a little way from it, there lay some large timber-trees, which had been cut down the summer before, and I suppose lay there for carriage. I drew our little company in among those trees, and placing ourselves in a line behind one long tree, I advised them all to alight, and keeping that tree before us for a breastwork, to stand in a triangle, or three fronts, enclosing our horses in the centre. We did so, and it was well we did, for never was a more furious charge than the creatures made upon us in this place. They came on with a growling kind of noise, and mounted the piece of timber, which, as I said, was our breastwork, as if they were only rushing upon their prey.

O, what a savage battle it was. My man Friday had his great wooden sword in one hand and a pistol in the other, and lay about him as a farmer does swing his scythe, cutting down wolves as the other cuts down grain. Etienne did fight as best he could with his pistols, yet his wounds made him slow and weak and he fell beneath fierce teeth and claws. The Portuguese youth, Dacosta, and his companion were dragg'd down and screamed for several minutes afore growing quiet.

Amidst all this, tho', I was keenly aware that no wolf would approach me. Even these starv'd creatures would not come near the beast. I bethought myself to turn this to our advantage, and yet even as I consider'd this did things take an e'en darker turn.

An awful howl rang in the night, as loud as a cannon or a strike of thunder. At this sound all the wolves did fall back, even those feasting upon our fallen company. A path open'd cross the pack and a fearsome animal did lope out from the wood. As it passed the wolves did snarl and cower, and I had no doubt this was the pack leader.

Truly it was a monster among the wolves, long in the fang and as high as my waist at the shoulder. Its jaw was a handspan and half again across, and each of its claws and fangs were the size of my thumb. A thick grey pelt cover'd it, streaked with white and silver in many places, for this great animal had no doubt ruled its small kingdom for many years.

It came to a halt a few yards from our breastwork and its eyes did pass back and forth over us as a cook's eyes pass over fresh wares at the market. Of our twelve strong company, there were but seven left, if I were to count Friday and myself, and there was little hope we would survive if the wolves attacked again with this huge animal at their fore.

On a sudden, the pack leader seem'd to single me out and sent many a snarl my way. One or two wolves began a low howl, and soon all of them fill'd our ears with their cries. The huge wolf growled and snarled at me, and its teeth did gnash at the air in a manner that could only be a threat to us. Or to me.

"He not want fight you, master," said Friday, who still stood at my side. "He want fight the beast. You here, the beast here, is challenge."

I look'd up at the night sky and the crescent moon above us, and ask'd Friday if he thought the great wolf would let us come back in two weeks, but my man did not laugh.

The wolf howled again, and a most frightful thing then happen'd. Deep under my skin, the beast stirr'd and woke. I cast my gaze upon the crescent moon again and tried to calm the dark thing in my soul, but it was to no avail. The wolf somehow saw the beast within my flesh and wish'd to fight, and the beast had look'd out thru my eyes and accept'd the challenge. Once before leaving the island I had set it free on a night not of the moon. Now it forced the change upon me the way one forces a ship against the current.

I threw off my gloves even as Friday helped me from my cloak and coats, for he saw the mantle of the beast settling upon me. Our companions did question my methods as I stripp'd off my cloathes, but then the beast was near enough they grew silent, except for one merchant's servant who did scream like a child, and was soon joined by the screams of all of them, and a sharp hiss from my man Friday.

For as I remov'd the cloathes I hated so, the great wolf reared back and stood on its hind legs like a man, and I saw knuckles where it had seem'd to have paws. And as the hood fell across my senses, my last clear thought was that I knew the thing that had call'd out the beast.

The fight was a brutal thing, and so much of it I saw thru the smok'd lens. The other, the *loup garou*, to use the French word for it, had years of strength and animal cunning. It hurt the beast as nothing ever had, and the beast grew more and more savage for it. For a moment I saw my man Friday, who lunged in at the *loup garou* with his wooden sword, but the beast lashed out at him, driving him back. This was its fight, and none other would rob it of victory. It was a deep challenge, a savage challenge, and soon all I could discern was pain and blood, tooth and claw, and flesh and howls.

I awoke with blood in my mouth which was not my own, and it did taste sharp and warm and sweet all at once. I spat it out as one does foul food.

The pack was gone. A last few wolves stood to watch me stand, and whimper'd at my stare, and fled to the wood with their tails down.

The rest of our company was dead or gone, with only three unaccount'd for. I never saw or heard word of them again, nor did I know if they escaped the wood. Nor did I care.

In the snow across from me was the uncloathed body of an old man, his throat torn away by savage teeth. His face was long and dirty, his beard thick and matted. It was a face that had not been made use of in many, many a long year. Not since long before my first voyage at sea. I look'd upon him and saw the high cheeks and strong nose of my father, while the dull eyes were the round ones I remember always on the face of my mother.

Friday was dead.

My man lay in the snow, his eyes wide to the night sky and his great wooden sword by his hand. A mighty cut had lain him open and spillt his innards, and tho' I tried hard to tell myself it was the work of the *loup garou*, I recalled the beast's great anger at having its challenge interrupted.

And as I held my man there on the plains of Languedoc and the tears fell from my eyes, I knew how damned and accursed I was, I who all in one night had kill'd the most loyal servant and friend ever known, and his own years-lost brother.

My lies, my last voyage,
back to my island

I n about three hours more I dragg'd my cold self to the town where we were to lodge, which I found in a terrible fright and all in arms. It seemed the night before the wolves had broke into the village and put them in such terror they were oblig'd to keep guard night and day, but especially in the night, to preserve their cattle, and, indeed, their people. None questioned my tale of the pack which had kill'd my companions, or asked of the great wooden sword I clutch'd to my bosom.

I was oblig'd to take a new guide here and go through Thoulouse to Gévaudan, where I found a warm climate, a fruitful pleasant country, and no snow, no wolves, nor any thing like them. When I told my story at Gévaudan, with certain restrictions, viz. my own nature and the fate of my friend and my companions, they told us it was nothing but what was ordinary in the great forest at the foot of the mountains when the snow lay on the ground. They inquired much what kind of a guide we had got, who would venture to bring us that way in such a severe season, and told us it was surprising even I escaped not devoured. When I told them how we placed our-selves, and the horses in the middle, they blamed us and told me it was fifty to one but we had been all destroyed. It was the sight of the horses which made the wolves so furious. At other times, they are afraid of a gun, but being excessive hungry, and raging on that account, the eagerness to come at the horses had made them sense-less of danger. They told me if we had stood all together and left our horses, the wolves would have been so eager to have devoured the horses we might have come off safe, having our fire-arms in our hands, and being so many in number. I could do naught but agree, and think to myself that very little could have gotten my friend off that mountain.

I have nothing uncommon to take notice of in my passage through France, nothing but what other travelers have given an account of, with much more advantage than I can. I spent a single moon in that country and then traveled from Gévaudan to Paris, and without any considerable stay came to Calais, and landed safe at Dover, the 14th of Jan. after having a severe cold season to travel in.

Having resolv'd to dispose of my plantation in the Brasils, I wrote to Captain Amaral at Lisbon. Having offered it to the two mer-chants, the survivors of my trustees, who lived in the Brasils, they accepted the offer.

And thus I have given the first part of a life of fortune and adven-ture. A life of Providence's chequer-work and of a variety which the world will seldom be able to show the like of.

Any one would think in this state of complicated good fortune and woes I was past running any more hazards, and so indeed I had been, if other circumstances had concur'd. But I was inured to a wandering life, had no family, nor many relations. Nor, how-ever rich, had I contracted much acquaintance. Tho' I had sold my estate in the Brasils, yet I could not keep that country out of my head and had a great mind to be upon the wing again. Especially I could not resist a strong inclination I had to see my island again, and to know how the villains had fared, and if the poor Spaniards were in being there.

Dear Amaral dissuaded me from it, and so far prevailed with me, that, for almost seven years, he prevented my running abroad before he went peacefully to meet his maker. During which time I took my two nephews into my care, tho' they had not received our family blood from my widowed sister, e'en though she had a she-beast of her own. The eldest, Richard Marsh, having something of his own, I bred up as a gentleman, and gave him a settlement of some addition to his estate, after my decease. The other, Ezekiel Marsh, I put out to a captain of a ship. After five years finding him a sensible, bold, enterprising young fellow, I put him into a good ship and sent him to sea. This young fellow afterwards drew me in, as old as I was, to farther adventures myself.

In the mean time, I in part settled myself here. First of all, I married a good woman, Guinevere, and had by her three children, two sons and one daughter, Lawrence, David, and dearest Katherine. All of these three did take on the family blood, and many good nights were spent teaching them as my father had taught me. They became very familiar with the beast, and it treated them as if they were its own pups, which they were, upon a fashion.

But my wife dying of consumption and my nephew, Ezekiel, coming home with good success from a voyage to Spain, my inclination to go abroad prevailed and engaged me to go in his ship as a private trader to the East Indies. This was in the year 1697.

In this voyage I visited my former home, the Island of Despair, and was both surprised and pleased to see all the men had survived and a full colony in place. I saw my old friend Olegario and the Spaniards, had the whole story of their lives, and of the mutineers I left there. How at first, influenced by the island, they insulted the poor Spaniards, how they afterwards agreed, disagreed, united, separated, and how at last the Spaniards were oblig'd to use violence with them. It was a history, if it were entered into, as full of variety and wonderful accidents as my own part. Particularly also as to their battles with the savages, who landed several times upon the island to reclaim their dark church, and as to the improvement they made upon the island itself. How five of them made an attempt upon the main land and brought away eleven men and five women prisoners. At my coming, I found about twenty young children on the island, and all of them did have the dusky skin and dark eyes of their mothers.

Here I stayed about 20 days, and even the beast was pleased to run cross its hills and thru its savannahs again, tho' it staid clear of the dark church, which still stood and was avoided by all, or so I was oft told. I left Olegario and his people supplies of all necessary things and two workmen which I brought from England with me, a carpenter and a smith. And upon the shore of my old creek I did bury the wooden sword I had carried with me all these years, and shed more than a few tears for my dear man Friday, who I miss'd even more being here again.

Having settled all things with them, and engaged them not to leave the place, I left them there, 'tho the next few years of the island were filled with many adventures of much interest. All these things, with an account how 300 savages came and invaded for their dark church, and how they brought monstrous things with them, and how the dream god did extend his influence to my nephew's youngest child, and with some very surprising new adventures of my own, I shall give a farther account of in another volume.

END OF VOL. 1

About the Author

PETER CLINES (@PeterClines) grew up in the Stephen King fallout zone of Maine and—fuelled by a love of comic books, *Star Wars*, and Saturday morning cartoons—started writing science fiction and dark fantasy stories at the age of eight with his "epic novel" *Lizard Men from the Center of the Earth*. He made his first writing sale at age seventeen and his first screenplay earned him an open door to pitch story ideas at *Star Trek: Deep Space Nine* and *Voyager*.

He is the author of *The Fold*, the bestselling and ongoing Ex-Heroes series, the acclaimed *14*, *The Junkie Quatrain*, numerous short stories, and countless articles about the film and television industry.

He currently lives and writes somewhere in southern California. If anyone knows exactly where, he would appreciate a few hints.

Moments with the
MASTER

WISDOM FOR THE JOURNEY

JOHN
THIELENHAUS

TATE PUBLISHING
AND ENTERPRISES, LLC

Published by Tate Publishing & Enterprises, LLC
127 E. Trade Center Terrace | Mustang, Oklahoma 73064 USA
1.888.361.9473 | www.tatepublishing.com

Tate Publishing is committed to excellence in the publishing industry. The company reflects the philosophy established by the founders, based on Psalm 68:11,
"The Lord gave the word and great was the company of those who published it."

Book design copyright © 2014 by Tate Publishing, LLC. All rights reserved.
Cover design by Ivan Charlem Igot
Interior design by Mary Jean Archival

Published in the United States of America

ISBN: 978-1-63367-574-2
Religion / Christian Life / Devotional
14.10.16

Now glory be to God! By his mighty power
at work within us, he is able to accomplish
infinitely more than we would ever dare to ask or hope.
May he be given glory in the church and in
Christ Jesus forever and ever through
endless ages.

—Ephesians 3:20-21

This book is dedicated to my wife Jane, who has been my friend for more than fifty-two years. She is the most precious gift the Lord has ever given to me. If given the chance, I'd marry her all over again!

To our son, Douglas, and his wife, Brenda, and to our daughter, Susan, and her husband, Eric, your presence and love has brought so much joy to our hearts and our home. And in honor of our grandchildren, Monica, Melinda, Zeke, Stephanie, Chris and Joshua who have filled our lives with laughter and hope for the future.

Thanks and Acknowledgments

I am filled with thanks and gratitude to God for allowing me to experience the incredible blessings of this project. I have never worked so hard nor felt God's presence with such clarity. Thanks to my dear wife Jane for her suggestions, help, and skill in this project. I would like to acknowledge my parents whose lives of devotion to Jesus Christ was the guiding light of my life. God placed in their hands the chisel that shaped every aspect of my life.

Furthermore, I would like to thank dedicated professors, mentors, coworkers, and congregations whom I have served for five decades of ministry. My deep thanks for so many people who, through their writings, sermons, and wise counsel, have greatly affected my life. I'm grateful for family and friends whose love and prayers have sustained me in my journey and been a constant source of strength and encouragement.

Finally, I thank the people who have passed through my life, who have become the fabric of God's great plan for my life. May the blessings of God rest upon each of you! Thanks for your love and grace—I will be forever indebted to you!

Thanks to Tate Publishing for believing in me and making my dream come true.

Introduction

Welcome to this exciting book, *Moments with the Master*—a collection of daily meditations from God's word that can facilitate your spiritual journey as you are equipped to live with God's perspective. Many of the devotionals are reflective of my "growing up" years spent on our Kansas farm and later from my pastoral ministry.

After you read each Scripture and the corresponding devotional, take a moment to reflect on what God is saying to you. Ask God to help you make the changes necessary to become the person God wants you to be. Do not allow your past to control your future. *Moments with the Master* will deepen your relationship with the Lord, giving you courage to face the challenges of each new day!

May God strengthen your walk with him! He cares deeply about you and wants to bless you more than you could possibly hope or imagine. Have a great year exploring his truth! When you follow God's instructions, you can be assured that the best is yet to come! *Moments with the Master* is a great way to discover the purposeful, joyful, and abundant life God created you to enjoy!

> And now just as you accepted Christ Jesus
> as your Lord, you must continue to
> live in obedience to him. Let your roots grow down into
> him and draw up nourishment from him, so you will grow
> in faith, strong and vigorous in the truth you were taught.
> Let your lives overflow with thanksgiving
> for all he has done.

—Colossians 2:6-7

Life Is a Parade

January 1
Joshua 1:1-9

America celebrates New Year's Day with the fabulous Tournament of Roses Parade from Pasadena. Every float is covered with flowers, about a hundred thousand blossoms! While admiring beautiful floats, we know life is not a "tournament of roses!" God never promised us a tournament of roses, but he turns mornings out of evenings and brings roses from thorns. It has been a real joy to trust him in last year's journey!

Despite troubles and challenges, we've been blessed throughout last year's journey. But today we are "on the other side of the Jordan"—a New Year! Each year sets new paths for our feet, new experiences, challenges, new joys and sorrows. We have not passed this way before, but confidently travel with faith in this New Year. The New Year may mean changes in our plans, some refocusing, retirement, a move, or a new job. But with Christ before us and his Spirit in us, we can travel with hope and genuine excitement. He who led in the past will be our abiding portion—the Eternal "I AM"—the One who is the same yesterday, today, and forever!

With confidence we move forward in the grace of a New Year. In 365 days, we need to be ready for the next "Tournament of Roses" Parade. That means, in every day ahead, followers of Jesus must help "build and decorate the float" whatever the cost, to the praise and glory of our Great God. Let's make the most of this year by living our lives as Godly disciples, redeeming the time until he returns and judges our "float!"

My moment of reflection...

Faith 101

January 2
Matthew 14:22-32

Facing a New Year is like the wild ride Peter faced one stormy night on the Sea of Galilee. The disciples thought it would be a routine commute to the other side, but Jesus knew it was going to be a pop quiz in "Faith 101!" My generation has grown up singing Andrae Crouch's song, "Through it all…I've learned to trust in Jesus, I've learned to trust in God." But have we? Is that really true? When bright skies turn black and waves are high and we don't see any help on the horizon, do we really trust him? That's what Peter had to do. That's what we must do throughout the year!

When Peter stepped out of the boat that unforgettable night, he was leading the way by faith. It wasn't John or Philip who climbed out of the boat. It was Peter, with eyes fixed on Jesus, who attempted the impossible! In that turbulent moment, Peter learned that he did have faith, but had so much further to go. There's nothing wrong with getting wet when we seek to walk on water or go "under" for a couple of seconds when the Lord is there to pull us up!

The "good news" is Peter reached a new level of faith that night. The only way you are going to grow and mature in faith is to reach your hand toward the Lord's outstretched hand and take one step while keeping your eyes on Jesus. It is with that kind of faith we get "out of the boat" and walk with him, joyfully accepting the challenges he places before us!

My moment of reflection…

I Won't Let You Fall

January 3
Psalm 90:1-17

A fire swept through the home of a couple with small children. They all managed to get out of the roaring inferno safely. Without warning, one of the boys dashed into the burning home to look for his dog. In his search for his dog, the boy found his way to an upstairs window when he heard his father yell, "Son, jump! I can catch you! Jump now!"

Filled with terror, the boy cried, "But daddy, I can't see you." Trusting his daddy's voice, the boy jumped blindly into the smoke and safely into his father's arms!

Many times we find ourselves on a dead-end street, full of hesitation and doubt. At a fork in the road, we don't know which way to turn. We are afraid because we can't see the hand of the Lord. We know he's there, somewhere, but it's so dark and we feel so alone! But listen to the Lord: "What really matters is I see you. I know what I'm doing! You can jump into my purposes for your life and I won't let you fall. Trust me!"

When you step out of your comfort zone and get out of a sinking boat, you will find the Father's arms strong enough to catch you and his grip firm enough to guide you wherever your path may lead. God gives us what we need and guides us with his grace. He will "…provide good things to eat when you are in the desert…You will be like a garden that has plenty of water or like a stream that never runs dry" (Isaiah 58:11, CEV).

My moment of reflection…

Your Finest Hour!

January 4
Proverbs 3:1-12

Preparing for Christian ministry, I chose Proverbs 3:5-6 as my life's verses: "With all your heart you must trust the Lord and not your own judgment. Always let him lead you, and he will clear the road for you to follow" (CEV). Solomon teaches there are three commitments in life that prepare one for the decisions of life—commitments that build a lifestyle that enjoys God's daily direction, no matter "what!" This is his instruction:

- Determine your Director—"Trust in the Lord with all your heart!"
- Detect your Detractor—"Lean not on your own understanding!"
- Declare your Delight—"In all your ways acknowledge him!"

It's simple: "Acknowledge him!" And the promise is, "God will direct your paths." Not that he might or should or could—but will! In this age of aimlessness, how can I experience God's will for my life today? When I come to the inevitable fork in the road, how can I know what decision God would have me make? Here is the wisdom: If you work on determining and detecting and declaring, God will direct!

Reflecting on my spiritual journey of more than fifty years, I have found that the Eternal God was present at every juncture of life. We make countless mistakes and our lives are haunted by past failures. But as sons of God, we have been redeemed and forgiven and Christ has become our spiritual identity. Today can be your "finest hour" as you determine to trust in the Lord with all your heart! Look forward with great anticipation today to see what God is going to do with you. It could be your "finest hour!"

My moment of reflection...

Standing Strong

January 5
Matthew 7:21-29

Jesus was a great story teller!

> Anyone who hears and obeys these teachings of mine is like a wise person who built a house on solid rock. Rain poured down, rivers flooded, and winds beat against that house. But it did not fall, because it was built on solid rock. Anyone who hears my teaching and doesn't obey them is like a foolish person who built a house on sand. The rain poured down, the rivers flooded, and the winds blew and beat against that house. Finally, it fell with a crash. (Mt 7:24-27, CEV)

Everyone has experienced storms in their life! Maybe you are in the middle of a storm today—a storm of sickness, depression, financial stress, or strife in a relationship. While storms can take many forms, they all share a common tendency: they tend to inhibit or stop progress toward God's wonderful plan for your life! Trouble comes, not because God is punishing you or trying to teach you a lesson, but because we live in a fallen world. Some storms are the result of pure disobedience, like Jonah, who ran from the presence of God.

As an obedient "doer" of the word, your house will not fall when a storm comes. However, failure to hear and "do the word" will leave you open to storms. But as a doer of the word, you will be in a position to walk in blessings, prosperity and success. So in the calm or in the storm, listen carefully to the words of the Master who says, "Be of good cheer…peace be still" (John 16:33; Mark 4:39, KJV).

My moment of reflection…

In His Time...

January 6
Ecclesiastes 3:1-22

The years seem to fly by, don't they? Years, months, weeks, hours, minutes, and seconds whip by—almost faster than you can see. We are cautioned in the word of God that our lives on earth are very short! Moses reminds us that our lives are like "tender grass" that is green in the morning and dried up by evening (Psalm 90:5-6), and James tells us our lives are short, like "a vapor" (James 4:14). Not only does God do all things in his time, Solomon writes that "God has made everything beautiful in its time" (Ecclesiastes 3:11, NIV).

Let these verses remind and encourage you that your time is in God's hands:

- "But as for me, I trust in Thee, O Lord, I say, "Thou art my God." My times are in Thy hand" (Psalm 31:14-15, NASB).
- "There is an appointed time for everything. And there is a time for every event under heaven" (Ecclesiastes 3:1, NASB).
- "Let us not lose heart in doing good, for in due time we will reap if we do not grow weary" (Galatians 6:9, NASB).
- "Therefore, be careful how you walk, not as unwise men, but as wise, making the most of your time" (Ephesians 5:15-16, NASB).

Your gift today is time—be careful how you spend it! Make the most of every opportunity to share God's grace with everyone you know. The next time you see a timer counting down, remember God's counter is running too. The time is short between this moment and when we shall see him face to face. Until then, continue to serve him with your whole being, with all that you are!

My moment of reflection...

Encouragement

January 7
Jeremiah 1:1-19

You can be or do or say anything God calls you to be or do or say! God came to Jeremiah and said, "Before you were born, I chose you to speak for me to the nations...I promise to be with you... so don't be afraid" (Jeremiah 1:5, 8, CEV). God had great plans for Jeremiah, and he has great plans for you—he has not changed! God knew what Jeremiah really needed at that moment was a word of encouragement, a word from someone who really believed in him! Many of us need someone who will say to us, "I believe in you!" Believers have such an encourager—the Lord! He sees possibilities within us we never dreamed possible. If we believe in him and his dream for our lives, we can accomplish more than we ever dreamed possible. A little girl was working with plasticine, a clay-like substance that can be used over and over because it does not harden. She formed a beautiful angel-like creature with wings but quickly molded the angel into a clay ball.

"What's this?" she asked.

"A ball," someone said.

"Nope," said the girl, "it's a hiding angel."

Some of us have within us "hiding angels," just waiting, longing to be released. You are released when you discover that you are a child of God! Before you were formed in the womb and before you were born, you were set apart for something good and beautiful. To believe that about ourselves is to unleash powers and possibilities beyond our imagination. Let God touch your lips and encourage you to release the "hiding angel" today!

My moment of reflection...

In the Presence of the All-Powerful

January 8
Luke 5:1-11

Peter had been fishing all night and caught nothing! Jesus tells Peter to fish in the deep waters. Soon their nets were so full their nets were breaking, and they needed help! Then it dawned on Peter: This Nazarene carpenter is more than a man! Peter reacts, "Lord, don't come near me! I am a sinner" (Luke 5:8, CEV). Some people don't know how to behave in God's presence because they haven't had much experience with God!

Remember Isaiah? He had the most notable confrontation with God in history! When King Uzziah died, he came to the temple and saw the Lord exalted, seated on a throne. Then he heard these words, "Holy, Holy, Holy, Lord All-powerful! The earth is filled with your glory." Isaiah cries out, "I'm doomed...I have seen the King, the Lord All-Powerful" (Isaiah 6:3-6, CEV). Sometimes, like Isaiah, we may not maintain a proper decorum in God's presence. We don't know how to act!

In the presence of the Divine, Isaiah and Peter realized they needed help. Both discovered they had a mission in life—to live the Jesus life. Isaiah said, "Here am I, send me." And Peter heard Jesus say, "Don't be afraid; from now on you will catch men." Their mission was to take Christ's love to folks who wouldn't know how to behave in church!

But here is the good news: God is here, right where you are this very moment! He is seeking to make his presence known to each of us. So how do you act in his presence? It's simple: don't be afraid, confess your need, and find your mission!

My moment of reflection...